Praise for

GLOW

Kirkus Reviews Best Books of 2017 Selection

★ "Bryant brilliantly lures readers into an engaging mystery, a page-turner that begins beneath layers revealed in both paintings and chapters. A riveting story of ambitious and self-sufficient women, both in the present and past."
—*Kirkus Reviews* starred review

★ "As each girl tells their story, the true events and stories of the real radium girls are brought to light. Bryant's novel will surely spur readers to learn more about this dark part of history."
—*SLJ* starred review

"This fictionalized take on the Radium Girls is by turns suspenseful, macabre, and, at points, quite gory. Bryant doesn't shy away from the true horrors that befell these women—and worse, the abject neglect from their male superiors, many of whom knew the true dangers of radium...An eye-opening window into a troubling moment in history."
—*Booklist*

"Readers who love the historic side of this genre will crave more of Lydia's story...gruesomely detailed and suspenseful."
—*VOYA*

"The historic and labor and —*The Horn I*

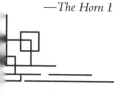

stry, medicine, : and tragedy."

GLOW

Megan E. Bryant

Albert Whitman and Company
Chicago, Illinois

Bryant, Megan E.

Glow / Megan E. Bryant

Summary: "When thrift-store aficionado Julie discovers a series
of antique paintings with hidden glowing images that are only
visible in the dark, she uncovers a century-old romance and the
haunting true story of the Radium Girls"—Provided by publisher.
Family life—New Jersey—Fiction. | Painting, Modern—Fiction. |
Radiation—Fiction. | Factories—Fiction. | Sisters—Fiction. |
Letters—Fiction. | New Jersey—History—20th century—Fiction.
PZ7.B8398 Glo 2017
[Fic]—dc23   2017031988

The quotation from Vera Brittain from *Letters from a Lost Generation*:
First World War Letters of Vera Brittain and Four Friends, edited by Alan Bishop
and Mark Bostridge, is included by permission of Mark Bostridge
and T.J. Brittain-Catlin, Literary Executors for the Vera Brittain Estate 1970.

Printed in the United States of America
10 9 8 7 6 5 4 3 2 1 LB 22 21 20 19 18

Design by Cynthia Fliege

For more information about Albert Whitman & Company,
visit our website at www.albertwhitman.com.

For Daniel–
mon amour est plus grand que les étoiles.

Life seems quite irradiated now when I think of the sweet hours that may be ahead—when I shall see once more "the things I strive to capture in vain..."

—Vera Brittain
December 7, 1915

CHAPTER 1

I used to worry about the dark. When it's dark, you can't see what's coming. Sometimes you can't even see what's right in front of you. When it's dark, your whole life can spiral out of control. When it's very dark, your dreams can slip away—and good luck getting them back.

It seems so much safer in the light. That's probably why it took me way too long to figure out that it wasn't the dark I needed to fear, never the dark, but a certain kind of light that lurks on the other side of it. This light calls to you on false pretense; it makes promises it never intends to keep. Things that happen in the dark—forbidden kisses, broken promises, buried secrets—are supposed to stay there, but that light will always expose them. Because that light is not kind. It's not innocent.

That light is hungry.

It wants to burrow inside you, haunting your hollow parts, shining in places that no light should ever brighten. It wants to bore tunnels through your bones. Unstoppable once it's been unleashed, more powerful than any other force of nature, that light is what you *should* be afraid of. Terrified, even. I wish I'd known that back when summer started, when my biggest problems were juggling two jobs and obsessing about all the ways my life had unraveled when I wasn't paying attention.

I would've been more careful, that's for sure.

✻ ✻ ✻

I wasn't supposed to be at work that day, and I definitely wasn't supposed to be working at Bed Bath & Beyond's East Hanover location. So I wasn't supposed to see my best friend, Lauren, shopping for stuff to deck out her dorm room. But there she was, biting her lip as she stared at her phone, her Kool-Aid red ponytail streaming down her back like a juice spill.

"Oh my God, Laure!" I said, grinning as I reached out and gave her ponytail a tug. "What are you doing here?"

"Julie!" she said, and even if I hadn't noticed the surprise in her voice, I couldn't miss the guilt in her eyes. So she was trying to avoid me. "I'm just…You know…What are you doing here?"

"Working." I pointed at my name tag. "You know I never say no to an extra shift. So what brings you to the one-stop shopping destination of Bed Bath and Beyond–East Hanover?"

"Oh, you know," she said. "Just…shopping."

I tilted down the plastic basket looped over her arm and peeked inside at the neon-purple shower caddy and extra-long twin-size sheets. "Are you getting stuff for your room at Parsons?"

"Well, yeah," Lauren replied. "Just a couple things. I know it's only June…probably way too early…"

Her eyes darted to the side, and I knew I had to fix it. I had opened this can of awkward, after all.

"No, that's really smart," I said right away. "I have been to hell, and it is Triple-B on a Sunday in August. God, can you imagine? The future frat boys of America plotting to sneak a mini-keg into the cart without their parents noticing?" I shuddered with horror, and Lauren laughed, to my relief.

"Come on. Let me help you shop." I pressed on, reaching for the list in her hand, somehow managing not to flinch when I noticed it was printed on official Parsons letterhead. The school must have sent it to all incoming first-year students. I would've gotten one too, if I hadn't turned down their offer of acceptance. Only a couple months ago, I was agonizing over whether I should study art at Parsons or major in premed at New York University. But that was back when I had choices. That was before I'd spent every penny of my college savings account to keep my mom's house out of foreclosure.

"No, Jules. It's cool," she replied. "I'm not getting anything else today. I'll probably just check out now."

"Let me use my employee discount! Do you have cash?"

"I was gonna use my mom's card."

"Go get some cash," I insisted. "Then I can use my discount for you."

"Can't you just use it with the card?"

I shook my head. "I'm not supposed to let other people use it. But if we get this stuff with cash, they won't know. Come on. I'll hold it at my register while you go to the bank."

"Ehhh...I'm here now," Lauren said. "What's your discount, any-way? Ten percent?"

"Fifteen."

She shrugged. "I'll just put it on my mom's card."

"Okay, whatever," I said, turning around quickly so Lauren wouldn't notice I was blushing. For weeks, I'd been wearing desperation like perfume, and I could tell that Lauren had just caught a whiff of it. *Who cares about your 15 percent discount?* I asked myself. *Stop acting like everyone else is as broke as you are.*

We didn't say anything as I rang her out.

"When are you off?" Lauren asked suddenly.

I glanced at the time stamp on the receipt before I handed it to her. "Hour and a half."

"I'll come back for you," she said. "We'll do something cool."

"No, you don't have to." I had to give her an out. It was bad enough that Lauren's eyes were full of pity whenever she looked at me. If we started hanging out only because she felt sorry for me, our friendship would be doomed.

"I'll be waiting out front," Lauren insisted, flashing the smile that almost always got her exactly what she wanted. "Be there."

"Okay." I gave in, pretending like I wasn't completely relieved. Besides, what else was I going to do with the long, hot afternoon stretching out ahead of me?

BB&B was not a store I wanted to work at—God, I never even wanted to shop there—but it was about a million times better than my other job at McDonald's, where I spent sweaty hours dodging grease splatters and Coke spills. No doubt I'd landed both jobs because, unlike practically everyone else my age, I wasn't looking for summer employment. No, I was there for the long haul—into autumn and beyond, as long as they'd have me.

Don't get me wrong. I was really grateful for the jobs. They were my best chance for going to college in a year or two, as soon as I'd saved up enough money for tuition, room and board, books, and everything else needed for Success in Life. No matter how you crunched the numbers, there was no denying that college was stupid expensive. *But worth it,* I reminded myself as I picked up a used Kleenex somebody had dropped in the aisle. *So worth it.*

Three o'clock came at last, and I bolted into the smothering air outside, where veils of heat shimmered off the sidewalk in a feverish haze that made me feel as slow and sticky as the tar oozing out of the blacktop. Lauren was waiting out front, just like she'd promised. Her emerald-green SUV sparkled under the relentless sun, an oasis in an asphalt desert. Her car looked as perfect as the day she'd gotten it as the world's best sweet-sixteen birthday present. I should know. I was there.

I yanked open the door and slipped into the front seat, aiming both AC vents directly at my face before I reached for my seat belt. "Hey, Claude." I sighed.

"Hey, Vince," Lauren replied. We'd been using those ridiculous nicknames since we first got into art in middle school, back when we thought Monet and Van Gogh were the standards by which all art should be measured. Though practically everything else had changed since then, I knew we'd still be calling each other Claude and Vince when we were wrinkly roomies in a nursing home.

"You're welcome," she continued, holding out a venti frappuccino.

"Awesome, Laure! You didn't have to do that. Thank you!" I exclaimed, sucking on the straw as if I were about to die of dehydration or, more accurately, caffeine withdrawal. I didn't offer to pay her back. The frappuccino was delicious, but not really worth it when I calculated the cost as equivalent to an hour of drudgery at Mickey D's. Besides, it's not like she would have taken the money anyway.

"It's my job to get you refreshed and recharged," Lauren said. "I have a big afternoon planned for us."

"The beach?" I asked as I glanced at the members-only parking decal for New Jersey's most exclusive beach in the corner of the windshield.

"This is better than the beach," Lauren said, and she actually bounced up and down a little. "Trust me!"

In about fifteen minutes, we were cruising the streets of West

Orange, past the overpriced boutiques and two-story brick office buildings, until Lauren turned onto a side street that was less cookie cutter than the rest. "Surprise!" she crowed. The street was cluttered with an assortment of indie stores. I knew right away why it had appealed to her.

"Shopping!" I said, trying—and failing—to match her enthusiasm. Lauren could tell I was faking it; she was already rolling her eyes at me.

"There's not just shopping. Look. We could get new piercings. I'm going to get a tattoo!"

"You are not."

"I am!" Lauren insisted. "I'm eighteen, and I have my ID, and there's a really cool tattoo place over there—"

"Can we look at this logically, please?" I asked. "Since your eighteenth birthday, we have gone to not one, not two, but three different tattoo places. And how many tattoos have you gotten?"

"None. But—"

"Have you even finished the design?"

"Well, no, but maybe I'll just go with something in the book."

I gave her my best are-you-even-kidding look. "Really? You want to be a Parsons student with a totally generic tattoo from the book? I don't think so. Please, Laure, you're better than—"

Lauren flicked her fingers toward my face, like I was some bug she could shoo away. "Just forget it," she interrupted me. "We can skip the tattoos and get psychic readings instead!"

I saw it then, just on the other side of the tattoo place: a small store with a neon crystal ball in the window. "I don't know…" I said slowly. "That's not really my thing."

"I'll pay," she declared, as if that was why I wanted nothing to do with a psychic reading. "Come on. It will be fun!"

I will never understand why people are into psychic readings. As if they weren't fake-fake-fake. As if what the future holds could only be wonderful—instead of totally devastating. But I didn't say any of that to Lauren. Instead, I shook my head and started grinding my teeth, a bad habit that had started as an involuntary reflex after my dad moved out seven years ago. Now, though, the repetitive force and familiar pressure in my jaw was almost comforting. Lauren cringed, clapping her hands over her ears.

"Stop! Stop!" she begged. "That's the worst sound in the world. God, you're giving me chills."

"You have chills because the AC is on high."

"No, it's that gross thing you do with your teeth."

There was a pause, and our eyes met. Then Lauren sighed and said, "Fine, no psychic today. But we can check out some of these stores, right? Jump out. I think I have to parallel park."

"Look out, world!" I cracked.

"Funny. Really hilariously funny," Lauren said, but I could tell she wasn't mad by the way she stuck out her tongue. Her forehead furrowed as she inched the SUV closer to the curb, while I guided her like an air traffic controller.

"Forward. Forward. Forward. Stop. Okay, move back. A little more. Not that much. Jesus, stop, Laure!"

"Stop freaking me out," she called through the open window. "How's that?"

"You're still three feet from the curb."

"Good enough!" Lauren said.

"So…where to?" I asked as she joined me on the sidewalk.

Lauren shrugged. "Let's just see what looks interesting."

Halfway down the street, an oven-hot breeze kicked up. It fluttered the maple leaves but not my stick-brown hair, which was stuck to the back of my neck with sweat. Instinctively, I reached for my sketchbook to see if I could capture the light filtering through the leaves before I remembered that I didn't have it. Lauren always used to joke that my sketchbook was my security blanket, and maybe it used to be. But that was a while ago. At this point, I couldn't even remember the last time I'd seen it.

At first, all the stores seemed the same, stocked with second-hand junk that had been cast off in hope that someone else would want it…or need it, which is not the same thing at all. For Lauren, shopping was like a competitive sport, and she was determined to medal by purchasing something at every store. I had already promised myself that I wouldn't spend a penny—every cent I earned went straight into my savings account—so I tried to coach her away from truly disastrous decisions, like the menorah made out of crayons and the oversize bumblebee-striped sunglasses. Let's just say that I was only partially successful.

Then we walked into a consignment store called Lost & Found, and everything changed. It was nestled at the end of the street beside a vacant lot, as if the building itself was an afterthought. Except for the sunlight streaming through the front window, the store was dim, lit only by small lamps with rose-colored shades. The pink light made the store seem more special than I suspected it was.

It was already too late though. We were both captivated. "Find something you love," Lauren whispered, her eyes staring beyond me with a hungry look. "I'll buy it for you."

"You don't have—" I began. But she had already wandered off toward a rack filled with gauzy dresses, leaving me alone. I started to follow her before I paused, then walked the other way. I already knew how it would go: crammed together in a fitting room, wearing unfamiliar dresses like a strange skin, fighting the same fight about whether or not she'd buy one for me. If money was like oxygen to Lauren, spending it was like breathing, an autonomous function requiring absolutely no thought. Sometimes her generosity was physically painful for me, every purchase a black hole that sucked me deeper and deeper into her debt. She might not have been keeping track, but I sure was.

I drifted toward the back of the store where there were shelves of old books and a doily-covered table with a quirky sign announcing NEW (OLD) RELEASES.

The sign was half right anyway.

All the books displayed on the table were by the same author, Charles Graham, who I'd never heard of. *Lost to the Light, Ghost Generation, Fallen and Forgotten.* He must've been real fun at parties.

After a couple of minutes, I abandoned the books for a bin filled with artwork. My fingers tingled as they grazed over the roughness of canvas and the grain of wooden frames. The paintings on top were…well, they were not good: crying clowns on black velvet; spackled sunsets as generic as a greeting card; creepy portraits of children whose proportions were just a little off, making them look more cursed than adorable.

Then I found it—or it found me. When I'm feeling especially superstitious, I let myself think it was waiting for me. I knelt before the painting and stared.

A tall wheat field, each stalk somehow unique yet blending into the one next to it, bending but not breaking; the wheat stretching off the canvas and into the background until it met the purple smudge of sunset. In the sky, a solitary aviator in an open cockpit with leather cap, goggles, and all. *Where is he going?* I wondered. *What is he flying away from?* And in that moment, I longed to be the pilot, to take off on my own solo flight across golden fields, racing the sun to tomorrow and the next day and the next with no end in sight. Only escape.

The frame was simple—unfinished pine with a smattering of dark wormholes, small enough that it fit easily in my arms—and yet within it, a whole world was contained. A cascade of choices had led the pilot to that moment—decisions forged despite all the unknowns, the details lost or perhaps invented by the artist—and yet you didn't need to know them to understand a fundamental truth: there were *always* options.

That's when I knew beyond all doubt that this painting would be mine. I had to have it. And the little round price tag gumming up the corner told me that I could.

"Look!" Lauren said, her voice effervescent in my ear. I spun around and saw her behind me. How long had she been standing there?

"College clothes!" she continued a little louder. She held up velvet blazers and poofy skirts with ironic petticoats and even a pair of fuchsia cracked-leather ankle boots that I already knew she would never, ever wear.

"Very cool," I said. "Very art school. You will look so unique."

"Just what I wanted," she said, extremely pleased. "Ready to go?"

I trailed behind Lauren as she made her way to the register. As if she'd heard the soft thud of that enormous pile of clothes landing on the counter, a woman suddenly appeared through a curtain in the back. She was somewhere between mom age and grandma age, with wiry red ringlets exploding from her head like fireworks. "Are you ladies ready?" she asked, her eyes glinting at the size of Lauren's pile.

"Oh my God, is this your store?" Lauren cried. "I love this place. I'm definitely coming back next week. I wish I had a store like this. I totally want to have a store like this someday!"

The woman smiled as she started to ring up all the clothes. If she saw through Lauren's gushy cheerleading, she didn't show it. Then she turned to me. "Just this?" she asked, pointing at my painting.

I nodded.

"I love this one," she said. "It's only been here a few days. Not surprised it's moving fast. Did you see there's a companion piece?"

"Um, no."

She squeezed around the counter and plucked it from the stack of paintings in the bin—a rendition of the New York City skyline in a matching pine frame. Then she waited expectantly for praise.

"Nice," I said.

"Should I wrap them together?"

I shook my head. "No, I'm just going to get the other one."

"I'll sell you both for eight dollars," she offered.

I thought about the crumpled ten in my pocket and shook my head again. It wasn't just the money holding me back. In my heart of hearts, I knew that I didn't need a reminder of the big city I couldn't even afford to visit, the place where my life might have begun.

"No thanks," I said, keeping my voice friendly. "Just one today."

"I'll buy it for you," Lauren piped up.

"I don't want it," I said, louder than I meant to be. "Just the airplane one. Please."

Then everyone was too quiet as the woman wrapped my painting in brown paper. "Thanks for shopping here, ladies," she said evenly. "Come back anytime!"

The silence lasted as Lauren and I walked back to her car. "Well, what do you think?" I finally asked. "Ready for that tattoo?"

"Oh, I'm just not sure." Lauren sighed. "I mean, I don't want to rush it. I kind of have it narrowed down to either my hip or my ankle. One of the two."

"If it's on your ankle, your mom will see it," I pointed out.

"Hip, then, I guess," she said, pushing a button on her key ring.

"What are you doing tonight?"

"Ugh. I have to babysit the Gruesome Twosome." Lauren groaned. "You want to come over? I could really use some help."

"Sure," I said, more grateful for the invite than I wanted to let on. I loved Lauren's brother and sister, fraternal twin tornadoes, almost as much as she did. Those kids could rip up a room in less time than it took to go pee, so I knew why she wanted my help. But beyond that, I was glad to have any reason to stay out. And from the way Lauren smiled at me, I knew she understood.

✳   ✳   ✳

Much later, there was a full moon gleaming in the sky when I pulled up in front of my house, but it was still dark enough that you could pretend not to notice the peeling paint, the dandelions spawning across the yard, the For Sale by Owner sign that had been on display for nearly a year. Even though my mom was obviously home—her car was in the driveway—the house had an air of emptiness, a lonely feeling like no one lived there, which had crept over it with such stealth that Mom and I hadn't noticed until it was too late to stop it. If I was quiet enough, I could get to my own room without waking her. I hoped.

With my paper-wrapped painting tucked under my arm, I tip-toed up the stairs, stepping over the creaky one like I still had a curfew. That was another thing that had snuck up on us: the end of my curfew. I think it died on the day I wrote that check to my mom, just over $200,000 after the penalty tax and administration fees. Anybody who can write a check that big is way too old for a curfew. The money was much more of a security blanket than my sketchbook; I used to wrap myself in thoughts of it, imagining paint-splattered studios or gleaming labs, the college education that would determine my entire future.

To think that there'd been a time when deciding which college to attend was the biggest problem I faced.

Stop dwelling, I scolded myself. It was better to think about my savings account, growing by dollars and cents every week. After all, my college dreams didn't have an expiration date. It was more like an unavoidable delay.

Then my room was right in front of me, the door closed, like always. I slipped inside and shut the door behind me, like always, and sighed. Success.

Or something like that.

I hung up my new painting before doing anything else, taking down the mirror over my dresser so I could hoist the frame up on the wall. (Really, I'd rather not see myself wearing my hideous work uniforms every day, thanks anyway.) The first hang was crooked, of course, and it would have been easier with someone to help. But this was a job I had to do by myself, easing the frame by degrees until it was at least a little centered.

I stood back to inspect my work. Yes. Centered. At least something around here was.

And then I was so tired—that full-body tired that made every inch of me leaden, heavy, dull. This kind of exhaustion was no stranger; sleep had been my favorite hiding place for months. I swapped a balled-up T-shirt on the floor for my polo. Brushing my teeth, washing my face could wait until morning.

I turned off the light. I fell into the bed.

And then I sat up.

In the seconds between turning off the light and getting into bed, something in my room had changed.

Something was not right.

My painting.

What had happened to it?

Suddenly I wasn't tired anymore, not even a little. I got out of bed and crept closer to the painting, which glowed with ghostly luminescence. Like a moth to the flame, I approached it without hesitation, my hand reaching to touch, violating every art museum's cardinal rule.

In the dark, the canvas had transformed. The empty sky now glittered with stars, each one shining brighter than the real stars out my window. The wheat field had morphed into an ancient rose garden just past full bloom. Wilting petals had started to fall, drifting past thorns that jutted from gnarled stems.

But the biggest change was that my solo aviator was no longer alone. Now there was a girl pressed behind him, her arms wrapped around his waist, her head resting on his back. Her scarf trailed behind her, fluttering in the wind. The expression on her face was what really intrigued me. That look of perfect peace, of utter contentment, of true love. The two people in the airplane were like puzzle pieces that had finally been found and fit together. Staring at her face, I wondered if anyone would ever look at me like that.

I stepped back from the painting and made my eyes slip out of focus so that it was just a glowing patch on the wall, with all the details blurred. When I focused my eyes again, I saw something else: a message written in the stars, correspondence by constellation.

It read: *Mon amour est plus grand que les étoiles.*

CHAPTER 2

September 5, 1917

Dearest Walter,

Scarcely twenty-four hours have passed since we parted, and yet already there is so much to tell you that I hardly know where to begin! I must apologize first for the scene I caused on the porch when we said good-bye. I had steeled myself to be bright and cheerful, that you might remember my fortitude and perhaps be strengthened by it during the long days that lie ahead. Instead, what have you to remember me by now? A blotchy face, a drippy nose, red-ringed eyes, and the dampness from my tears that soaked right through your smart new uniform. I do believe—for I do believe in you—that you will return to me safe and sound, once this dreadful war is over. Think of me sitting in the same moonlight that shines down on you, wherever you may be. The world is not so very large that this distance between us is insurmountable.

After my disgraceful farewell to you, I expected to hide away in my room and cry and cry until I could cry no more, but that only lasted for the first fifteen hours—and then Liza came clattering up the stairs at noontime, which was strange because Liza always takes her midday meal with the other girls. She flew into our room, snapping her fingers at me and crying, "Up! Up! Get up, you layabout. You're doing no one any good by lounging away the day!"

Before I could protest, Liza continued: "Edna Parsons is ill and not coming back to work for likely quite some time, so you've got to hurry now to meet the foreman before word spreads about the position! The line outside the factory tonight will have fifty girls if it has one, and there's not a moment to lose. I wouldn't be surprised if the break room is empty right now with all the other girls doing what I'm doing, so up! Get up!"

Liza dove into the closet and emerged with one of her dresses—not one of mine, which were neatly pressed and ready for wearing, but her aubergine serge, the one with the edging of lace at the collar and the very straight skirt that skims right over the hips to the ankles with hardly a hint of petticoat.

"I won't wear your dress," I said, finally getting out of bed.

"You will," she said firmly as she grabbed a brush from the bureau and began attacking my hair with it. "None of your dresses fit well enough."

Not everyone wants to dress as forwardly as Liza, though of course styles must change to conserve fabric for the war. It's safe to say, however, that Liza's motivations for dressing as she does have little to do with patriotic sacrifice.

In the matter of the dress, Liza would not budge, and her exuberance was infectious. Suddenly I was arranging my hair and, without even asking, Liza took Charlotte's Sunday hat from her room and pinned it right onto my head. Hardly ten minutes after she'd burst into my room, we were outside. (Liza herself wore no hat, truly a testament to the haste with which she'd rushed from the factory!)

It was such a gray and lonesome sky, Walter, looking as if it would rain, and I regretted leaving home at all. But as Liza and I ran to the factory, the grayness seemed to lose its oppressive character, and I wondered if perhaps the sun would shine after all.

At the far end of Dover Street, we saw Minnie Johnson and her sister, Eugenie, and they were heading straight to the factory as well! Liza and I didn't say a word, but she grabbed my hand, and we ran even faster, our heels clacking on the cobblestones. Once Minnie and Eugenie saw us running, they started running too. Well! What do you think happened next? Liza nearly yanked my arm from its socket, and we were the first to reach the heavy metal gates. She pulled them closed behind us with a clang so loud I could feel it in my teeth.

My other piece of luck was that Eugenie's shoe fell off. (Now I wonder if it was Minnie's shoe she was wearing, and if Minnie was trying to make her over as Liza had done to me. Really, why else would Eugenie wear such dainty shoes, with those sweet little buckles, given her current place of employ? And with those dreadful Womanalls she's forced to wear, poor dear!) Eugenie lost a few moments trying to put her shoe back on, moments of which Liza and I took full advantage as we raced up the stairs to the foreman's office.

Just outside, Liza paused and turned me to face her. She stared at me with a critical eye, then adjusted my hat and pinched my cheeks three times, though I don't know why. Looking at Liza is generally like looking in a mirror, and if my cheeks were half so flushed as hers, I must have been looking very cheery indeed, despite all the tears I'd shed.

The foreman was finishing what smelled like a liver sandwich from his tin pail. He did not look pleased to see us.

"Was I not clear, girlie, that I'm not to be disturbed during my lunch?" he snapped at Liza, not even glancing in my direction. Her head ducked down as in a moment of bashfulness, entirely put on, because when she looked back up, her eyes were snapping merrily.

"Your lunch looks nearly finished to me," Liza said impertinently, and I felt my cheeks flush even more at her boldness. But—and here I realized why she had insisted that I wear her dress—his wide, shiny face broke into a smile that I did not like one bit.

Liza leaned forward and placed a cookie on his desk, one that she must have nicked from the kitchen on our way out. "Mr. Mills, you ought to meet my sister," she said. "At least to eat this cookie she made. Lydia's first rate in the kitchen, you know. And other places."

(Are you smiling, Walter, as you read this? I know you think Liza's brashness is quite a joke, but I was embarrassed by her as always. In the assigning of qualities, I seem to have been blessed with enough modesty for both of us, while she lacks the slightest sense of propriety.)

"Is she now?" Mr. Mills asked, turning to me with that odd smile. His glance roamed toward the floor, where I looked too, and saw nothing of interest but the toes of my shoes. "Then why is she such a skinny, small thing?"

"She's just sixteen, but she's a hard worker," Liza said in a rush.

"Oh?" Mr. Mills asked as his eyes traveled back up to my face. "And what work do you do, girlie?"

Liza nudged me, and I tried to find my voice.

"I'm a laundress," I finally said softly.

Mr. Mills' smile vanished. "Thank you anyway," he said, reaching for his coffee.

Liza's eyes were flashing with fury, and I knew the moment we were outside she would light into me. But I didn't know what I'd done wrong.

"No, no, no," she said loudly. "That's not right at all. She does a little laundry from time to time, but she's actually an artist!"

Mr. Mills laughed, not unkindly—at least it didn't sound unkind. "An artist like you?" he asked Liza.

"Even better," Liza announced, and only I knew how much it pained her to say that.

Mr. Mills looked at her sharply, then turned back to me. "Let me see your hands," he ordered.

My hands! My pride and my shame! I gave Liza a pleading look, but she was still so angry at me that, under her fierce gaze, I knew I had no choice but to pull off my gloves.

I suppose I should be grateful for my vanity, because I know my hands would be much the worse if I didn't coat them in warm beeswax every evening and wear soft cotton gloves while I sleep. I knew that helping Mother with the laundry would eventually wreck my hands as it has wrecked hers, but I've tried so hard to protect them. At least I have succeeded in part, because there is just the one burn on my right wrist, and they are not nearly so cracked and scaly as Mother's hands.

Mr. Mills's eyes narrowed as he examined my hands. "Wiggle your fingers."

I did and felt ashamed that a stranger was paying such close attention to me.

"What type of art?" he asked.

"She's a p—" Liza began.

"I'll hear it from her mouth, thank you," he interrupted her.

"I paint," I told him. "Oils, mainly, when I can buy the paint. Sometimes I mix tempera, if there's egg to spare for binding the pigment." I did not add that there usually isn't.

He nodded, almost to himself. "Well, those are the finest-looking hands I've ever seen on a laundress," Mr. Mills finally said. "Which leaves me to think you're not quite as hard a worker as your sister would have me believe."

Oh! The way I blushed again, and my ears were burning.

"But perhaps you've been protecting your hands in the service of your art," he continued. "In which case, all the better for me, provided that you're as capable as your sister in that area."

Liza's shoulders went a touch straighter, which was an encouraging sign.

"You'll have a provisionary period," he said, "to make sure you can do this work. It's very important work, you know. We hire only the best girls to do it, and I can assure you there are many more who'd be happy to take your place. I just have to put the word out, and they'll come running."

Liza's foot brushed against mine.

"Yes, sir," I said right away. "Thank you, sir. I'll work very hard for you. I promise."

"Tomorrow at seven, with your sister, and you'll start your training. Now let me finish my lunch in peace," Mr. Mills said, reaching for the cookie Liza had dropped on his desk. We hurried out of his office and passed by Minnie and Eugenie, and my, their faces were sour!

I waited until we were outside before I threw my arms around Liza's neck. "Thank you, Liza. Thank you, thank you!" I cried.

"You nearly ruined it all, you know," she scolded me. "A laundress! Shame on you!"

"Some warning might have been nice," I retorted. "You never told me not to say that."

Liza shrugged away from me, and just as quickly her face was beaming again, all sunshine and roses. "Just wait till Mother finds out you got yourself a position at ARC!" she crowed.

A horrible thought hit me then. "But who will help Mother with the washing?"

"Oh, Charlotte will, or we'll hire someone," Liza said, dismissing my worries with a wave of her hand. "You won't be making what I'm making, of course—you're not experienced enough—but you'll still earn double what you're earning now. Mother will be thrilled!"

Liza glanced at the clock atop the factory's tallest tower. "I don't have time to walk you home, little sister," she said. "Be a good girl and take in all your dresses at the bust. An inch or two ought to do it. And ready yourself for your last afternoon as a laundress!"

Liza kissed me on the cheek, and I squeezed her hand, hard, to tell her how grateful I was. Just as she skipped back into the factory, a very sullen Eugenie emerged. At that, I hurried on my way. I had no desire to exchange words with Eugenie, and the clouds above had started to crack apart, dissolving across the sky so that the sun could shine through. It seemed like a very favorable omen indeed.

Our apartment smelled of wet linens and lye. Mother and Charlotte were home, and the great steel tub was already burbling on the stove. Quickly I changed into my work dress so that I could relieve Charlotte; from her grateful smile, I knew she'd scurry off to work on her poems. Somehow I managed not to speak of my new position. I was certain that Liza would want to be there to take full credit, which she surely deserved. Mother knew at once that something had happened—here I was, out of bed, with a smile flitting across my face when I least expected it, and yet still so sorely grieved in missing you.

Near seven o'clock, though we hadn't finished wringing the wash, I convinced Charlotte to help me carry the basket up to the roof so we could hang some of it up to dry. When the church clock struck seven, I turned so that I could see the gates of ARC open, and like they did six nights a week, the girls streamed out, finished with the day's work. How many times had I stood on this roof, watching them with longing and envy? Admiring how beautiful they were in the darkness, glowing like luminous snowflakes as they drifted through the streets of Orange? How much I had wanted to be one, and now I was. Tomorrow I would be among them, shining for everyone to see that I, too, was one of the lucky ones.

It was only then that I realized I had never asked Liza what was ailing Edna Parsons. What could possibly make her so ill as to leave her job at ARC, knowing full well that it would not be held for her?

Then I realized that I didn't really want to know.

Over supper, I allowed Liza to share my good news. Oh, Walter! It was the happiest supper we've had since Father passed. Mother and Charlotte were so thrilled for me—for all of us, really, because Liza was absolutely right. It's no secret that ARC pays better than any other factory, even the girls! And the work isn't bad, either, so Liza says. I will find out for myself tomorrow.

I can hear Liza washing her face, so I'd best finish this and seal it in an envelope, or else I just know she will read it while I sleep. I vowed to have a letter to you in the post today and have clearly failed, but I thought it was important to tell you everything—everything!—that happened. Still, it pains me to think of you not hearing from me at the first possible opportunity and wondering if I've already broken faith. But I haven't and never will.

My darling Walter, it's difficult to believe that just twenty-four hours ago you took me in your arms and kissed away my tears, and now I don't even know where you are—if you are spending a night at the docks, or in some lonely barracks somewhere, or if you have already set sail for war-torn shores, with only the vast ocean swirling around your ship for as far as your eyes can see. I look up at the stars and make our secret wish, just as we promised. Perhaps, at this very moment, you are doing the same. Your handkerchief is tucked away beneath my pillow. I am counting the moments until I can press it to my face, to feel you as close as you can be tonight, and to dream of the day when you will come back to me.

I remain, ever most faithfully yours,

Lydia

CHAPTER 3

I woke up scratchy-eyed the next morning. My alarm had already been beeping for ten minutes by the time I was conscious enough to smack it silent. The room was obscenely bright, the curtains stretched wide apart. I must have forgotten to close them before I finally fell asleep.

I sat up and looked at my painting. With so much sunlight streaming into the room, there was no sign of its glow-in-the-dark secrets, but it was enough for me to know that they were there. They had to be, right? I hadn't stayed up until four a.m., searching the canvas, researching what I'd found, for nothing, right?

Like that French, for example: *mon amour est plus grand que les étoiles.* Well. Who'd have thought that four years of high-school Spanish would fail me so soon after graduation—especially ironic since I'd snubbed French as a waste of time. I could speculate that the phrase had something to do with love. Infinite love, maybe? But what did I know?

The Internet saved me, offering a translation of "My love is infinitely greater than the stars." It was pretty, almost poetic—but more than that, it was personal. Whoever it was intended for, the message had to be a clue.

A clue to what? Maybe to the purpose behind the painting or the reason I'd needed it so badly, or maybe even to the artist's identity. Her initials (for some reason I was sure the artist was a girl) glowed in the dark, a lacy *LG* looped together in the lower left corner like strands of cobweb. I had traced her initials again and again overnight, so surprised by her choice to make her identity disappear in the day. That would make it more difficult to find any other paintings, but I was up to the challenge—starting with the one I'd left behind, with its New York skyline. I needed the next chapter in this story.

The owner of Lost & Found raised an eyebrow when I walked into the store, but I didn't care as I hurried back to the art section. I spotted the New York painting right away. The street was lined with little shops. I could make out a florist's window crowded with roses and a hat shop full of adorable old-fashioned hats. There was a bakery. A post office. A dentist. Each building was made of rough strokes, thick with texture and dried paint, and one corner of the painting had been damaged so that the bare canvas was exposed. Only later, after what I saw in the dark, did I stop assuming that was an accident and start wondering if it had been a deliberate artistic choice.

Even without the Empire State Building towering above the streets (and, as I looked again, I noticed that there was no Chrysler Building, either), I could tell that this city scene was a snippet of old New York. The focal point was the Flatiron Building, an awkwardly beautiful triangular tower jutting into the middle of street as if it had every right to be there. I recognized it from my visit for the prospective-student tours at Parsons and NYU last summer. Afterward, my mom and I had wandered up Fifth Avenue and sat in a park across from the Flatiron. It was so stunning, so unique and unusual and unexpected, that I thought, *If this is what New York City can do with a building, what could it do with me?*

That felt like a long time ago, now.

"So I changed my mind," I told the woman as I hoisted the painting onto the counter. "I'm going to buy this one too."

A grin spread across her face. "I knew you would!" she said proudly—smugly?—as she reached for the roll of brown paper. "I knew those two couldn't be apart. That'll be ten dollars, hon."

"Ten?" I repeated. "But…it was five yesterday. Actually, you offered me a discount if I bought both."

"Oh, well, that was yesterday," she said as she turned on the cash register, punching in her password with a stubby finger. "Sale's over now."

"But why did the price go up?"

Her eyes were wide, phony innocent, as she looked at me. "You know. Supply and demand."

My stomach clenched. How had I screwed this up? Why hadn't I just bought it yesterday? *Because I never expected to want it—to need it. Because I never expected her to be so greedy,* I thought.

But the truth was that for me, making the wrong choice had become an art.

I smiled weakly. "Please," I said. "Will you sell it for the original price? Please? I came all the way back just to buy this painting."

"Sorry, hon," she said. "It might be just five dollars to you, but a five-dollar loss is a big deal to a small-business owner like me."

Stupid hot tears filled my eyes, and I blinked fast, willing my eyeballs to absorb them. But she could see the extra shine in my eyes, I think. Something softened in her face, and I went for it, all the way, even though I knew how ashamed I'd feel later. I put my sweaty, wrinkly money on the counter and looked directly in her eyes. "Please," I said one more time, a perfectly controlled waver in my voice. "This is all the money I have."

It was true, after all.

She sighed as she bent over to count the crumpled bills. "You really need this painting?"

"Yes," I said, nodding like a little kid. "I really do."

"Okay, then. But next time—no discounts."

"Thank you so much," I said. "I really, really appreciate it."

When the painting was wrapped, she slid it back across the counter to me, then placed something in my hand. "Here's my card, hon. I have a feeling you'll be back."

I glanced down at the card and read:

LOST & FOUND
Antiques and Oddities, Sold on Consignment
Andrea Spinelli, Owner

I smiled really big to make sure she couldn't read my secret thought: *Why would I come back after you made me beg?*

* * *

Work dragged even more slowly than usual. When nine o'clock came, I was the first one out. I was glad that the painting was wrapped in paper; I didn't want to catch a glimpse of its glow-in-the-dark secrets in the trunk of my car—not when I could hang it in my room and do it right.

Only after my bedroom was blazing with light did I unwrap the new painting. I wondered how it would change in the dark. Would there be people in the streets? In the shops? Why, I wondered, were the streets so empty? Where was everybody? Even back then, New York was the city that never slept, right?

Suddenly, the house seemed too quiet. I turned away from the painting, fast, and turned off the lights.

Click.

"Jesus," I breathed, shoving my fingers into my eyes as if I could erase what I'd seen, hoping for a half second that I was hallucinating, or dreaming, or just wrong about the nightmare next to my bed. My hand hovered near the light switch for a moment; then, against all my better instincts, I moved toward the canvas instead.

What was painted there was so gruesome that it seared into my brain instantly, and I knew I could never scrub the memory from my mind. I wanted to look away. I needed to look away. I should have looked away, but I couldn't.

Each building had become a face, and each face was in agony, each mouth pocked with crumbling and missing teeth, each eyeball rattling in a yawning socket, each hollow cheek reduced to nothing but skin stretched over skull. It was a row of prisoners, of victims, of ghouls, and each one seemed to be groaning, to be screaming.

Then I noticed a message written in the starless sky:

Ça vient pour moi, je crois.

I wasn't scared—not really scared, anyway—so I don't know why my fingers were trembling as I typed the words into my phone.

I think it comes for me.

If the first message was personal, this one was even more so: a warning, a threat, a cry for help.

And here I was, all alone, hearing it how many years later?

It was impossible to tell.

What happened to you? I longed to ask the artist. Instead, I took the painting off the wall and carried it to my closet.

Then I changed my mind and leaned it against the wall, right next to the first painting. They belonged together, after all. I sat in front of the paintings and forced myself to stare at the terrible one until it became familiar, the way bad things can be absorbed until you forget just how awful they really are.

After all, she had been brave enough to paint it.

I could at least be brave enough to look.

* * *

When I got home from work the next afternoon, Mom was standing in the kitchen, staring at the dishwasher as if she could fix it through mind power. First the microwave, then the dishwasher, then the-freezer-but-not-the-fridge-thank-God. Ignoring their brokenness was a big part of pretending everything here was just fine.

"Hey, Mom," I said, rummaging through the mail on the table, secretly hoping to see my dad's handwriting even though the monthly envelopes had stopped coming last fall. He used to send exactly twelve a year, with two checks in each: one for child support and alimony, one for my college savings account. His last envelope had also contained a terse note, half apologetic and half defensive, saying that he'd be in touch when he could. It took us two months to realize what he should have said: no more support checks, despite the court order. At least he'd sent the note. Otherwise, we might have thought he was dead.

"Hey, sunshine. Have a good day?"

I shrugged. "Good enough. And I'm not scheduled at McDonald's tonight, so Lauren's coming over."

"Oh good!" Mom said, suddenly perky. "I haven't seen her in a while. I was afraid you two had a fight."

"Nope. Just busy," I said. "Working." I shifted my weight from one leg to the other, trying to figure out how to say this next part. "So I heard these guys talking in the break room today. There's a job fair in Hillcrest next week."

She turned away from me and plunged her hands into the sink to tackle two days' worth of dishes. "Oh? Are you planning to go?"

Not me. You, I thought. But what I said was, "Maybe we could both go! It's for that new factory—"

"A factory?" Mom interrupted me. "Assembly lines? I'm not qualified for anything like that."

"But there's got to be, you know, administrative positions. Office stuff. You could totally do that!"

She didn't say anything, but could I stop myself? Nope.

"Come on. I'll take the day off and go with you. They said you need to get there early, like six a.m." I plowed on. "I know you could get an office job there. I bet there will even be benefits!"

"I can go by myself," she finally said.

"Okay," I said, trying not to sigh. I'd take the day off anyway, just in case she changed her mind. I had no idea why she made it so hard to talk about this stuff. I was only trying to help.

Then, thank God, the side door opened. Lauren had arrived to rescue me. I swear I was never so happy to see her before.

"I'm starving," she announced. "What do you want... Oh hey, Mrs. Chase."

"Hi, Lauren," my mom said. "Good to see you, honey!"

"You too! How's, um, the, um, job thing?"

Abort. Abort. Abort, I radioed Lauren with my mind. It was bad enough when *I* tried to talk to my mom about her never-ending job search.

"Still looking," my mom replied, without any wavers in her voice or eyes. "I'm sure something will come along soon."

"Yeah," Lauren said, nodding her head as their conversation tumbled from normal to excruciating.

"I'm starving too," I said loudly to Lauren. "You want to grab some wraps or something? Go to Panera?"

"Yes. Absolutely."

Mom wiped her hands on a dish towel, and I wondered suddenly if she wanted us to stay and eat with her. But if that's what she was thinking, she didn't say it. Instead, she fumbled in her purse and handed me a ten-dollar bill. "Take this," she said.

"Are you sure?"

"Of course, Julie. Go. Have fun. I'll see you later."

"Thanks, Mom," I said, hesitating as I decided between a quick hug and a quick kiss. I went with a quick kiss.

Lauren followed me upstairs so I could change out of my work shirt. She plunked down at my desk and started rummaging through my jewelry box.

"You didn't text me back last night," she said as she tried on my favorite earrings. Without asking.

I turned to face the wall, hiding my frown while I stripped off my polo. "Sorry," I replied. "I was busy."

"With what?" she asked, reaching for my eye shadow.

I don't know why I showed her the second painting. It wasn't something I'd planned to do. And with it tucked away in the corner, she never would've noticed it on her own.

"What's that?" she asked eagerly. "Did you go back to Lost and Found? I can't believe you went back and you didn't tell me! You made such a scene about not buying that painting. How come you changed your mind?"

"You are not going to believe this," I began.

Of course as soon as Lauren knew there were secret images in the paintings, she had to see them. Despite my warnings, she insisted on taking them into the darkness of the closet. I wasn't surprised when she shrieked and ran right back out.

"That is seriously messed up!" she cried. There was something so voyeuristic about her reaction, like she was watching a horror movie and reveling in all the gore, that I immediately regretted showing her at all.

"Yeah. I don't know," I said. "So where do you want to eat?"

Lauren waved away my question. "Seriously, these are conceptually insane," she continued. "I can't believe you didn't text me right away. You know, it's kind of genius. I wonder how the artist did it?"

"I actually have no idea," I replied. "Did you notice that you can't see the glowing part at all in the light? That doesn't make sense to me. Shouldn't it—"

"Definitely." Lauren interrupted me. "If she painted the glowing layer over the original image, you'd always see some of it on the canvas. I know you would. So she must have…"

"Painted *over* the glow," we said at the same time.

In the pause that followed, we exchanged a smile. It had been a while since we'd finished each other's sentences like that, but at least we didn't "jinx" each other anymore.

"And if she painted over the glow, then how come we can see it at all?" Lauren added. "I mean, this is oil, isn't it? We shouldn't be able to see anything under it. The opacity."

I nodded. These were the thoughts that had been keeping me up at night. "And why was she painting over it?" I asked. "What was she trying to hide?"

"Or cover up?"

We stared at the paintings, silent.

"It kind of blows my mind, the amount of thought that went into them. God, I wish I knew what they mean. I can't stop thinking about them."

"Totally," Lauren said, circling them like a shark, her eyes narrow and focused. "Of course you can't. They're amazing."

Then I made one of those impulsive, split-second decisions. "This is it," I said. "This is going to be my summer project."

Lauren's perfectly plucked eyebrows arched so high they looked like umbrellas. "What do you mean?"

"Well, the paintings first," I said, figuring it out as I spoke. "I've got to find out if there are more. And find out who painted them. And then...and then I'm going to find out how."

"How?" she repeated.

"How she painted them," I explained. "I'm going to figure out her technique. Oh my God, Laure, it's perfect! I mean, it would be exhibit-worthy, don't you think? If I could figure it out? And replicate it?"

She didn't answer.

"I still have plenty of canvases from senior art seminar, and the leftover acrylics and oils. I don't need to buy anything besides some glow-in-the-dark paint!" I babbled on. "And I bet they sell that at Utrecht, or even Michaels—"

"Or Toys 'R' Us," Lauren said a little snidely, like my project was so immature that it would only appeal to kids. There was something very weird in her voice. I'd heard it before—when I told her all about my first date and when I'd been accepted to NYU. But it almost always vanished as quickly as it appeared, and this time was no exception. A sudden smile spread across her face, and her eyes gleamed with genuine enthusiasm.

"It sounds really great," Lauren continued. "Really cool. So... what next?"

There was still something in her voice that wasn't quite right, but I didn't know what to do about it. I didn't want to answer her question, either, but there was no way to dodge it. "I'm going back to Lost and Found tomorrow. Hopefully I can find out who brought them there…and if there are more."

"Cool. I'll come with," she said. "If that's okay?"

"Sure," I replied.

What else could I say?

CHAPTER 4

September 26, 1917

Dear Walter,

I have so many questions: How are you, and where are you, and what occupies your days? Every evening I race home from the factory in hope that I will find a letter from you. My eagerness has impressed upon me how you—how all our boys overseas, so far from home—must long for letters.

My last letter left you with the news that I have found work at ARC, where Liza has worked for the last two years. On the first day of my training, I was so nervous that my hands were trembling, but on our way to the factory, dear Liza chatted so merrily that there was very little room in my mind for nerves as we approached the iron gates. The other girls streaming in for the day's work greeted me with such cheer that I was sure we'd all become fast friends, especially as Liza is so well liked. Only Minnie Johnson was stone-faced, which I suppose I can understand, for she must have wished she was accompanying her own little sister. Poor Eugenie, facing another grueling day at the munitions plant, but I cannot feel too badly for her as munitions work is rather well paying too, for all the heat and danger it entails.

Inside the factory, Liza showed me where to hang my coat and hat before leading me to the dial-painting studio. (The second floor is reserved for offices and the laboratory.) Such a bright and airy room, Walter, with the biggest windows I've ever seen! It is a rather dusty place, though. All the surfaces are coated with a fine layer of powder, so that it is impossible to move about the room without acquiring a good deal of the stuff on one's clothes. I suppose that is why the girls glow when they leave the factory at night.

The girls began to gather their supplies, and in all the bustle, I was left behind. By the time the clock struck seven, the girls were perched on tall chairs at dark wooden tables, ready to begin. I hung back, unsure, until Liza beckoned me to her workstation. There was just one chair, so I was standing there awkwardly when Mr. Mills arrived. His smile was unsettling as he approached us.

"Well, Lydia, look at you today," he said so loudly that everyone turned to see. "So fresh-faced and ready for a hard day's work!"

To my dismay, he made a great show of dragging a chair to the opposite end of the table, far from Liza. Once I was seated, the other girls took up their paintbrushes and began to work. Their quiet chatting was a low hum that filled the room like so many bees buzzing about a hive. Mr. Mills sat close enough that I could smell the pomade slicked through his hair. He placed several items on the table: a small vessel shaped like an eggcup, a sheet of paper with several watch faces drawn on it, a dish of gritty powder, a jar of paste, and another jar with three of the queerest paintbrushes I've ever seen. They have long wooden handles and a thin brass strip to hold the camel-hair bristles in place—what bristles there were, I should say, since they only had three or four thin hairs. How, I wondered, is anyone expected to paint with these?

Yet all around me the other girls managed, so I resolved to find a way.

First, Mr. Mills showed me how to mix the paste and powder together to make the paint, thinning it with a few drops of water. He cautioned me against placing the brush in the water cup too many times, so as not to waste the paint. It was a pale shade, with yellowish undertones, and it had a luminous quality in even the starkest daylight. The paint was quite tacky on account of the glue base, but a bit of water helped it to flow more freely—but not too freely, because then the miniature hash marks on the watch dial would be impossible to paint.

How strange these newfangled trench watches are! I cannot imagine that men will abandon the pocket watch for one to be worn around the wrist. But Mr. Mills explained how our boys in the trenches are fighting at night and must have a quick and ready way to know the time, even in the dark, to coordinate their movements. So progress has filled a void through the invention of the trench watch and this miraculous powder, this Lumi-Nite as they call it, that can make anything give off illumination.

I took care to steady my hands when Mr. Mills decided that it was time for me to practice painting. The paper faces seemed so impossibly tiny, with faintly traced numbers that were barely visible. Now I understood why the brushes had so few bristles. Any more, and it would be impossible to paint those miniature numbers.

I bit my lip and dipped the brush into the paint. After painting the simplest number (the one), I smiled, full of pride, until I realized that the tip of my brush was flattened—ruined! I knew I would have to pay for it before I'd even earned a cent.

"A little less pressure next time," Mr. Mills said kindly, and then he leaned very close to my face. "Watch carefully. I'm going to teach you how to tip."

He puckered his lips, as if he'd sucked on a lemon, and looked so odd that it took all my composure not to laugh, but I watched carefully as he placed the brush between his lips and—well, here I begin to blush—kissed it so that it took shape again. The damp warmth of his mouth shaped the bristles as if they'd never been flattened.

I snuck a glance around the workroom and saw the other girls doing the same—painting, then pursing their lips and tipping their brushes. Later, Liza explained that it's called lip-pointing. The girls who'd had previous jobs painting fine bone china had taught everyone else how to do it. It saves more paint than washing the brush after each application and also saves the step of drying the brush—an advantage since we are paid by the piece and time is of the essence.

I spent the morning on sample watch faces, soon learning that the six and the eight, with lines as thin as a hairbreadth, are the most difficult to master. By the midday break, I was still struggling with uncooperative blobs obscuring the thinnest part of the eight, and fighting frustration with the paint, the brushes, and myself in equal measure. I was even a bit sullen as I sat next to Liza in the break room so we could share our lunch from the pail.

But the other girls cheered me with stories of how long it took them to learn. Jennie Mercer told me about painting doll-baby eyes with paint so thin it ran down the doll-baby's face like tears, and how then she herself started to cry, smearing her own face with paint and tears so that she and the doll-baby were both wet-faced with tears that glowed in the dark. By the time she finished her story, we were all laughing so loudly I nearly forgot my vexation.

It grew quiet all of a sudden, and then Minnie asked, "Did anyone call at Edna Parson's last night?"

The silence deepened until it was quite clear that no one had.

"I was just wondering how she's doing," Minnie pressed on. "I would've gone myself, but Eugenie was all out of sorts with disappointment, so I stayed home with her."

"What's ailing Edna?" I asked.

Liza's hand fluttered up near her face. "Fevers. And some problem with her complexion," she said. Her voice was strange to me.

"That's all?" I asked. "Why would she leave her job over a trifle like that?"

"Because she's nearly as vain as you are!" Liza teased me. "Truthfully, the spot on her face is hideous. Even Mr. Mills remarked on it once. I can't blame her for never wanting to come back!"

"You needn't be cruel," Mary Jane spoke up, and even Liza looked abashed. You see, Mary Jane is the oldest of us all, twenty-two and married. Her husband is stationed overseas so I suspect she works to pass the time.

Liza's closest friend, Helen, then said, "Lydia, shouldn't you be practicing?"

I started with alarm, wondering if trainees were allowed to enjoy a break for lunch, but then she pushed a small jar of glowing paint and a paintbrush toward me. She slapped her hands, palms down, on the table. "Care to do my nails?" she asked, her eyes twinkling. "Robert is taking me to the pictures tonight, and I thought I'd surprise him!"

Everyone cooed in the way girls do when one is talking about her sweetheart. I picked up the brush but hesitated for a moment. "Are we allowed?" I asked. "To use the company's paint?"

I was embarrassed when the others laughed, but Liza was kind and protective as only a sister can be. "Hush," she said to them. Then, to me: "You wouldn't think it, but ARC considers it practice to improve our skills."

Well, I was eager to continue my practice, even in a task as frivolous as painting Helen's nails. It was a relief to work with a larger brush, and there was certainly less pressure without Mr. Mills hovering over my shoulder, waiting for me to err.

I finished the day with yet more practice watch faces, to my chagrin, but I am determined to succeed, and perhaps tomorrow Mr. Mills will give me a real watch face to paint. It must happen eventually, I know, if I am to keep my position.

Now I must end this letter, so I may help Mother and Charlotte with the laundry. My days are full, as they should be, and yet they seem to pass so slowly, with all the waiting and wondering I am doing, while I miss you and hope that you are well and safe—wherever you are and whatever you're doing.

As always, I send my greatest hopes that the Almighty will protect you.

And my fondest affection,

Lydia

CHAPTER 5

Lauren and I met up the next morning at Lost & Found. Andrea Spinelli, the owner, grinned when she saw us. "Welcome back," she said. "Just browsing today, ladies, or is there anything I can help you with?"

"Actually, yeah," I replied. "Do you have any more paintings like the ones I bought?"

"Sorry, hon," she said, shaking her head. "I just took the best two. He did bring some other things—mostly World War One memorabilia. You might be interested in this…"

Andrea unlocked a case behind the counter and pulled out an old wristwatch. The leather band was deeply cracked, with a scorch mark on one side, and despite the protective cover of a brass case that resembled a birdcage, the glass face was pretty scratched.

"Cool," I said. "Kind of steampunk." But the watch wasn't a painting, and despite the damage, it cost three hundred dollars, so I carefully handed it back to her.

"I want to see," Lauren complained, pushing past me to take the watch. "I like it. What do you think, Jules?"

I shrugged. "It's got that dirty metal feel," I replied. "Would you really want to wear it?"

"What if I took it apart?" she asked. "I could make, like, a found objects collage. I bet it has cool gears inside."

You don't have to buy every single thing that's for sale, I thought with a flicker of annoyance. But all I said was, "That seems like a lot of money to pay for something you're going to destroy."

Then I turned back to Andrea. "Did you say the best two paintings? Are there more?"

"Oh yeah, there were at least five or six more," Andrea said. The skin around her eyes crinkled, like she thought the whole thing was funny. "Why? Did you find part of a treasure map or something?"

I forced myself to laugh. "No. I just like the style. I'm, um, redoing my bedroom, and I was hoping to get a couple more. So…if you don't have them, do you know who does?"

"I only take what I'm sure I can sell," Andrea explained. "Otherwise, I'm wasting everybody's time. But not everyone in the consignment business is as choosy as I am. I couldn't tell you where those paintings are, but if he tried to sell them here, I'm betting he tried to unload them elsewhere."

"He?" Lauren spoke up. "He who? Do you know how we could contact this guy?"

Andrea paused. "It was an older gentleman who brought them in," she finally said. "But I can't share his contact information with you. That wouldn't be right."

"Do you have his name?" I asked too eagerly. "Or know how we could get in touch with him? I just want to ask him some questions—"

Andrea's look was piercing. "I just told you that I can't share his contact information. I have to respect my clients' privacy. If I start violating their trust, they'll stop bringing me their treasures."

"Did he pick up his cut?" Lauren said.

"No. Not yet," Andrea said after a moment.

"Then could we leave a message for him?" continued Lauren. "So he could, like, get in touch with us if he wanted to? See, we're going to Parsons in the fall, and one of the techniques used in those paintings is really impressive, and we just wanted to ask him some questions about it. For our studies."

This is not your thing! I thought, wishing there was a way to tell Lauren to back off. Instead, I nodded like everything she said was the simple truth.

"Oh," Andrea replied. "Why didn't you say so? You girls go ahead and write that note. I'll be sure to give it to him when he comes in."

Lauren and I crouched in the corner of the store as we composed the message, finally settling on this:

Dear Sir,

I am an aspiring art student who bought the two paintings you sold through Lost & Found. I have some questions about the technique used in these paintings. Would you please call me as soon as you can?

Sincerely,

Julie Chase

I added my phone number, gave the note to Andrea, and said, "Thanks so much for passing this on. I know it's kind of weird."

"Weird?" She laughed. "Listen, I run a consignment shop. You would not believe the *weird* that has come into this room. Good luck with your school stuff, girls."

"One more thing?" I asked Andrea. "If he comes back and has more paintings, would you put them aside for me? I'll buy them all."

Andrea nodded, but from her smile, I could tell she was humoring me. "Sure thing, hon. Leave your number so I can call you if he brings anything else."

We were halfway to the door when she called after us: "Wait!"

I spun around.

"I almost forgot," Andrea said as she crossed the store. "There was one more thing...a diary..."

I tried not to get too excited. I mean, maybe the diary was connected to the paintings. But there was no guarantee.

The book Andrea gave me was slender, with a cover the color of garnets. It looked almost new. I scanned the first page and read:

> 8 March
> Charlotte has given me this diary with her first paycheck
> as a pastime for my convalescence, which shows how lit-
> tle she truly knows me. I'm sure she feels very important
> to have some spending money of her own now, though
> why she'd waste it on blank books and inkpots, I can't
> explain. Do I sound quarrelsome and ungrateful? Good,
> because that's how I feel.

I turned the book over in my hands, pretending to examine the endpapers when I was really looking for the price tag. It was seven dollars—worth it, I decided, just in case it was connected to the artist. Seven dollars: what a small price to pay for the opportunity to read someone's most secret thoughts.

"Thank you," I said. "I'll take it."

While Andrea rang me out, my phone buzzed with a text from Jazmine, one of the assistant managers at Bed Bath & Beyond. I crossed my fingers, hoping for an extra shift...but no such luck.

Julezzz. I think I left my thumb drive at work, and it's got a paper on it that's due today. Can you bring it to me?

no prob. where are you?

you are the best. ever. admissions office, Newark University. work-study job

gotcha. on my way.

"Who are you texting?" Lauren finally asked.

I looked up. "Sorry, Laure. I have to go. My manager left something at the store, and I need to bring it to her at Newark University."

She scrunched up her face. "No! We're supposed to hang out today!"

"What can I do?" I said, holding up my hands. "She's my boss." The truth was I would've done it anyway, but Lauren didn't need to know that. "You can come with me, if you want. It shouldn't take too long."

"I don't know," Lauren said slowly. She glanced warily at the sky. "Do you think it's going to rain? Because I'd go to the beach, but not if it's going to rain."

I shrugged. "Don't know."

"Maybe I'll risk it," Lauren said. "When's your next day off?"

"Not sure."

"Well, whenever it is, you're hanging out with me, got it? We'll shop for more paintings."

"Got it," I replied as I slid into my car and started rolling down the windows. I watched Lauren cross the street and climb into her gorgeous SUV, adjusting the air and messing with her phone. She already had *everything*, but it wasn't enough. Now she wanted to glom on to my painting project too. It was hard—really hard—not to feel jealous. But that wasn't the kind of friend I wanted to be.

It took an hour to swing by the store, find Jazmine's thumb drive at the bottom of her locker, and drive out to NU. I hadn't been on a college campus since all those tours last summer, and the thought of how much had changed since then was enough to kick off a parade of unwelcome memories: the desperate deep cleaning of the house when Mom suddenly realized that selling it was her only option, the hope for a magical buyer who never materialized, the excruciating conversation when she told me that the bank was going to take everything, the way turning over my college account was a choice that never felt like one.

Mom went so crazy when it all started to unravel, and my college savings disappeared into her debt. She called every college financial aid department and submitted dozens of forms, but we were too late—way too late. Aid had already been requested and granted, and the meager merit scholarships tossed at me were more embarrassing than useful. Even if private loans, with their ridiculous administrative fees and sky-high interest rates, were an option, I would've refused them. What Mom went through—what we both went through—had showed me just how easy it was to drown in a rising tide of debt. If I got in over my head, who would save me?

So I filled out job applications instead of acceptance forms. *A minor setback,* I told myself. *I'll work hard and save every single penny and start college a little late, that's all.* I could even pretend I was taking a gap year, like a cool rich kid. After all, I'd spent years getting ready for college—SAT prep classes, campus visits, countless drafts of application essays. I was not about to throw all that away.

I don't give up that easily became my mantra, a refrain that I repeated daily—hourly, sometimes. Even now, driving into one of Newark University's enormous parking lots, the words soothed me. Newark University had never been part of my plans, so there was certainly no reason for its campus to inspire this unexpected flicker of envy. Of longing.

The concrete campus was quiet, practically deserted, the perfect setup for some kind of brain-eating zombie invasion. Every boxy building was the same, so I approached the quad in the middle of them all, hoping to find a directory. The concrete path led to a concrete courtyard studded with benches made from concrete slabs. What was *with* all the concrete? They couldn't afford any other materials? The whole place looked more like a parking lot than a university.

There was only one person on the quad, a guy reading a book and eating something from a paper bag. Even from a distance, I noticed his olive skin with golden undertones, jet-black hair as dark as deep space, and shoulders that were straight and strong. There was something else, though, something beyond his physical features, that caught my attention. I think it was the way he stared at that book with such intensity, such unbroken focus that I wondered for the briefest moment what it would feel like if he looked at *me* that way.

"Hey," I said, walking up to him. "I'm sorry to bother you, but—"

"Blueberry?" he asked.

I blinked. "Sorry?"

"You want a blueberry?" he said, shaking the bag in my direction.

"Uh, no, I'm good," I said. "Do you know where the admissions office is?"

"I do," he replied. "Are you looking for it?"

"Yeah. Can you tell me how to get there?"

He shoved the book and the blueberries into his backpack and stood up. "I can take you there."

"No, don't worry about it," I said quickly. "Just point me in the right direction, and I'll figure it out."

"It's no worry," he said and stood there, waiting for me to join him.

So I did.

"Grad student?" he asked as we started to walk.

I laughed.

"Okay. Transfer?"

I shook my head.

"First year? Really?" He seemed genuinely surprised. "You don't seem like a first year."

"I'm…I'm not," I said awkwardly. "I don't go here. I'm just dropping something off for a friend."

"Oh. I see."

The way he looked at me right then, with those dark and deep-set eyes, made me all flustered, like there was something more behind his words, a hidden meaning I couldn't quite catch. I stared straight ahead, tried to shake it off, and vowed to ignore this sudden urge I had to look, really look, into his eyes.

"My name is Luke," he continued. "I'm in the grad program. Chemistry."

"Wow," I said, impressed. "My favorite. Of course, anything's better than physics. Man, the *hours* I spent staring at wave tanks—"

He laughed. "So are you a science major, then? Wherever you go?"

"Uh, no," I said. "I haven't decided." Which was technically true. If I wasn't even enrolled in college, I sure didn't need to have a major declared.

"What else are you thinking of?"

"Art." He was so good at asking questions that we were halfway across campus before I realized that I'd given up the short form of my autobiography. *You don't owe him all this information,* I told myself.

It's not like you're ever going to see him again.

I glanced at Luke out of the corner of my eye. His hair was sort of brushed off to the side, a definite Supercuts special that somehow worked over his nose, which was, I have to say, perfect—delicate and straight, with enough definition to be really masculine without taking over his face.

I checked myself and looked away before he could catch me staring.

"I don't think I got your name," he said, guiding me around a corner.

"That's because I didn't say it," I replied. "It's Julie."

Luke nodded. "Here we are," he said abruptly, reaching past me to open the door. I tried to hide my smile. He was so funny, opening the door for me like it was 1955 or something. After I slipped through the door, I turned to thank him and say good-bye.

But Luke walked right in behind me. Like he had no intention of leaving me there.

"Admissions is this way," he said, continuing down the hall. Very little natural light made it through the narrow windows. The fluorescent lights above were working overtime and buzzing loud enough to make sure you noticed.

"Thanks again," I told Luke with a distinct note of finality as I spotted Jazmine behind the counter.

"You're welcome," he replied, falling back so that I was pretty sure he got the hint.

I walked up to Jaz's window. "Special delivery," I announced, dropping her thumb drive on the counter.

"Jubilee to the rescue!" she replied.

I gave her a look. "You promised you wouldn't call me that." Since Jazmine was a manager, she'd seen my job application—which meant she knew my real name.

"Fine, all right." She sighed. "It's the best name, though. You should own it. Jubilee, bringing happiness wherever she goes."

"Or something like that." I laughed.

"Seriously, though, thank you for this," Jazmine said as she pocketed her thumb drive. "You have saved my life."

I shrugged off her thanks. "It was nothing. So this is your other job? Seems pretty nice."

Jaz shrugged. "It could be worse, that's for sure." Then she glanced over my shoulder at Luke. "Who's that?" she asked in a low voice. "Somebody special?"

"Him? Oh God, no," I replied. "I just met him. He showed me how to get here."

"Ahhh," Jazmine said knowingly. "So you made a new friend."

"Not exactly."

She raised an eyebrow. "A new stalker?"

I shook my head. "No, he's fine. Harmless."

An older woman who must've been Jazmine's boss approached us. "Everything okay?" she asked lightly, but it was obvious she knew I wasn't here on any kind of official business.

"I was just leaving," I said. "Bye, Jazmine."

"Bye, Julie," she replied. "Thanks again. I really appreciate it."

I was turning around to trudge back through the concrete wonderland when, to my surprise, I saw that guy—Luke—still standing there, staring intently at a bunch of brochures stuffed into a plastic display.

"Oh hey, Jubilee," he said, acting all surprised to see me, but there was this completely insufferable twinkle in his eyes.

"Don't," I said. "It's not my fault my mom gave me an incredibly stupid name."

Luke held up his hands. "You don't have to tell me. My mom

named me Lucien."

"Lucien?" I repeated, cracking a smile.

"Yeah, she spends one summer in Paris, and I get stuck with a pompous name that nobody can pronounce," he replied. "'Lu-chee-en? Loo-see-en?'"

He shuddered, and I had to laugh.

"That's why I go by Luke," he finished. "But I like Jubilee. It's pretty."

"Not to me."

"So I was wondering," he began. "Do you want to get dinner sometime?"

"My schedule's really crazy," I said automatically. It was true—but the minute the words were out of my mouth, I realized that they sounded like a total dismissal.

"Ohhh," Luke replied, nodding. "Got it."

"No, that's not…I'm juggling two jobs," I said, feeling stupider with every syllable. "So…it really *is* crazy…"

He took a brochure out of the display and scrawled something on it—something that was too long to be just a phone number. "Call me sometime. Or not. Either way."

We pushed through the double doors at the same time.

"Thanks again…Lucien," I said, being careful to pronounce the name exactly as he had. *Loo-shen.*

"Any time…Jubilee," he replied, raising two fingers to his temple and giving this ridiculous little salute.

He was so *different*…but at least he was genuine about it, honest in his eccentricities, and not different in some show-offy, *ooh-look-how-alternative-I-am* way. As Luke walked toward the quad, I watched him, but he never looked back.

I glanced down at the brochure Luke had handed me. A large

photo of a toolbox jammed with hammers and screwdrivers was plastered on the front of it. "Add more TOOLS to your TOOLBOX at Newark University!" the headline screamed.

Under that, Luke had written:

> They paid someone to make this flyer. Paid them money. Thank God it wasn't me. Luke, unlicensed Newark University tour guide, at your service, twenty-four hours on call.

And then his phone number.

CHAPTER 6

October 16, 1917

Dearest Walter,

Your letter was waiting for me when I came home from work—
what joy! My fingers still glowed, and I smiled to think of my glowing fingerprints mingling with your invisible ones, as if even across
thousands of miles our hands might touch.

Mother found some task in the kitchen to occupy my sisters to
give me a few quiet moments to read your letter before sharing its
contents—some of its contents—with the rest of the family. My
sisters are nearly as fond of you as I am. They already consider you
the brother they never had. We have been so eager for news that I
was sorry to see some unfeeling censor has obliterated so many of
your words. I understand the need for secrecy and sacrifice, but it
would be a comfort to find your location on the globe, to mark your
position in my mind, to know under which sky you rest your head
at night.

I believe I mentioned before that I am indebted not just to Liza
for my job, but also to Edna Parsons, who vacated it due to illness.
I am not especially close to Edna; she was a few years ahead of me

at school, so Liza knows her better. Anyway, the girls at the factory have been taking turns visiting her, and recently Helen decided that I might be included in this rotation as well.

Edna's apartment is just a block past the gasoline factory, and the fumes were most unpleasant as I approached. The odor lingered even in her building, where it mixed with cooking smells and a sort of stagnant air that cannot be healthful. The windows were painted shut, but with the gasoline factory so nearby, I'm sure opening them would only worsen the situation. I wondered how long Edna would expect me to stay.

She has lived with her older brother, Albert, ever since their parents died some years ago. Their apartment is just two rooms, with a shared bath down the hall. The table was set with a tatted doily, on which sat a plate of crackers and a bowl of tinned peaches. I realized with a dreadful turn that I should have brought something for Edna—cake or bread or perhaps a basket of fruit.

"Would you care for some tea?" Edna asked me.

"Oh, certainly," I told her. "Please allow me to fix it. You should rest."

Edna was already halfway to the kitchen. "Nonsense! I've rested all day!" she exclaimed.

I wondered about Edna's illness. Though rather thin, she looked well; there was high color in her face and a sparkle to her eyes. Perhaps she still suffered from a fever. I noticed a frenetic intensity to her movements. She moved, spoke, laughed very fast and sudden, as if afraid the opportunity to do so would pass her by. Her beautiful auburn hair was swept up on just the left side of her head. It was a strange style, the likes of which I've not seen before; it suggested interruptions and unfinished business. Only later did I realize that her hair was partially down to conceal a bandage on the right side of her face.

Soon Edna returned with the tea set—two cups and a teapot decorated with delicate wreaths of forget-me-nots.

"How sweet!" I cried as I examined the fine work on my cup. "Did you paint these?"

"Oh, I did, yes," Edna said modestly. "I worked at Hedgecomb before ARC opened its factory. I mainly painted plates, but tea sets were my favorites. Such a happy thought to think of fine ladies enjoying afternoon tea from one of my sets."

"How skilled you are," I said, looking closer at the forget-me-nots and feeling discouraged about my own abilities.

Perhaps Edna sensed my thoughts because, after a pause, she asked, "Are you enjoying the dial painting?"

I had worried that this exchange would come to pass, but it was clear to me that she harbored no resentment. My thoughts flailed about for a moment before I replied with a question: "It is tricky, isn't it? I am perhaps too clumsy for such fine work."

Edna clucked at me. "You'll get there," she promised. "When I started at Hedgecomb, they only let me edge the plates for such a long time! I thought my fingers would be gold forever!" She examined her hands ruefully, as if golden fingers could benefit her now. "But enough of that! Tell me, tell me everything from ARC. I want to hear all the news!"

I cannot imagine that there was much news since Helen's visit the night before, but we had a pleasant time chatting. As the hour grew late, I realized that Albert had not come home, and I asked about his whereabouts.

"He heard about work in Pennsylvania," Edna said, "and went to make inquiries."

I felt sorry for Edna then, though I tried not to show it. She must be aware that I know why Albert travels so far to seek work. After all, any young and able-bodied man who has not volunteered for service is viewed with suspicion. At least now, with Edna's ailment, he has an excuse for his abstention from the war, since there is no one else to care for her. How sad that made me. If I were to fall ill, Mother and Liza and even Charlotte would surely dote on me.

"Are you all right by yourself?" I asked Edna. "Is there anything you need?"

"I am quite all right, thank you," she replied. "I am sure he will be home tomorrow or the next day."

I smiled at Edna as I returned my little teacup to its saucer. "Thank you so much for this lovely supper," I told her as I prepared to make my exit. "I had such a pleasant visit."

"Oh, must you go?" Edna cried, unable to conceal the desperation creeping into her voice. "So soon? I had hoped—"

She caught herself then, and I was not sure what to do. But the thought of Edna spending the long night by her lonesome moved me to stay a few minutes more. With one frail hand on my wrist, as if to hold me there, she reached under the love seat and pulled out a scrapbook of sorts. Edna was silent as she carefully opened the book; then she placed it in my lap.

"There is something that I need," she said softly, and the artifice of her enthusiasm faded away. She seemed suddenly very tired, and I was certain then that I had overstayed my welcome.

With quiet reverence, Edna turned the pages of her scrapbook. Each page was a work of art; a wish for the life she longs to resume. I would not be surprised to learn that this exquisite scrapbook is her only pastime during her convalescence.

There were two advertisements that Edna had pasted into the book. I cannot re-create for you their exact wording, but it was something akin to this:

I did not understand why Edna showed me these advertisements until she tapped the bottom of one. There, in fine print, I read the name and address of my employer! Her meaning began to dawn on me.

"This Evr-Brite," I said carefully. "It sounds miraculous."

Edna nodded. "I know it could help me. See, Lydia, I asked Helen...I asked for you, specifically...You see, I always remembered your kindness...I knew that you would help me."

Walter, how can I describe what was in her eyes when she said this? A strange hybrid of urgency and expectation, and I realized that for all her fawning charm, Edna believes that she is owed...and that I am the one who owes her.

"If you would just pop upstairs tomorrow," Edna said in a rush. "Perhaps one of the chemists would be willing to give you a sample of Evr-Brite. I shouldn't need much, I think. Just a vial or two."

"And what does your physician say about it?"

"Physician?" she repeated. "What physician? We cannot aff...But you see, it isn't necessary. I just need some Evr-Brite, Lydia. If half these claims are true—"

"If," I interrupted her.

"It would certainly improve my circumstances!"

I must have paused too long because Edna grabbed my arm. There was wildness in her eyes as she pleaded. "Please, Lydia, please, I know it could help me! See? You see?"

Edna ripped the bandage from her face, revealing—well, Walter, I shouldn't like to describe it here. Suffice it to say that the wound on Edna's face festers in a most unwholesome way; the size, shape, and color of a rotting crab apple. Oh, the smell of it…Tears filled her eyes, though from pain or shame, or both, I can't say.

"Of course I will try," I whispered. I forced myself to move slowly as I closed the book and returned it to Edna's lap. I patted her hand in hopes of reassuring her. Then I measured my steps to the door, and then I ran from Edna's apartment—from the gasoline fumes and the stench of decay—all the way home.

What a wakeful night I spent, Walter. I worried about Edna, who seemed so unwell by the time I left her apartment, and about the promise she forced me to make. I had little choice but to see it through, but I dreaded the thought of paying an uninvited visit to the laboratories upstairs. I resolved to go first thing in the morning and be done with it.

On the second floor, the chemists wear smart white coats like men of medicine and work at long tables that are cluttered with glass—vials and beakers in all shapes and sizing, fragile tubes and pipes. I noticed, too, that most surfaces are covered in the same fine powder as the dial-painting studio downstairs. I suppose it comes with the industry, but one might expect better hygiene where medicine is compounded.

Of course my presence as a girl was noticed immediately, and all the men grew silent and turned in my direction. All but one, whose workstation was nearest to the stairs, and so to me. Unlike the others, he worked behind some sort of improvised screen, standing as far as he could from the materials. Indeed, he even handled the vials with a pair of tongs! And yet his supplies were the same as any other chemist on the floor. He did not seem to be working with anything dangerous or corrosive. But I had no further time to ponder. All the attention in the room was on me, a small fish very much out of water.

"I am sorry to interrupt," I said. "But I was...do...do you make Evr-Brite here?"

"We do, miss," said a large redheaded man, quite obviously enjoying my discomfiture.

I wished I could speak to one of the chemists in private and not here in the open. But I had no choice but to press on.

"Would it be possible for me to...procure a small amount?" I said in a rush. "I have a friend—who used to work downstairs—who believes that she would benefit from a dose or two."

"'Course you can get her some," he replied. "They sell it at most every druggist."

Was my meaning so unclear to him? I think not, because he continued. "Does Mr. Mills know about this errand for your friend?"

"N-no," I stammered.

"Then you'd best be off before he finds out!"

How heartily they guffawed at that! I was a joke to them. I know there are worse things than being laughed at, Walter, but at that moment, I would've been hard-pressed to think of one. I was about to make my red-faced exit when the strange chemist near me, who had been stone silent to this point, leaned out from behind his shield and caught my eye. I thought perhaps he would take pity and give me some Evr-Brite after all.

"You have no business here," he said. "Go on, now. And don't come back."

Well! As if that wasn't evident!

So I did as he said and quickly. At noon I found Miriam, whose turn it was to visit Edna that evening and gave her a message to relay: I was unable to procure what she sought. Though I tried my best, I remain unsettled by this entire course of events. Edna is not my responsibility, and yet her circumstances tug at my heart. She should be able to see a doctor, Walter, and she should have whatever medicine she needs. I even popped into the druggist on my way home, but Evr-Brite, in its pretty glass bottle, is too dear for my purse. I tried, though. I did try. Perhaps Albert will find work soon, and then Edna can have the care she deserves.

The hour has grown late, so I must conclude my letter here, dear Walter. It is astonishing to me how slowly the time passes since you left. I wonder if it would be easier to bear your absence if only I knew how long it could be—or, even better, if your safety and well-being could be guaranteed. How sweet it will be when we are reunited once more! Until then, carry my love with you always, as it will always be yours.

Love,

Lydia

CHAPTER 7

My shift was unexpectedly canceled on Monday morning, giving me the chance to mess around with the cheap glow-in-the-dark poster paint I'd bought. My sophomore-year painting final, a sailboat bobbing on an azure sea, had been living under the bed for two years. It had earned me an A–, but looking at it now, I could so clearly see all the painting's shortcomings, all the large and small ways in which I'd failed to capture the incandescent mystery of light on the water, the invisible power of wind in the sky. I didn't have a problem testing the glow paint on this canvas; I couldn't possibly make it worse.

First, I swirled some paint around in my palm. It was sandpaper-rough, full of particles that were suspended in a sticky medium, probably glue-based. The roughness indicated that the particles were relatively large, which meant they must have been really weak to glow so faintly. I'd need some pretty sophisticated equipment to find out just what was making the paint glow, but if the Internet was right, it was probably zinc sulfide with a copper activator. For some weird reason, glow-in-the-dark formulas were guarded almost as carefully as state secrets, but the zinc-and-copper combo had been around for a long time. It was found everywhere from glow sticks to those plastic stars you could stick on the ceiling, the ones that shined so much brighter on the package than they did in real life.

So there I was, dabbing poster paint onto the waves around my sailboat, thinking that at the very least I could get some interesting luminosity out of this, like those phosphorescent waters off tropical islands in the Caribbean. But the paint was too gritty; too pasty. I tried thinning it with a little water, but that just made a runny mess that pooled across the canvas. I'd thought I couldn't make my painting look any worse, but I was so wrong. The globs of glow paint looked like seagull crap bobbing on the waves. It was a disaster. Even the faintest application was completely visible in the light.

This paint sucks, I thought, wishing I could get my four dollars back. I should've known that I wouldn't be able to re-create LG's magic with this cheap gunk. Already I was calculating how many hours I'd have to work to buy that cool glow paint I'd seen on the Internet.

I turned away from my artistic disaster to look at the two paintings I'd purchased from Lost & Found. In the morning light, there was no trace of the glowing images, but I knew they were there, especially those secret initials. *Who are you, LG?* I wondered. The paintings were old—that much was obvious—but she might still be alive. Maybe I could find her. Maybe she lived in a nursing home, and I could visit her, bringing cookies along with my questions. Maybe we'd have long afternoon chats…Maybe we'd even paint together…But first I had to find her. How?

Newark University must have an art history department, I thought, remembering my visit to campus. *Maybe one of the professors knows how to find a local artist.* LG could've had shows in the area or taught at an art school, even. She could be known.

In less than a minute, the art department secretary answered the phone.

"I'd like to schedule an appointment with a professor," I said.

"Are you a student?" she asked.

"Uh..." I had to think fast. "Prospective student. I'm thinking of applying."

"Oh. Well, we have a departmental open house for prospective students in the first week of October," she said.

"But...that's three months away," I replied. "Isn't there anyone I could meet with sooner?"

"Hold on just a minute," she said.

I flopped back on my bed and frowned up at the ceiling. *Look at me, sleuthing,* I thought. I could already tell it was going to be one of those things that seemed so much easier on TV. Real life, like always, was ready to throw a bunch of stupid obstacles in the way.

Then the secretary was back. "Most professors don't hold office hours during the summer," she said. "But Professor Maxwell is in today, and he said he could meet with you any time before one o'clock."

"That's great!" I exclaimed. "Thank you so much!"

By the time I rinsed my brush, it was already after eleven. As I was on my way out, a voice called from the kitchen. I stopped, hand on the doorknob, considering for the briefest moment whether I could just crash out the front door, make a lot of noise, and pretend that I hadn't heard her. If I was going to do it, I should've just done it. Because in that pause, my mom called my name again.

Now there was no escape.

"What's up?" I asked.

"Good morning, sweetie," she said, looking up from her coffee.

She was still wearing her bathrobe. "Where are you off to?"

"Newark University. I have an appointment."

Mom's eyes widened. I should've known she was going to make a huge deal out of it. "Oh, Julie, is it an interview?" she asked breathlessly. "Did you apply for admission?"

"No, of course not," I told her. "I'm still going to Parsons someday. Or NYU."

She sighed and took off her glasses. "I wish you would consider other options," she said. "Just because your first choice is out of reach—"

"It's not out of reach," I interrupted her. "It's delayed. There's a difference."

"You shouldn't put your life on pause, Julie," she urged.

My life is on pause? I thought. *You're the one who barely leaves the house.* I had to be careful; there was no point in getting angry. Yet that was exactly what would happen if I didn't leave. "I should go, or I'll be late."

My mom swallowed funny, like she was holding back something she wanted to say. "Julie. I don't think you need to be so hostile to me."

"I'm not being hostile, Mom. I just have to go. I can't talk about this now." *Or ever.*

"I don't understand why you're treating me like this, Julie. It was only a suggestion. You don't want to go to college? You don't have to. No one's going to force you. You had so many dreams, honey. It breaks my heart to see you walk away from them."

Incredible. She seemed to actually believe the words coming out of her mouth.

"Don't talk to me about walking away from dreams," I said. Then I escaped before she—or I—had a chance to say anything else. It was better that way. We hadn't even gotten started, my mom and me; we hadn't even scratched the surface. Her know-it-all tendencies, her tedious lectures, her outdated advice: she didn't know half as much as she thought she did. About me. About life. About anything. If she did, she never would've gotten us into this mess.

Even so, remorse started crawling over me before I pulled away from the curb. I imagined her sitting on the couch all by herself, with no one to notice if she was lonely, no one to care if she was sad. But I couldn't bring myself to go back inside and talk to her. So what if her feelings were hurt? My whole *life* hurt. I had *nothing* to apologize for.

To prove it, I played the radio really loudly for the entire drive, but it still couldn't compete with the wind howling through the open windows. By the time I parked, my hair was a ratty mess, but it was worth it. And it felt good, too, fighting all those snarls, yanking a brush through the tangles until my eyes stung with tears.

A few minutes later, I found myself sitting across from Professor Maxwell in the art department. He peered at me through gold-rimmed glasses as if my appearance in his office was a puzzle that he couldn't quite figure out.

"What can I do for you, Miss Chase?" he asked.

"I have some questions about how to identify an anonymous artist," I began. "I have these old paintings that are marked only with the artist's initials, LG. And I was wondering if you have any advice on figuring out who she is."

I fumbled for my phone. "Here," I said. "I took some pictures."

Professor Maxwell barely glanced at the screen. "These look very amateurish to me," he said. "Where did you get them?"

"Thrift stores, consignment shops...that kind of thing."

His knowing smile made me bristle. "So you're a fan of *Antiques Roadshow*."

"Sorry?" I said, confused.

"Listen, I'm not an appraiser, but I don't think they have much value," he continued.

"I wasn't asking about their value," I said. "I want to know who the artist is. There's a fascinating technique used here… These paintings glow in the dark—"

Professor Maxwell winced. "Oh, how unfortunate," he said. "A gimmick like that is generally used to mask a talent deficit."

I stared at Professor Maxwell for a moment. *He can't hear me,* I thought. There wasn't a single thing I could say that would make him listen. He'd judged the paintings without even seeing them, and that judgment had seeped into his perception of me too. I saw myself as he saw me: insignificant, trivial, childish. He clearly thought I was as worthless as the paintings.

Wrong on all counts, I thought. "Thanks for your time," I said, before walking out of Professor Maxwell's office. *Jerk,* I thought, shoving through the doors into the blinding sunshine. *Of course they have value. They're valuable to me.* My steps were hard and purposeful, as if I could stomp out the professor's condescension, my mother's inertia, and—especially—my own inadequacies.

If only it were that easy.

I glanced around the empty quad. I knew what I was looking for, but I didn't want to admit it, not even to myself. And still I lingered, waiting, as if by wanting to see him I could make it happen.

If the quad hadn't been made of concrete, if the sun wasn't so high and so hot, if I could have sat down casually, like I had a reason to be there, I might have been more patient. I might have left things up to chance. I definitely wouldn't have texted him.

Hey, it's Julie. Remember me? From admissions office?

Julie? I know a lot of Julies

But I only know one Jubilee

Yes, that's me

Good to hear from you, Jubilee

Don't

I mean it

OK

Julie

So what's up?

I'm standing in the quad, wondering where my tour guide is

Moi?

No, the other guy who told me he was at my service 24/7

I regretted that one after I sent it. Did it make me sound slutty? I couldn't tell.

Whoa, now. Didn't know I had so much competition

Ugh. So it did.

ANYWAY

Want to give me a tour?

Of course I do

But I can't

I scrunched up my face as I read Luke's text. He *can't*? After he was the one asking me to dinner? Um, okay.

I'm in the lab monitoring an experiment and can't leave

Care to join me?

Really? That's allowed?

The moment I sent that, I groaned. What a dumb thing to say.

Sure. If you bring the coffee

Think I can handle that. How do you like it?

I'm pretty sure I'd like anything that you brought me

But since you're asking, milk, no sugar would be perfect

Done. And where are you?

Bldg B—science. 5th floor chem lab. Can't miss it

I'll be waiting for you

I pocketed my phone, then realized that I didn't have a clue where to buy coffee on campus—and I wasn't even sure that I had enough money to pay for it. It took me an embarrassingly long time—twenty minutes!—to track down the dining hall, get the coffees, and make the hard choices like hot or iced. By the time I located Building B and took a slow ride on the creaky old elevator to the fifth floor, I wasn't sure what I was doing anymore. But I wasn't going to let that stop me.

When I peeked through the narrow glass window in the door, I saw Luke, his head bent low as he scribbled in a notebook. His hair was so dark, so shiny, that I wondered what it would feel like between my fingers.

I shook the thought from my mind and knocked with my foot on the door. I wasn't trying to kick it in or anything, but I realized—too late—that was probably what it sounded like.

He looked up at once, his eyes bright and intense from behind a pair of safety goggles. A slow smile spread across his face as he crossed the room and swung open the door.

"Delivery," I said, holding up the two coffees.

"Thank you, Jubil...Julie," he corrected himself quickly.

"No problem."

Luke hovered in the doorway for a moment, and I suddenly thought: *I'm not supposed to be here after all. Now he doesn't want to let me in.*

"I can go—"

"Oh no," he said. "It's just...I have to ask you to put on some goggles. Safety first and all."

"Sure. Whatever."

Luke led me into a small room off the side of the lab, where I put on a pair of goggles and glanced up at him through plastic lenses. "What do you think?" I asked. "Am I working the mad scientist look or what?"

"All you need is a white coat," he replied.

"Actually, what I need is an elastic," I said, gesturing toward my hair. The old rules from high school chem lab were kicking in.

"Oh right," Luke said. "Sorry. Didn't even occur to me."

He was back in a moment with a rubber band, the kind that would pinch when I pulled my ponytail out later. Then the weirdest thing happened. As I held out my hands to give him the coffees, Luke—well, I think this is what he was trying to do—reached for me, as if he would pull my hair back by himself. It was just a moment, but there was something there, a dangerous wobble in my world. Something had shifted on its axis, and I wasn't sure how to put it right again.

With exaggerated formality, Luke took the coffees from me and dropped the rubber band in my palm. I raked my hair back and twisted it into a knot that thumped against my neck. Then I followed Luke into the lab, racking my brain for anything to say—anything that might diffuse whatever had just passed between us. But Luke beat me to it.

"What are you doing here?" he said. "Visiting your friend?"

I shook my head. "Not today. The more interesting question, I think, is what are you doing here?" I said, glancing at Luke's workstation. The glass wall of the hood was only up about four inches, just high enough for his hands to reach through and conduct experiments within it. A 50 mL flask, crowned with a condenser, rested in an oil bath beneath the vent. The oil shimmered as it warmed, approaching 50 °C which was—give me a second to do the math—about 120 °F.

Just like that, I was transported back to senior-year science lab. I was surprised by how eager I was to run an experiment. At graduation, I didn't think I'd miss anything from high school.

"It's a kinetics reaction," Luke explained as he sipped his coffee. (He went with hot.)

"Oh," I said, trying to keep up. "For, um, what? I mean, what purpose?"

"Well," he said, pausing dramatically, "I'm going to cure cancer."

"Good," I replied. "It's about time somebody got on that."

"No kidding," he said wryly. "To be honest, though, my experiment so far is doing an excellent job of finding substances that don't cure cancer. But, you know, maybe this one will be the one, right?"

"So why cancer?" I asked. "Of all the diseases out there? Isn't everybody trying to cure cancer?"

"Actually, I'm more interested in combinatorial chemistry," Luke began.

"Making something out of nothing," I said, quoting my old chem teacher, Mr. Reese. Pretty much everybody would roll their eyes and die of secondhand embarrassment when he got started—he was just so earnest about science and how much he loved it—but his giddy enthusiasm had made a big impression, I guess. He'd done this whole PowerPoint presentation about careers in science, trying to dazzle us with state-of-the-art technology and the promise of discovery.

I glanced around the NU lab and realized that I was finally in a place where I could publicly geek out as much as Mr. Reese—maybe even more—and nobody would judge me for it. In fact, everybody else in the lab wanted to be here. They'd probably be geeking out too.

"Yeah, or actually making something new out of other somethings," Luke corrected me. "But all the money is going to biochem these days. So I'm just being practical, really. This way I can get funding for my combinatorial chem. And if one of these compounds proves to have some medicinal benefits, well, God, that would be amazing."

"So…" I said, hoping I wasn't about to make a total fool of myself, "do you have a nuclear magnetic resonance spectrometer? In this building?"

"You bet we do," Luke replied. "It's in the basement. I definitely get my exercise. Six flights down to the NMR, five flights down to the ice machine in the student lounge…"

"So not the best design."

"No." He laughed. "Not really. But at least I never need to go to the gym. Except to shower and stuff."

I must have given him an odd look because he turned away fast and made a big show of checking the thermometers. "Almost there," he said. "When this hits sixty, I'll plunge it in the ice bath—"

"Wait a sec," I interrupted. "Why would you go to the gym just to shower?"

"Well, because the emergency decontamination station in the corner only has cold water," he cracked.

"Do you live here?" I asked, keeping my voice as even as I could. "In the lab?"

"That, uh, depends on your perspective," Luke replied. "Is that more or less weird than living out of my car?"

I tried to smile like normal, but I don't think I pulled it off.

"No, don't look at me like that," he said quickly. "I had an apartment all set up for the summer, see, but it fell through at the last minute, so I was kind of camping out here for a few days while I tried to find something else, and then I realized, well, this isn't so bad. Why spend two thousand dollars to rent an apartment for the

71

summer when I wasn't going to spend any time in it anyway?"

Oh my God, I thought. But Luke didn't pause, not even for a fraction of a second.

"I know how it sounds," he continued. He was talking really fast. "But, you know, I'm here for at least twelve hours a day anyway, and the dining hall is open all summer, and I can shower in the gym and sleep downstairs in the student lounge. It's not so bad."

I knew all the feints and fake-outs of being poor. I knew how vital it was to hide the absolute soul-crushing worst of it. I didn't know Luke that well, but to show him that I was shocked—I mean, he had just told me that he was technically homeless—would have been devastating. It was obvious that he wanted to act like it was no big deal, and the kindest thing I could do was pretend along with him.

"Hey, whatever," I said with a shrug. "Whatever works for you, right?" I leaned close to the thermometer and said, "Almost sixty. What happens next? The ice bath?"

"The ice bath," he confirmed.

"To stop the reaction?"

"Exactly!" he said, and I saw a small spark light up his eyes before he yawned, covering his mouth with his hand at the last minute.

"I'm sorry," I said, laughing. "Am I keeping you up?"

Luke shook his head and looked a little embarrassed. "Sorry. I've been here all night."

"For real?"

"Yeah. We're coming into hour...sixteen," he replied, squinting at the clock on the wall. "Only two to four left."

"Isn't there anybody who could take over for a while?" I pointed across the lab to where another guy worked under another hood, ignoring us so completely that I wasn't sure he'd even heard me come in. "So you could get some sleep?"

"Like I'd let him!" Luke laughed. "No, this experiment is all mine. It was my idea, I wrote the grant, I got the funding, and I'm running it. And hopefully I'll have something publishable by the end of summer."

"Wow," I said, and I couldn't help sounding impressed.

"Yeah, well, we'll see," he said, suddenly modest. "It might amount to nothing. I just don't know yet."

We sat quietly for a few minutes, sipping our coffees as we watched the warning-red glow of the hot plate and the viscous oil swirling around the flask. I couldn't tell if our silence was tipping into awkwardness, so I glanced at the clock. "I should go."

Luke followed me to the door. "Thanks for the coffee, Julie," he said as I took off my goggles. "And the visit. Sometimes these long experiments can get pretty—"

"Boring?" I suggested.

"Lonely," he said at the same time. And then, I'm not even kidding, he blushed.

"Well, good luck with it," I said. "I hope you get the results you're looking for."

"Me too. And if not, I'll just skew the data. No, I'm kidding. I would never do that."

"I didn't think you would."

And then, hiding my smile, I walked away...without looking back.

CHAPTER 8

November 12, 1917

Dearest Walter,

I have heard that for some soldiers, the novelty of war loses its appeal once they undertake the actual fighting of it. I see from your letter that this is not the case for you. There is a great sense of excitement in your letter, and I wish I could muster some on your behalf. In truth—and no doubt I'll regret posting this letter—I cannot see this cause with such vivid clarity as you do. To know that you walk close to death in all your waking hours makes it hard for me. I can neither breathe nor sleep nor fully be of this world, with all our ease of living, until you are back in it with me.

The year is in decline. The blazing glory of autumn succumbs to the grim gray sweep of winter. Already it is so cold, and yet not nearly so cold as it will get. I see mud in the gutter and think of mud in the trenches; I see frost on the pavement and think of soldiers shivering in ice-crusted woolens. I take no satisfaction from the comforts of my simple life, not when so many suffer without end and without cause. How much longer, how much more can we all endure? For months, we were promised that the war's duration would be but a matter of days. Now there seems to be no end on the horizon. I worry that this war will drag the whole world to hell with it.

I am gloomy tonight; I apologize. I set out to write a letter full of cheerful news from home. But I am under a pall—we all are—because Edna Parsons died yesterday. It was not entirely unexpected, I suppose, as she has been too ill to receive visitors for several days now. And yet it is sobering to know that a chum can slip away so suddenly. It is never far from my mind that I have usurped her— taken her position at the factory, where I sit in her chair and hold her paintbrush—when Edna should have enjoyed a great many more years on this earth.

And oh, Walter, I should not even write of it, but the way she died…The girls spoke of it all day long in terrible whispers, as if speaking the words in a hush could somehow diminish their horror. That complexion problem that troubled her…Well, that pustule on her chin swelled and swelled, filled with a toxin so foul that it ate a festering crater through her skin, right to the bone of her jaw, and she died from it. Oh, of all the many miserable ways to die!

Edna's funeral is in two days, and I do not expect that I will attend. As I said, I didn't know her well. I am also hesitant to be away from the factory, even for half a day, when I am still so new and inexperienced. And, I can admit to you alone that I am haunted by how I failed poor Edna. What if—what if—the Evr-Brite might have saved her? I tried to get some for her, and now I fear I should have tried harder.

I try to remind myself that there were many things that could have contributed to Edna's demise. The unhealthful air. The lack of good, nourishing food. Albert's long absences. Would one small bottle of Evr-Brite have helped?

I suppose we will never know.

I can redeem this letter with at least a little good news. My speed continues to increase, and so does my pay. I find myself quite at home in the dial-painting studio, though I don't like the liberties that Mr. Mills takes with the other girls. A leering smile here, a sneering remark there, even a pinch from time to time! He hasn't tried any such indignities with me, thank heavens, but I guard against it. I do not smile when he is near, lest he think I encourage such behavior. Some of the girls try to match wits with him, tit-for-tat—and of these, my own Liza is the worst! The way she thrusts up her chin and stares into his eyes as if they are equals. It is positively a disgrace.

I am more vexed with Liza than usual, as you've no doubt noted, even as I marvel at her dial-painting skills. She is so very fast that I wonder how she ever got so good, and she won't tell me, which I think is very small and mean-spirited of her, don't you? I know some of her secrets, though. I know that she paints her name and address inside the back of each watch that crosses her workstation, in hopes that a lonesome soldier overseas will find her message and send her a letter. You will tell me if one of her watches should pass through your hands, won't you? I will try not to be cross that you did not receive one of mine instead. (I have a confession: should one open my watches they will find my initials glowing on the back. I don't want letters from any other soldier than you, but I would be ever so pleased if one of my watches did somehow find its way to you, and now you will know if one has.)

And I know another of Liza's secrets: she has six jars of Lumi-Nite powder hidden beneath her bed. I awoke in the night from an unsettling dream, and I could see the light they cast while she slept. I crept across the room with as much stealth as I could muster to confirm my suspicions. The light is so enchanting, Walter. It even transforms the dust beneath Liza's bed into an otherworldly wonderment. Not even her buzzard snores could shatter my reverie. I would like to bask in this light always. It is somehow soft and yet bright, casting a warm glow though it is cool to the touch, and it brings gentle comfort as it illuminates the darkness. I can't fault Liza for wanting some for herself. I would like a jar to call my own as well.

I would never tell Mr. Mills that she has pinched some Lumi-Nite from the factory. But I wonder what Mother would say. This is a secret I will keep to myself...for now.

As I am now paid for my painting, Mother is taking in less laundry than before. I strive so that our little family may no longer engage in such work. One might expect Charlotte to be grateful, but something troubles her. She has always been a sweet girl, yet she's become moody, retreating to her room and her writing whenever she has the chance. I should shower her with extra affection now that I am so often away from home. She has always looked to me, more than Liza, for guidance and support. I see in Charlotte the glimmer of great things to come, Walter, and consider it my duty and my privilege to give her all that she requires to achieve them.

Know that I work to make you as proud of me as I am of you. That no matter how dreary or despairing my days, there is one thought that ever brings a smile to my face: your safe return.

Love,
Lydia

CHAPTER 9

It should've been simple. I mean, we'd very clearly agreed that Lauren would text me on Thursday morning when she got up, and we'd search for more glowing paintings. Not that I really needed her input—I had already googled every consignment and secondhand store within fifty miles and plotted them on a map, using colored pencils and India ink to mark each one. I already knew where we were headed, just as soon as Lauren got up. So I waited. And waited. And waited for her text.

But it didn't come.

While I waited, I sat down to paint. The night before, I had started a brand-new canvas. Acrylics, quick to dry and easy to clean, were the obvious choice for the next stage of my glow-paint experiment. A sandy shore, speckled with gold, a twilight of indigo and amethyst, rose-tinged wisps of cloud in the sky. Real sand was more beige, but I wasn't interested in realism right now. I wanted to paint a candy-colored romance, something bright and sweet and irresistible. The special glow-in-the-dark paint I'd ordered would arrive any day now. When it did, I wanted to be ready for it.

Lost in my art, the morning slipped away from me until I suddenly glanced at the clock and realized it was lunchtime—and I still hadn't heard from Lauren. She'd left me no choice but to set off on my little expedition without her. I shrugged off the twinge of guilt by reminding myself that I didn't have the luxury of wasting my day while Lauren slept in. And foraging for paintings all by myself was definitely faster. I went straight to the art section in each store and left immediately if I didn't find anything.

The first two stops were wastes of my time—worse than wastes, because they brewed a new worry in me: that there were no more paintings, that I'd missed the chance to buy the ones that Andrea had told me about. *This is hopeless,* I thought. *This is worse than searching for a needle in a haystack. They could have been sold, or maybe the person who had them changed his mind—kept them for himself—*

Stop, I told myself. *Focus. Breathe.*

My luck changed at a used bookstore, of all places, where the air was perfumed with the scent of yellowed paper and crumbling adhesive. I found exactly what I was searching for: the same simple frame, the same bold strokes. On the canvas, streamers twirled across the ceiling of a cavernous hall, where half a dozen couples danced together. The guys were in uniform and the girls had ribbons in their hair, toy soldiers waltzing with china dolls. Despite their old-fashioned clothes and high-button boots, they hardly seemed dated at all. Looking at them—the girls, especially—I got the feeling they were depictions of real people the artist must have known, or at least seen before. One girl had high cheekbones and arching brows. Her face was long and hollow like her angular body. Another girl's nose turned up just a touch, matching the joy in her grin and the crinkles of happiness around her eyes. These girls could've been my friends. I could've been painted into this scene.

Only one person wasn't dancing, a girl who hovered in the

doorway, watching, as if she was reluctant to join in. I looked for a single guy—maybe her date?—but didn't see him; I wondered if she'd gone alone. Did girls do that back then? If so, who had given her the delicate rose corsage that was twined around her wrist?

This was not a complex composition: people in the foreground, a pop of color in the streamers to catch the eye. Even so, I couldn't stop staring, wondering what would appear in the dark, on the dance floor, among all those starry-eyed couples.

There was only one way to find out.

I wasn't going to rush home to the darkness of my closet without checking for anything else from the original owner. If I could find a name, a date—*anything*—

"Anything," I repeated to the guy behind the counter. I couldn't tell if he was stoned or just terminally bored, but my presence seemed to be a major inconvenience for him. He didn't even bother to stifle his sigh as he punched a few numbers into the computer.

"This client is also selling a box," the clerk replied. "And a silver-plated brush-and-mirror set."

"Can I see them?" I asked. I tried to act chill, but inside I was all *A box! A box!* Who knew what it might contain?

But the guy shook his head. "The set sold," he replied.

"And the box?" I prompted him.

He peered at the computer and sighed again. "Still here," he said. "Hang on."

A few minutes later, he placed a wooden box on the counter. It was as plain as the paintings' frames, with no decoration except a tarnished clasp. My hands felt too big, too clumsy as I coaxed the hook out of the latch and pried open to the lid to discover...

"These are recipes," I said, flipping through the yellowed cards inside the box. "It's a recipe box."

"I said it was a box," he replied like an idiot.

I ignored him as I glanced at the cards. There was a recipe for pea soup; one for fish croquettes; one for potato bread; one for war cake, which sounded like a pitiful attempt to make the best out of a very bad situation. The pudding recipe was the most tattered of all, with enough stains to prove it had been used a lot. I turned it over in my hands, imagining a young mother, maybe not much older than me, dishing up pudding for her kids after they choked down fish croquettes and potato bread.

But that was pure speculation. They were only recipe cards, after all; there wasn't a name or a date or a single identifier on them. War cake, though...that was worth looking into. If it was a recipe from wartime, when staples like eggs and milk and sugar were rationed, that might help me narrow down the time period. I was about to take a picture with my phone when I realized it was dead. Naturally.

"I'll just get the painting," I told the guy as I put the recipe cards back in the box.

The new painting fit, barely, in the trunk of my car, and I made a mental note to start stocking some sheets or blankets so that I could start treating the paintings better than they'd been treated so far. I plugged in my phone to charge it. When it powered up, I realized that I had a ton of missed calls and texts—all from Lauren. Uh-oh.

Hey! When did you get up?

Her reply was fast.

Where have you been? I've been waiting for two hours!

I didn't notice that I'd started grinding my teeth until I caught the edge of my tongue between them. The pain was fierce and immediate, followed instantly by the tang of iron as blood seeped through my mouth. I yelped in surprise, glad there were no witnesses to such a moment of sheer stupidity.

I had to play this carefully with Lauren, who hated to be kept waiting. She practically took it as an insult.

Sorry! I didn't want to wake you up. Had to get out of my house

I was sure she'd understand that, after everything that had happened with Mom. I pushed my swollen tongue into the hollow of my cheek as I waited for the pain to subside. I kept texting, my thumbs skittering across the screen so fast that Lauren would have to wait to respond.

So I went shopping

Guess what?!?!

Found a new one!!!!!!!!

You went without me?

I frowned at the phone; it was hard to tell over text if she was really mad or not, so I decided to grovel a little. But Lauren wasn't done yet.

How could you do that? You knew I wanted to go

Please please please don't be mad. I'm sorry!

A pause. Longer than it should've been. Then, finally:

I'm getting ready for the beach.

Thought we'd go look for more paintings?

You already did that, didn't you?

Yikes. It was time to give her a call.

Lauren answered on the fifth ring. "What's up?"

"I'm soooo sorry," I said. "Don't be mad. I just…You know, stuff with my mom. I had to get out of there. And I really didn't want to wake you."

"So what's up with your mom?"

Lauren's question hung there as I squinted out the spotty window. After how careful I'd been all spring, so artfully changing the

82

subject whenever my mom came up, answering her now was a little too complicated—especially for a day so blindingly bright. I suddenly wanted to crawl into some cool, dark place and stay there, alone, for as long as it took for this day, this summer, this time in my life to pass.

"Do you still want to hang out?" I asked Lauren abruptly. "You can come over and see the painting, I guess."

There was another pause before she replied. "I'm going to the beach," she finally said. "You want to come?"

Now it was my turn to hesitate. I thought about my legs, which I hadn't shaved in four days. I thought about the double indignities of last year's bikini, which simultaneously crawled up my butt while offering way less support than any of my bras.

And I thought about the painting in the trunk of my car, and whatever secrets it would reveal in the dark.

"I can't," I replied. "I need to—"

"Okay." She cut me off. "Bye."

I stared at my phone as she hung up on me. Now I had another mess to deal with, all because—what? Because I didn't sit around all day waiting for Princess Lauren to roll out of bed? Because I didn't feel like going to her private beach club where everyone knew I didn't belong? Why did she always get to be in charge?

On the drive home, I forced myself to push Lauren from my mind and let my thoughts focus on the glow paintings and the mysterious artist behind them. LG. There were so many things I still didn't know: *Who was she? Where did she get that paint? Why was she using it? What were her secrets? What was she trying to say...and what was she trying to hide?*

And underneath them all: *How did she do it?*

By the time I got home, I didn't want to wait another minute to see the painting in the dark. I certainly wasn't going to wait for a late-summer sunset. I took the stairs two at a time. My closet wasn't huge, but it was big enough to squeeze inside with the painting. I closed my eyes, savoring all the exquisite anticipation. What, what, *what* would be revealed?

I was ready to find out.

When I opened my eyes, the blackness was all-consuming, just a thin sliver of light slipping in from under the door. I didn't need to adjust to the darkness, though, because the painting—and yes, oh yes, it was one of them—glowed like a beacon calling me to it.

I'd tried to prepare myself, but there was no way to be ready for what appeared on the canvas. In the dark, the couples had been stripped of their clothes and their skin; their skeletons gleamed, bones glowing as they danced in a fevered frenzy. What had been a charming scene, old-fashioned and romantic, was now ghastly.

And it got worse.

Because as I looked closer—and I had to look closer; I could not look away—I realized that their bones were broken. Not every bone, maybe not even most of them, but here and there—femurs and tibias, ribs and radii—I saw everything from hairline fractures to jagged compound breaks where needle-sharp shards of bone would've ripped through muscle and flesh.

If any muscle and flesh had remained.

The damage was catastrophic. And there were…there were *teeth* scattered across the dance floor. Glowing teeth, root and all, as if the skeletons had opened their mouths—perhaps to smile, perhaps to kiss—and their teeth had crumbled, tumbled to the floor.

My fingers traced the skeletons, frozen in their grotesque dances, to feel the breaks in the bones. Whenever I moved, I could feel something brush against my head, my cheek—*clothes,* I reminded myself, *not ghosts or specters or whatever.*

That's when I saw the words painted in the floorboards: *Avant la rupture, on voit les fissures.* My phone had just enough charge to translate.

Before you break, the cracks will show.

I whispered the words aloud, letting them slither into the heavy stillness pressing down on me. Until that moment, I'd nearly forgotten about my bitten tongue. Still sore, still swollen, it throbbed when I spoke. Was that the taste of blood again?

Get out of here, I told myself, flinging the door open so I could scramble into the light.

The diary I'd bought at Lost & Found was on my bedside table. I reached for it almost by instinct, still hoping that there might be something, anything, written inside it that could connect the author to the paintings. There weren't many entries, though, and they were all so short.

10 July

Tomorrow! Tomorrow! Lydia is taking me to New York City! I think I shall buy a new hat. I almost asked Lydia to buy me one in advance of our departure, but decided against it. How much better to have bought the hat myself in New York City. Not many girls here can boast of owning a hat made in New York. Besides, Lydia always picks the plainest of hats.

I turned each page slowly, methodically, until I reached the back cover. One corner of the endpaper had started to peel away from the cover, just enough to bother me. I had some acid-free glue in my desk...It would be an easy fix...

Wait.

Was there something under it?

I didn't need acid-free glue. I needed a razor blade.

As the blade sliced through the endpaper, I felt like I should apologize. It was never my intention to deface the diary, which had obviously survived for decades before it fell into my hands. I shook the book, just a gentle shake...

A thin edge of paper appeared.

My fingers weren't nimble enough to coax it out, but I was able to grasp it with a pair of tweezers. It was a letter—no, not even a letter, a note: short and sweet and deeply romantic.

ARC
482 DOVER STREET, ORANGE, NEW JERSEY

My love,

The factory is full as always, but empty without you.

I'm surrounded by time: clocks ticking, watches watching, each second an eternity, because you are not here.

I want to see your eyes.

Touch your face.

Kiss your lips.

When?

Name the time and I will be there, roses in my hands, love in my heart.

I have a very important question to ask you.

—E. M.

At last, I thought with dizzying glee. I had been stumbling blindly, grasping in the dark for a clue, a sign, *anything* besides the enormous void of my ignorance. Now I had so much—so much! Initials. Letterhead. An address!

I reached for my keys.

CHAPTER 10

December 24, 1917

Dearest Walter,

Christmas Eve, my love, and if not a joyful one, at least it is rich with promise that this wearisome war will end so that we may pick up the loose strands of our lives and weave them together once more.

I have had a bit of trouble at my job, which I'm ashamed even to admit to you. Mr. Mills isn't pleased with my work. He gave me such a dressing-down about the state of my dials that I nearly cried in front of him. With quivering voice, I asked how I might improve.

"All the numbers must have a crispness to them, and none of these bleary smudges I'm seeing on your dials, girlie."

"The paint," I said miserably. "It's too hard to work with."

"I taught you how to tip, did I not?"

"And I do tip my brushes," I said.

"Then tip them more," he snapped as if I am simple.

I am not fond of this practice! The paint is pasty and gritty, and though the taste is bland, the texture in my mouth is so unappealing.

"Might I use the little cup of water instead?" I asked.

"For what purpose? To rinse your mouth?"

"No, sir," I replied. "To rinse the brush after each numeral."

There was a long silence while he looked at me with incredulity. "Exactly how much Lumi-Nite would you like us to pour down the drain?" he finally asked.

"I'm sorry?"

"If you want to rinse your brush in water after each numeral you paint—poorly, I might add—then you might as well pour the paint directly down the drain," he said. "So I would appreciate an estimate from you as to how much paint you would like to waste."

"None, sir. I apologize."

Here, Walter, I was gravely afraid that I was to be let go, and I think my eyes cast about with great desperation, because once again Mr. Mills's voice turned kind.

"You needn't worry about consuming the paint," he said. "It's a boon to your health, is what it is. You should thank us. That same powder that makes the paint glow is used medicinally all over the world."

I nodded, remembering the advertisements that Edna had so carefully saved in her scrapbook. Since that night, I have seen signs in the druggist's window making similar claims. One would have to live in a cave to be unaware of Evr-Brite's amazing healing powers.

"And here you have a daily dose free of charge! With our compliments! We pay you for the privilege!" Mr. Mills said, his hearty laugh booming through the office. "Surely you've noticed some positive effects on your health already, Lydia?"

I wondered at this for a moment. I cannot say that I have, but I have been so reluctant to tip my brush that perhaps I haven't benefited as I might have.

"I know your sister has," he continued with a strange sort of smile.

Liza is certainly the picture of health. And now that I think on it, she looks very well lately. Her face has the luminosity of a pearlescent moon. Though she is a bit pale, that is more likely due to the grayness of winter.

"Tip more," Mr. Mills said with a finality that told me I was excused. "Practice at home. I expect to see improvement within the week."

Practice at home, Mr. Mills ordered me, but with what? This paint is unlike any I have ever used before. How should I have it at home without Liza learning that I'd snooped under her bed? But as you'll see, I figured out a solution.

After my meeting with Mr. Mills, I felt too upset to join the girls in the lunchroom, but I had no other place to go. Fortunately, by the time I arrived, Liza was commanding all the attention, reading her latest letter aloud for all to enjoy.

Oh! Perhaps I have forgotten to tell you! Liza has been writing a serviceman overseas who wears one of her watches. His name is Captain Reginald Lawson, and he is a pilot. It seems to me that the war serves as a fiery catalyst for declarations of love, inflaming passions that would otherwise burn slowly. Though they have corresponded only a few weeks, Liza and her captain already exchange an intimacy that should make her blush. If I sound annoyed, it's only because she compares her circumstances to my own. As if a flirtation of a few weeks' duration could ever compare to what you and I have! Even Charlotte is sick of the way Liza carries on, but I suspect she also wishes she were old enough for a sweetheart of her own.

That reminds me of a sorry exchange I had with Charlotte three nights ago. She slipped into my room and sat on the edge of my bed, as she used to do every night. I was glad to see her, calling her my pet and brushing her hair the way she always used to love. But after a few moments, Charlotte turned to face me with moon-shaped eyes and tremulous hope in her voice.

"Lydia, there's a factory set to open in the new year," she began. At that, I knew what she was going to say: that she wanted a job outside the home, longed for the independence of working on her own. Of course, at thirteen years old, Charlotte is not too young for factory work, but as she is the baby of the family, we have all taken special pains to coddle her. Perhaps these indulgences have gone on for too long. Anyway, as I listened to my little sister, I vowed to take her part however I could.

I soon realized I had misunderstood the purpose of our conversation.

"The factory will make masks," she continued. "For the soldiers. The special kind for use in a chemical attack."

I shuddered then to hear her words; I shudder now to write them to you. I am so afraid of these terrible poisons, concocted in chemists' labs, that blister the lungs and larynx. When you think that war cannot become more horrifying, the men in charge find a way to make it so. How can they find honor in the poisoning of soldiers? Or is honor now counted in the number of incapacitated troops?

Change is so rapid in these modern times, perhaps too rapid, I fear. Do the scientists ever pause to consider the consequences of their alchemy? Or does technological progress require the momentum of a locomotive? But these are dizzying times for us. The lab that churns out barrels of toxic mustard gas for harmful purposes is a close cousin to the lab that purifies a powder that not only makes watch dials glow, but cures cancer and holds astonishing regenerative properties. It is the way of the world, I suppose, that goodness so frequently conceals a dark side.

But I digress. As I was preparing to praise Charlotte's

91

industriousness and encourage her to get a job at the mask factory, she spoke again.

"They will only hire girls with a loved one in the war," she said all in a rush. "A husband or a brother or a sweetheart. And I have none of these."

"But why, Charlotte?" I asked, dreading her answer. "Why should that matter?"

"Because the work is so very delicate and important," she replied. "They believe a girl will show greater care if she knows the mask she makes might cover the face of a man she loves."

I stayed silent in hope Charlotte wouldn't continue the conversation, but she pressed on.

"Lydia, you could apply for work there," she said. "And then I could have your job at ARC. I know they would take you on at the factory. I know it. Your hands are so fine for such work, and considering you and Walter—"

"No, Charlotte," I said, and my voice was not as gentle as it might have been. "I will not do what you ask. I cannot."

She looked as if I had slapped her in the mouth. "Why, Lydia?" she burst out plaintively. "They won't have me! I am of no use to them! But you, you could work there, and then we would be the only ones to know that you were leaving ARC. I know that Liza would take me to meet Mr. Mills, and I am sure they would bring me on. Then I could work at ARC with Liza, and you would have a fine position at the other factory, serving the war effort."

"There are other factories," I told her. "Other factories that have no such strident eligibility requirements for their girls. I would rather see you return to school, but if what you desire is work outside this apartment, I will support you when you make your case to Mother. But I will not leave my position at ARC so that you may take it."

Her eyes were full of such reproach, Walter, that I turned away and began to tidy the bureau, hoping to signify that the conversation was over. It worked; Charlotte slipped out of my room.

What I share with you in confidence, Walter, and what Charlotte could never know, is that those masks have haunted me since I saw them in a newsreel at the picture show. In my dreams, a monstrous army marches onward, masked with unblinking fly's-eye goggles and elephantine hoses swinging in the wind that swirls poison gas around them. I wake, gasping, as if I, too, were surrounded by clouds of oily droplets in shades of decay: foul greens and browns and yellows.

I could not assume the burden of making these masks if I were the only one in the world who could do it. I cannot bear the responsibility. If I should err in my work—if my clumsy hands should misalign the filters or insert the goggle glass too loosely—the calamity that could result is more than I can bear. Surely our soldiers deserve better. I can hardly paint a watch dial to satisfy a man as oafish as Mr. Mills. Something as critical as a gas mask should be left to more capable hands than mine. That is my cowardly confession to you.

You keep so many of my secrets these days, Walter. Here is one more that I alluded to earlier. There is something between Liza and Mr. Mills. I stumbled upon them in a stairwell, locked in a tender embrace. His thick and calloused hand, pressed to her chest, held a petite bundle of mistletoe. Oh, my high-spirited sister, with the wildness and temperament of a runaway horse! What mischief has she engaged in now, and with someone so uncouth as the foreman at ARC? In our room that night, I confronted her. She gave denials, but I could tell from the hollowness of her voice that they were false. Finally, she acquiesced and asked me what I intended to do with my knowledge of the affair.

"That is not the issue," I told her. "I want to know why, Liza. Why on earth would you involve yourself with Mr. Mills?"

From the length of the silence that followed, I thought she wouldn't answer, but at last, she spoke.

"He makes me laugh," she said simply. "I know he is too coarse for your highbred sensibilities, but he makes me laugh. And he pays attention to me like no one else ever has."

"For shame," I hissed. "And you leading on that poor captain overseas!"

"Who could be writing to dozen different girls just like me!" she retorted. "Really, Lyddie, your mouth is all puckered like a prune. There's no need to age yourself just to express your contempt of me. I will live my life while I can, regardless of whether or not it pleases you."

"Or Mother," I said, just to be quarrelsome.

At last, I had Liza's attention. "You mustn't tell her, Lydia."

Now it was my turn to be silent. And in a sudden and brilliant flash, I knew exactly how to get what I needed.

"I want some of your Lumi-Nite," I told her. "The stash under your bed. I want some."

"You goose," she said, laughing. "Where do you think I got it from? Who do you think gave it to me?"

"I don't care," I said. "But give me some, and I want to know how you paint with such speed too."

"And you won't tell Mother?"

"I promise," I said. (But she never made me promise not to tell you, Walter.)

"Tip more," she said. "After every stroke."

"That much?"

"Yes."

Then Liza approached my bed. "Open your mouth," she ordered.

She peered into my mouth as if I were a thoroughbred on inspection. At last, she found what she was looking for and plunged her hand into my mouth. I twisted away from her, but she moved with me.

"Right here," she said, tapping two teeth on the lower left side of my jaw. "Tip your brush in this space between your teeth."

I must have looked at her quizzically because she grinned and pulled down her lower lip so that she looked like a baboon in the zoo. "I have it too," she said. "That same space between the teeth. It is even more effective than lip-pointing the brush."

"And how much of the Lumi-Nite?" I asked greedily. "How much of that will you give me?"

"As much as you want," Liza said with such a lack of care that I might as well have asked her for the dust beneath her bed. "I'm glad you know about it. Now I can put it to use."

"To what use?" I asked.

Then Liza, eyes shining, shut off the light. She shoved me aside in the bed and clambered in next to me, both of us huddled beneath the blankets like we were small girls again. "A mural!" she said. "A celestial nightscape across our walls and ceiling. Oh, Lyddie, wouldn't it be lovely?"

I could see it at once: our walls as plain as they have ever been by day, but in the darkness, great swirls of glowing galaxies, an endless cosmos of gentle light, and stars to shine sweetly on us while we sleep.

"I would need your help, of course," Liza continued, as if my silence was a sign of reluctance rather than wonder.

"You'll be able to get enough Lumi-Nite?" I asked. The walls, suddenly, seemed very large.

"He'll give me as much as I want," Liza replied.

95

"I want my own supply."

"For what?"

"For canvases. To paint them in the modern style."

The words tumbled out of my mouth before I understood them; it was the sort of brilliant inspiration that reveals itself wholly formed. How enchanting it would be, I thought; self-lighting artwork, and I knew with the most delicious certainty that no one has yet attempted such a thing.

"I am sure that can be arranged," Liza said.

And as we reached this agreement, the bonds of our sisterhood were strengthened as they had never been before. We have already begun to paint, starting with the ceiling over Liza's bed, of course; but I can still see it from where I lie.

So I conclude this letter, Walter, with much optimism for my own small days and nights: that they shall be filled with painting and practice, and that I—that Liza and I—will create something beautiful. In our war-weary world, beauty is in such short supply, and the growing darkness makes it hard to find the light. If every person living strove to create something beautiful, mightn't we brighten the world enough so that all could see the path to peace?

We have passed the shortest and darkest day of the year, and I take comfort knowing that from now on there will be more light—just a little, every day, and then a little more, and then a little more after that. I pray that this coming new year will bring peace. It cannot possibly bring more suffering.

In my mind's eye, this is what I see: two chairs by the fireplace, a small evergreen gleaming with strands of golden tinsel, carols playing softly on the wireless, and your hand in mine. Next year, let it be so.

All my love,

Lydia

CHAPTER 11

One urgent text and ten minutes later, I pulled up at Lauren's house. She was perched on the hood of her car with her beach bag slung over her shoulder.

"I'm sorry," I said in a big rush. "I wasn't trying to blow you off. It's my only day off for, like, a week. It was slipping away from me. I *had* to go."

She didn't say anything.

"But look," I said, holding out the note. "Look what I found! It was hidden in the diary. It has an address!"

Lauren glanced down to read the note. Since I couldn't see her eyes, there was no way to guess what she might be thinking. At last, she said, "Where?"

"Where what?"

"This address," she said. "Where is it?"

I gestured to my car. "Let's find out."

"Now?" Lauren asked. "You want to just…go there?"

"Why not?" I said. "Please come with me, Laure. You can go to the beach any day. But this is really…I think it's really important!"

Her eyes shifted back and forth a little as she weighed her options.

Then she gazed warily at the sun. "It *is* getting kind of late for the beach," she finally said.

"Come on!" I said, jangling the keys in my hand.

"In your car?" She shook her head. "Let's just take mine."

"I can drive," I offered.

"But wouldn't you rather go in mine?"

What could I say to that? Sorry, Lauren, that I'm too poor to drive anything nicer? Sorry that you're too good to go anywhere in my car?

I locked up my hatchback and climbed into the passenger seat of Lauren's SUV, wondering where the GPS would lead us. A mansion or an apartment building? A factory or an office complex? Or, worst of all, a parking lot, a place where history had been paved over like it had never even happened?

This part of Orange was not like West Orange, not even close. There were no overpriced boutiques here, no sidewalks washed daily, no perfectly manicured trees. From the passenger seat, I saw twenty-four-hour day cares and check-cashing joints. I saw weeds proving their dominance over cracked concrete. I saw barred windows and graffitied bricks. We were getting closer—and closer—

"It should be on the right," I said.

Lauren pulled over to parallel park, which was easy since there were hardly any cars on the street. I tried to pretend that wasn't a bad sign.

"Jules," she said. "Where *are* we?"

"I'm not sure," I admitted. "Let's take a closer look."

I could tell she didn't want to get out of the car, but I pushed ahead anyway. A tall chain-link fence surrounded a large brick building, two stories tall, with walls and walls of windows and a clock tower that had clearly stopped ticking long ago. Even from a distance, two things were clear: its function was industrial, and it was deserted.

"What do you think that building was used for?" I asked Lauren. "A factory, maybe?"

"I have no idea," she replied.

"I'm going in."

"Are you nuts?" she asked. "What about the fence?"

I shrugged. "I've climbed fences before."

"Julie! That was back in fifth grade!" Lauren exclaimed. "This is trespassing. You don't even know what's in there. It could be a gang headquarters or...or...a colony of homeless druggies."

I shot her a look. "Don't be like that. It's obviously abandoned. And if it's not, we'll come right back."

"We?" she repeated incredulously. "Oh no. No, no, no. You could not pay me money to go in there."

"Good, because I'm broke," I said. Then I slipped my toes into one of the holes in the fence. As I hoisted myself up, I felt like Cinderella. The hollow place in the fence fit my foot perfectly.

Lauren grabbed my ankle. "Please," she said. "Please don't do this. I'm really nervous."

"I'll be five minutes," I replied, wriggling free and scaling the fence before she could hold me back again.

"What am I supposed to do?" Lauren asked with a pout.

"Be a lookout?" I suggested. "Text me if there's anything sketchy I should know about."

That suggestion only made her face more pinched. "Be quick, okay?"

"I will," I promised.

I flung my legs over the top of the fence, then dropped onto the dry dirt on the other side. I was completely exposed as I hurried over to the building. Anyone who gave even a passing glance would know that I definitely didn't belong here. The doors were chained shut, and that might've been the end of it except for the windows. More than a few of them were broken, the frames a gaping, glassless portal that was plenty big enough for me to climb through. At first, I just peeked inside. There was a thick layer of dust on everything— and I mean everything—which made it immediately obvious that no one was around. I couldn't even see mouse tracks.

I glanced over my shoulder at Lauren, who was staring at her phone. She wouldn't notice if I slipped inside for a minute or two. I barely had to duck my head to clear the window frame.

I had every intention of staying objective—until I found myself in a large, open room, where the air itself seemed enchanted. Miniscule particles drifted on unseen currents, glittering in the late-afternoon sun that streamed through the windows. I could swoop my hand through the air, and they would dance in response: fairy dust, gold motes, snippets of stars swirling in a microscopic universe. When I stepped forward, they parted for me, opening a path even as they helped to fill the emptiness of the room.

There wasn't much to see besides long tables that had been bolted to the floor, too cumbersome or inconvenient to steal, I guess. Had there once been chairs? Benches? Rickety stools perched on too-tall legs? Even the overhead lights were gone. Only a tangle of dead wires remained, looming in the rafters like a nest of snakes.

This must have been a factory, I thought, looking at the tables and all that dust. The wires overhead meant this place had electricity, but there were no signs of machinery. Maybe the work that happened here was done by hand, tasks too delicate for machines that were just as likely to mangle flesh as metal.

All that light, though—those enormous windows and the artificial illumination overhead. It was the perfect place to create art. I stood at one of the long tables and imagined myself here with an easel and palette. I was about to write my initials in the dust on the table when I thought better of it. Instead, I made the letters *L* and *G*. "Were you here?" I whispered into the emptiness.

If so, she'd left no trace.

Crumbling stairs in the corner had once led to the second floor, but the wooden planks had since rotted to splintery weakness. That ruled out a trip upstairs—but there was a door on the other side of the room, and I could think of no reason why I shouldn't open it.

I reached for the tarnished handle and eased open the door. Without the bank of floor-to-ceiling windows, it was considerably darker inside the little room, but there was just enough light that I could see rows of hooks lining the wall and several midsize cupboards, their doors dangling from rusted hinges. Unlike in the open, ethereal workroom, the air in here was close and confining. It wasn't just the battered cupboards that left me feeling claustrophobic. There was a deeper sense of something…*bad*. A thing that could not be spoken or known, just sensed in ways that were both intuitive and untrustworthy.

What happened here? I wondered.

I had no proof that something had gone wrong. There was nothing overt to make me feel so alarmed. So I steadied myself and continued to observe. A long bench, bolted to the floor just like the tables, ran through the middle of the room. Against the wall stood a tiny sink with a splotched mirror hanging over it. Was this a storage room—or maybe a break room?

My footsteps made no noise as I explored the room, peeking into each compartment. Nothing had been left behind, of course—or if it had, it was looted long ago—but it would've been stupid not to check. I tried to imagine what it would've been like to work here, how I would've walked into this room every morning.

Here's where I would hang my coat, I thought. *And here's where I would stash my bag.* I crossed the room to the sink. *And here's where I would wash my hands.*

I reached for the faucet handle, which was cold in my hand as I tried to turn it. I didn't expect anything to happen when suddenly a tremor rushed through the pipes, followed by a rattling howl deep within the walls. A spurt of brown sludge burst from the tap, startling me so much that I jumped—

And glimpsed a glowing face watching me from the mirror.

I would've screamed, but shock closed my throat. I would've run, but terror froze my legs. The seconds were impenetrable—that *face,* her eyes wide with fear, her features incandescent as they cast haunting shadows over the rest of her—

Then, in a jolt of understanding, I recognized that face.

The girl in the mirror was me.

I laughed, a loud bark of relief and embarrassment, and so did my reflection. *This is what happens when you stop being objective,* I scolded myself. But a smaller, stronger part of me disagreed. Losing my objectivity, even for the briefest of moments, made it personal. Made it real. Now I knew—I *knew*—they were all connected: the paintings and the diary and the love note and this old, hollow place that was both empty and full, reverberating with history and memory and secrets I was determined to learn.

"Lauren!" I yelled as I ran out of the factory. "Lauren!"

"Julie!" she screamed.

"It *is* connected!" I cried as I started climbing the fence. "I went in…and I saw…What? What's wrong?"

Lauren's face was streaked with tears. "You have been gone for an hour!" she said, punctuating each word with an exclamation point of outrage. "I didn't know what to do!"

I shook my head. "No way," I said. "Maybe ten minutes. Fifteen, at the most."

In response, Lauren thrust her phone in my face.

One glance at the time proved that she was right.

"I—I have no idea how that happened," I stammered. "It only felt like a few minutes. Why didn't you text me?"

"I did. Like a hundred times," she said.

"I forgot to even check! I'm so sorry," I said, so heartfelt that Lauren's face softened, anger morphing into disapproval. With a critical frown, she reached over and ruffled my hair.

"You are *filthy*," she said, but I didn't take offense. "Yuck. What were you doing—rolling around in a crawl space?"

"It's just dust," I assured her. "Nobody's been in there for a long time. But listen, it's definitely the right place. That dust, Lauren… It glows! It has to be connected to the paintings. I mean, what are the odds?"

"I don't know," she replied. "Maybe you can calculate them while you clean up. Let's go. It's getting dark."

As we trudged back to her car, we saw the sign at the same time.
WARNING: HAZARDOUS MATERIALS PRESENT. NO TRESPASSING.

I swallowed, and my skin started to itch, as if each individual speck of dust was vibrating. "How did we miss that?" I asked.

"I have no idea," she replied. "Did you…in there—"

"No, nothing," I cut her off. "It was just dust. I'm fine."

Neither one of us had much to say after that. I noticed Lauren kept her distance as I slapped at my clothes, my arms, my hair, trying to shake the dust off as best as I could. On the way home, I googled furiously on Lauren's phone, but none of my searches could answer the question of what exactly had been located at 482 Dover Street.

The address was one of many in New Jersey that had been slated for remediation. I wasn't entirely sure what that meant. My parents tried mediation before their divorce reached levels of epic hostility, but this seemed different.

Far more promising was the online archive of the *New Jersey Sentinel*. There were at least a dozen articles that included the address, most of them by some guy named Charles Graham.

"Okay!" I said. "Now we're getting somewhere." I tapped the first article—"Cowardly Capitalists Turn Tail and Flee to Europe"—but before it could load, a pop-up blocked the screen:

Please log in to access this article. Memberships to the *Sentinel* archives are available for $100 per year.

"Are you even kidding?" I groaned.

"What?" asked Lauren, who tried to glance at my phone. Her car swerved a bit before she overcorrected.

"You drive. I'll research," I ordered her. "I almost found something. I think. But it's behind a stupid paywall."

"Weak."

"The weakest. Why are they charging a hundred dollars for a bunch of old newspaper articles? Like, seriously, is there *that* much demand?" I asked. Then I sucked in my breath. "The library!"

"Huh?"

"I bet you a million dollars that the library has old newspapers on microfilm! Tomorrow! Let's do it," I exclaimed. "No, wait. I'm working. Damn it! But you could go. Would you go, Laure? Would you investigate? It's the *New Jersey Sentinel*...Looks like the articles are from the 1920s...You could find out what used to be there, find out what exactly was happening at that fac—"

"Okay." She cut me off. "I'll...look into it."

Was I babbling? Probably. If I talked a lot, talked nonstop so that there wasn't a pause or even a breath for doubt or fear to creep in, maybe we could both pretend that we hadn't seen that sign.

"Do you want to hang out for a while?" I asked as Lauren pulled up behind my car.

"Uh... I can't..." she replied slowly. "I think I need to help with the twins."

"Oh. Okay."

Lauren walked me to my car and stood by my window while I rolled it down. "Thanks for coming with me," I said. "If you find out anything, you'll text me immediately, right?"

"Yeah. Of course," Lauren said. "See you later, Jules."

Rolling up the window felt like raising a glass wall between us. We could still see each other through it, but that was all. I couldn't wait to get out of there. It was a stinging slap, the way Lauren clearly didn't want to hang out with me. I couldn't remember that happening before, not in the long and legendary history of our friendship. Was I too annoying to be around? Didn't she like me anymore?

As I drove away, Lauren stood on the curb, bouncing on her tiptoes with her arm held high in a motionless wave. I could see her in my rearview all the way to Park Street. It was no different from all the other times I'd driven away from her house, no different from when my mom used to drive me home, except back then Lauren used to wave really big, her long, thin arm arcing through the air. Suddenly it dawned on me. Soon that image—Lauren, grinning, waving from the curb—was something I wouldn't see anymore. She'd be living in New York, building an entirely new life for herself. Maybe she'd come home once in a while—for holidays or the occasional weekend—but why would she want to?

Lauren had been dreaming of living in the big city ever since freshman year, when we'd tried so hard to make lace knee socks happen before we finally realized that nothing new or original or interesting could happen in this town. It was so clear to me now that once Lauren was gone, there wouldn't be anything left for her here, not when the city sparkled all around her. Lauren herself had started to shine, like she was somehow already reflecting all the glittering promise of New York, and I thought, *How stupid I've been, how stupid, how didn't I notice it before?*

I was going to miss her so much, in so many small and ordinary ways. I set my teeth hard so that I wouldn't cry, grimacing at the pain in my jaw. But it was worth it, that deep ache nagging at the bone, because I honestly feared that if I ever started crying—about everything I'd lost, about everything I was losing—I might never stop.

CHAPTER 12

February 16, 1918

Dearest Walter,

What calamity has befallen us these past few weeks! You remember, I am sure, that Liza's Captain Lawson was wounded in duty shortly after the new year. Word came that he would be sent home to convalesce. It turns out his grandfather is a political figure of some renown, which might have something to do with his return. Some might think that he is lucky that a foot wound is the only price he pays to be released from his obligations to this country.

Well! Liza expressed such a range of emotions, Walter—from her despair upon learning that he had been injured, to her relief that the injury appeared minor, to her joy that he would be returning home. And then her utter thrill upon being invited to a homecoming party held in his honor at his grandparents' brownstone in New York City!

Most astonishing was Liza's sudden burst of energy upon receiving the invitation. Since the first news of Captain Lawson's injury, Liza has been wan and withdrawn, retreating to our room for a crying spell that inevitably transforms into a nap. Mother has indulged her, but sometimes I have been so cross with Liza that I've nearly snapped at her. There is always a great deal of work to do here, and one person's idleness increases the burden on the rest. Little did I know that all that was needed to restore Liza's vitality was an invitation to an elegant soiree!

"Oh, I hope there will be dancing!" Liza cried. Her eyes sparkled like sapphires, and there was a rosy glow in her cheeks that, I realized suddenly, had been absent for some time.

"Dancing?" I asked in disbelief. "Why would there be dancing to honor a man with a wounded foot?"

"I am sure there will be dancing," she replied. "And if he cannot dance, then at least he can watch!"

Mother was not especially pleased by the invitation, but of course there was no stopping Liza. It was decided that I should accompany her, which I was loath to do. Whatever the nature of this party, what reason do I have to celebrate until your return, Walter?

But I knew that I could at least remind Liza of her better judgment. Especially when I saw the modifications she'd made to her glass-green velvet gown: a swooping neckline that revealed so much of her décolletage that she fashioned a removable lace panel so that Mother could not see how exposed she would be. It would've been quite clever if it wasn't so outrageous. Oh, that brazen sister of mine!

Before we left for the train station, Liza asked me to paint jewelry across her skin in hopes that she and Captain Lawson might retire somewhere dark. She wanted to surprise him, she said, but I would have no part of it. So she sat before the mirror and did it herself: three beaded bands of increasing length around her neck, the longest one with a glowing pendant, and a lovely little heart on each earlobe. Charlotte lurked in the doorway, sorely vexed to be staying home, so Liza invited her in and painted some jewelry on her as well.

I watched Liza at the mirror with an odd combination of envy and admiration. I should never want to be so bold as Liza, but she must feel very free, and on occasion, I wish that I could be so free too.

"Minnie paints her teeth before she goes to the pictures with Ralph," Liza said. "Shall I give it a go?"

"Not for a first meeting. The jewelry you've painted is more than enough. Besides, we'll miss the train if we don't leave now."

"I wish I could go!" Charlotte exclaimed. So I told her, "Sleep in my bed tonight, Lottie, and we'll wake you up and tell you all about it the moment we return!"

When we arrived at our destination, Liza paused on the corner to remove her lace inset despite the bitter chill. Upon entering the Lawson home, though, I saw that Liza's and my best dresses were no match for the high fashion swirling around us. And I also knew that her plunging neckline was a poor choice. Along with our plainer gowns, she looked very unsophisticated, indeed, a mere girl playing dress-up in her mother's closet.

If Liza noticed any of this, she gave no indication. She simply shrugged her coat in my general direction—I had to scramble to catch it—and swept up the oaken staircase, which was polished to such a high shine that Liza's reflection in the glossy wood kept pace with her every movement.

At the top of the stairs, I took a moment to marvel at the opulence around me. It was so very elegant, Walter, with velvet drapes dripping down the walls, finely cut crystals glittering from each lamp, and the gleam of gold wherever I looked. Across from us, at the far end of the room, Captain Lawson—very sharply attired in a crisp uniform—reclined on a plush armchair, looking none too pleased to be part of the festivities. A quartet was playing a pretty melody in the corner, and a small number of people were dancing. My last thought, before it happened, was: Liza was right about the dancing.

She stepped into the room, with her head high as could be and a toss of her curls so that they might catch the light. And then she fell—oh! so terribly undignified, Walter!—poor Liza, a crumpled and ungainly heap on the floor, with all those eyes fixed upon her.

It looked like a clumsy misstep but was far more serious. I think what I will remember most is not the ashen shock on Liza's face, but the sound of the bone as it shattered. Of all the breakable things in this world, how many people have heard the sound of a bone? Have you heard such sounds in your duty, Walter?

To me, it registered somewhere between a distant crack of thunder and a branch breaking under the weight of wet snow, a sound that was sudden and over as quickly as it had begun, a sound that was not too terribly loud and yet was horrible to hear because it resonated through my body, as if my own bones understood what had happened and clenched in sympathy.

I rushed to Liza, of course, as did all those people in their fine clothes. Even Captain Lawson hobbled to her side with a cane. That this should be their first meeting! It was endearing, I must say, Liza looking up at him with tears sparkling on her lashes, and the concern writ on his face. I could tell at once that he had surrendered to her charms.

Captain Lawson is quite a bit older than I had assumed, probably close to Mother's age, with the wrinkles to prove it. He was so attentive to Liza, who was in such a great deal of pain that I doubt she noticed the odor wafting faintly from his injured foot, a sweetish stench of decay. I would not say it to Liza, but I doubt he can keep that foot for much longer.

Liza was very brave, Walter, and the picture of quiet suffering while we waited for a doctor. I tried to stay in the hall, feigning great interest in a series of antique family portraits, so that she and Captain Lawson might have a few private moments in which to become better acquainted. The doctor soon arrived and gave Liza a strong dose of morphine, which lessened the pain etched into her face, but did nothing to relieve its spectral whiteness.

Her leg was stabilized with a splint, and after Liza and Captain Lawson's tender parting, his driver brought us home in a fine automobile. There was great dreaminess in Liza's eyes for the whole ride home, due in no small part to the morphine, I am sure, but I know Liza. She was making plans. Even in that addled, pain-racked state, Liza was scheming to further her ambitions.

As for me, I was preoccupied during our ride with dread thoughts of the doctor's bill, as well as the great burden on me alone now that Liza will not be able to work until her leg has healed.

There was, of course, quite the commotion upon our return home. I did not remember to remove Liza's painted jewelry before we arrived, and so in the dim light, as Mother and I undressed her, the telltale glow was revealed. In her stupor, Liza was not aware of the high disapproval of Mother's gaze, but I certainly was, especially when her ire was turned on me. As if I might have persuaded Liza from offering up such a spectacle. Well! We both know that thought is a folly!

And so I did not have the opportunity to pay much attention to Charlotte. Otherwise I might have noticed that she too, was making plans. In the morning, I found her waiting at my door, dressed in her best outfit, wearing the same Sunday hat Liza made me wear to the factory for my very first visit. She had fixed a new ribbon to it—a thick band of garnet-colored satin—and I had to wonder how late Charlotte had toiled to accomplish this. The hat did look very handsome.

"Lydia, you'll take me to the factory, won't you?" Charlotte said urgently. "No one else knows about Liza yet. Surely I'll have first crack at her position—not to keep, just to hold for her!"

Smart little Charlotte! I thought as I gave her my warmest smile. Of course there was no reason why we should not attempt to secure Liza's position until she could return to it. Though I do wish that Charlotte could return to school instead. I want for her an expansive life, one filled with adventures that take her far beyond the modest walls of this apartment. When we took a leave of absence from school after Father's death, it was never meant to be permanent, though I suppose it's only practical to delay Charlotte's return a little longer, given what happened to Liza.

For all of our morning walk to the factory, which was frosty because the sun rose yet failed to offer even a modicum of warmth, I marveled at my little sister. Charlotte had her heart set on a dial-painting position, and through a combination of good fortune and assertiveness, she was about to get precisely what she wanted. There is a lesson to be found in that, I am sure.

The other girls streaming through the factory gates regarded us curiously, no doubt wondering why Charlotte had taken Liza's place by my side. Mr. Mills also looked upon Charlotte and me with suspicion, and I said to him in a low voice, "Might we have a word in your office, Mr. Mills?" He complied at once. I think Liza must have told him about what I saw transpire between them, because he now treats me with the utmost respect, using the manners of a perfect gentleman.

In Mr. Mills's office, I explained—as simply as I could and without undue embellishment—the details of Liza's injury. I watched him closely throughout my speech, and, Walter, I think he has genuine feelings for Liza! I was almost embarrassed for him, but that I knew Charlotte would never notice. After I assured Mr. Mills that Liza would make a full recovery, I explained to him that we all—Liza, especially—hoped that Charlotte may hold the position for her. Given Mr. Mills's affection for Liza, he was, of course, immediately amenable to our plan. And little Charlotte played her part exceedingly well, looking up at him with such especially large eyes all shining with hope, and her tiny hands fluttered birdlike with excitement when he acquiesced.

Perhaps Charlotte is not as young as I thought.

Well. She is the youngest of all the dial-painters, and so instantly became the pet of all the girls. There was a great outpouring of support and encouragement, in which Charlotte basked like an eager puppy. She was quite the center of attention, and to be honest, I was surprised by how much she enjoyed it. Charlotte now has no shortage of "big sisters" to advise her in all that she does.

Shortly before the end of the day, Mr. Mills called me into his office. I was concerned, of course, because I thought my painting had improved, and I feared that he had found new fault with me. However, I soon discerned that I was wrong in my assumptions about the nature of our meeting. He wasted no time on pleasantries.

"I should like regular reports on how Liza fares," he said with his customary bluntness.

"Yes, sir," I replied.

Then he paused, as if unsure of himself.

"I should...I should like to see her."

Walter, I could hardly conceal my surprise! Imagine Mr. Mills calling on Liza like a suitor, and she confined to her bed, wearing her nightclothes. Oh, Walter, Mother would never allow it, and even if she did, what would everyone think? A factory foreman paying a visit to Liza during her convalescence? There would be no doubt in anyone's mind that they had come to a particular understanding, and I knew that Liza had no interest in such a thing…especially not after her visit to New York.

"That will not be possible," I told him—oh, so rashly, before I quite comprehended the earnestness in his expression. The way his face fell, Walter, and the light in his eyes darkened. I continued with more care. "Not when she is in such great pain."

He seemed genuinely distraught to think of Liza suffering.

"Of course, I could relay a message to her," I told him.

He nodded without speaking and sat at his desk, where he wrote a short note. Then Mr. Mills opened a drawer and removed a large jar of Lumi-Nite powder. He proceeded to spoon some into a smaller vessel.

"When she is well enough to paint, she may enjoy this," he said as he pressed it into my hands.

"Thank you," I said. "I will see that she receives your letter as soon as I return."

Charlotte and I hurried home that evening, both anxious to see how Liza fared. We did not expect to find her in a terrible temper. Before we even had a chance to explain that Charlotte would hold the position at ARC until Liza could return, she flung out an accusatory arm and pointed at the ceiling.

"What right did you have?" she cried. "I wanted to finish it myself!"

I looked where Liza pointed and noticed, for the first time, that our celestial mural was complete. I turned to Charlotte in surprise. "You did this?" I asked.

Charlotte nodded, dumbstruck. "L-last night," she stammered. "I—I…You've both been working so hard, and I—I—"

"Out with it!" Liza snapped.

"I missed you!" Charlotte exclaimed. "All you do is paint. I thought if I finished the mural while you were at the party, you wouldn't have to spend all your time holed up in here."

I hugged my sweet little sister, who'd been made so lonesome by our preoccupation with the paint. "You should have asked, Lottie," I said gently. Then I turned to Liza. "Be glad of the favor she did for you because you won't be able to climb a ladder and paint the ceiling for weeks to come."

But Liza would not be placated. "I still wanted to do it myself," she grumbled. "And it's poorly done besides."

I wrapped my arm around Charlotte protectively. "I think it looks fine," I said firmly—though in truth, Charlotte's talents have always been literary, not artistic, much to her dismay.

Rather than close this letter on such a bleak note, I can share that I've made great progress at the factory, though it is due less to my many hours of practice than to the secret tricks Liza shared with me. Even when I sleep, my fingers curl toward my thumb as if clutching an invisible paintbrush, so much have I painted in these last weeks. I find that I grow accustomed to the taste and texture of the Lumi-Nite paint and mind it less than I used to, and I feel its effects on my general state of health, as Mr. Mills promised I would. Even Mother remarked on how well I am looking these days! Hurry home, my dear Walter, so that you may see for yourself. I count the days until your return, not knowing their number, but knowing as surely as I know anything that this terrible absence, like this terrible war, must in time come to an end.

All my love, always,

Lydia

PS: Did you, perhaps, venture to read my last letter in the dark? If not, please do so. More than that I will not tell you, for I should hate to ruin the surprise.

CHAPTER 13

Picture me like this: pupils dilated, shoulders hunched, paintbrush in hand, a nocturnal creature doing what can only be done in the dark. The sole light in my room came from the jar of glowing paint that had finally arrived. We'd met up at a pivotal moment, the paint, my painting, and me. What I did next would either solve the mystery of how LG made her paintings or ruin one of my own.

It had been days since we'd been to the factory, and to my extreme annoyance, Lauren still hadn't managed to find out a single thing about it. If I wasn't pulling doubles every day, I would've gone to the library myself, but budget cuts forced the library to close early during the summer. Lauren kept promising she'd check it out soon—and short of losing a day's pay, I had no choice but to believe her.

Whenever I had an evening off, I continued searching thrift stores for paintings. The latest one I'd found was propped against the wall over my desk. Dozens of stars gleamed over a lonesome landscape where nothing grew, not even scrubby pines or brambly tumbleweeds or those determined dandelions that will bury us all. When the lights were out, the stars started falling, except they weren't stars anymore. They were glowing teeth—molars and incisors and canines and cuspids—plummeting through the sky, planting themselves in the dirt so that they became tombstones with roots, covered with creeping vines and worm-eaten roses. I'd already looked up the French, *Rien de bon peut en résulter,* a more ominous message than usual: *Nothing good can come from this.*

But sitting there with a paintbrush in my hand, I had to disagree. I was getting closer every day. It was only a matter of time before I knew the truth.

I took a deep breath, dipped my brush in the glowing paint, and dabbed it on with quick, sure strokes, until two people magically appeared on the canvas, holding each other like they'd never let go. It was tricky to paint them entwined using only the glow paint; I relied on the power of empty space to reveal their arms, legs, heads. Hands. The paint I'd bought was some of the strongest stuff available, and it was worth every penny. They glowed beautifully. Brilliantly.

Then I snapped on the light…and realized that they were still completely visible.

"Damn it," I whispered, before shaking off my frustration. There was no reason to be discouraged; this was a misstep in the right direction, a failure that surely pushed me closer to success. I knew now, without a doubt, that the only solution would be to paint the glowing image first, then layer a background on top of it. That must have been how LG had done it so long ago.

Which meant that I was going to need stronger paint.

Success or failure would all depend on the particle size, I figured. Too large, and the paint would glow just the way I wanted—but it would be visible even under a thick coat of oil. Too small, and the layer of glowing paint would disappear completely.

Firecracker inspiration struck in the form of an explosive idea:

what if I made my own glow-in-the-dark paint? I could do my own little combinatorial chemistry experiments, adjusting the particle size, the binder, even the amount of catalyst. Everything! With that kind of control, I was sure that I could figure out LG's technique. That was all it took for me to abandon my artwork for my laptop.

After some research, I decided that I wouldn't waste my time with the old zinc sulfate and copper formulas. No, strontium nitrate with a europium catalyst would be way more powerful. There were premixed powders that I could buy online, but I had a better idea. It didn't take long to find his email listed on the Newark University website.

> Hey Luke,
> So this is probably going to sound kind of weird, but I was wondering if you could do me a big favor. Can you hook me up with some strontium nitrate and a little bit of europium and a couple other compounds? I'm working on this art project, and I want to make my own glow-in-the-dark paint. Anyway, let me know if you have any in the lab or if you can order it. Without some special license, I can't get it on my own. (Like strontium nitrate is dangerous, right? Ridiculous.)
> Thanks,
> Julie

As an afterthought, I included the formula and the website where I'd found it.

He responded in minutes.

J—

Glad you clarified re: strontium *nitrate*, otherwise I might've worried that you were concocting something nefarious. Some of strontium's isotopes are not quite so benign, as I'm sure you know.

Short answer, yes, I can "hook you up." You know where to find me.

L

I'm on my way.
Julie

*   *   *

Luke swung open the door to the lab before I had a chance to knock, like he'd been watching for me.

"And here you are," he said. "Come in."

"Thank you so much," I said right away. "Seriously, thank you. This is so huge."

Luke shrugged like it was no big deal, but I could tell he was pleased. "Actually, this sounds kind of fun," he replied. "I haven't done combustion synthesis in a while."

"Combustion?" I repeated.

"Oh, yeah. Let's go blow stuff up."

After we put on goggles, Luke led me past his usual workstation to the back of the lab. The hood there was entirely sealed, with two openings attached to long, rubbery gloves.

"I checked out the site you sent," Luke said. "This seems like a pretty straightforward reaction. You could just wear gloves, but I thought it would be better to use the glove box."

"Why? Is it dangerous?"

"It could be," he replied. "If you were careless or stupid. But you're not. Anyway, I've set up everything you'll need…You've got your strontium nitrate, your europium nitrate, your aluminum nitrate, a beaker of distilled water…The other materials are in the back. There's an analytical balance in there too. You'll want precise measurements, of course."

"Of course," I said. I already felt like I was in way over my head. "So I just…" I gestured toward the openings of the glove box.

"Yeah, by all means, go ahead," Luke replied. "Do you mind if I hang out?"

"Sure," I said, relief flooding my voice. "I mean, if you don't have anything better to do."

"No, I'm happy to assist," he said. The thought of *Luke* assisting *me* in an experiment was hilarious, but to his credit, he didn't laugh at all.

Be cool. I tried to psych myself up. *You've got this. It's just like chem lab, but with way better equipment. Equipment that costs more than your car. No. Stop. Be cool. And don't break anything.*

I took a deep breath and plunged my arms into the gloves. It was the weirdest feeling, my hands all clumsy and thick, like I was wearing a space suit or something. I was only distracted for a moment when Luke moved toward the glove box. I'm sure he was just trying to get a better look at the scale, but he was standing so close that there wasn't more than a fraction of air circulating in the space between us. Then I forced myself to focus on the experiment. As I started measuring the compounds, I realized that I was right: It really was like AP chem.

Measuring such minute amounts of rare-earth metals took a while, but eventually I was ready to dissolve the compounds in the distilled water. The water turned cloudy as I swirled and swirled it until there was no trace of the solids.

"Okay," I finally said. "I think it's good."

"Excellent," Luke replied. "Let's blow it up."

He removed the sample as I pulled my arms out of the gloves. My palms were crazy sweaty. I tried to wipe them off on my shorts without him noticing.

"You're not really going to blow it up, are you?"

"Just a little," Luke said with a grin as he slid open the glass panel to a fume hood.

"Is that a…microwave?" I asked.

Luke nodded. "Yeah. It's slightly more sophisticated than the kind you'd use to heat up a frozen dinner, but they both operate on the same basic technology. Not that you'd want to put food in here. It's full of contaminates."

Luke carefully placed the sample in the microwave, set the timer, and said, "Stand back."

I watched the timer run down, second by second, waiting. Luke was so chill about it, but I was twitchy with expectation. Then tendrils of smoke started unfurling through the fume hood.

"Is that supposed to happen?" I asked.

"Not to worry," Luke replied. His eyes never left the microwave. "The hood's got exterior ventilation."

Suddenly, there was a series of insanely bright flashes in rapid succession, explosions in miniature: combustion synthesis. I was expecting it, but I flinched all the same. A few seconds later, the microwave beeped. The reaction was complete.

Luke pulled up the glass panel of the hood and opened the door of the microwave. The clear liquid in the beaker had transformed into a crystallized mass, or perhaps I should say a crystallized mess. It looked like a clump of dirty snow that had been flung from the treads of a plow. I have to admit I was disappointed. But Luke seemed pretty pleased.

"Nice," he said, nodding in approval.

"Is it…it doesn't…It's not really what I expected."

"Really?" he asked. "What did you expect?"

"I don't know," I said, stalling. If he didn't see what was missing—the mysterious glow, the otherworldly strangeness—how could I explain it to him?

But maybe I was wrong. Maybe he did understand. I thought his voice was reassuring as he said, "You'll want to let that cool before you touch it. Then…what are you thinking?"

"Crush it, I guess. Into a powder that I can mix into some paint. And…is it okay if I make a couple more samples? I was thinking I'd play around with the proportions, maybe use a little more europium…"

"Absolutely. Go right ahead," Luke said. "Holler if you need anything."

I spent the next two hours mixing my samples and keeping careful notes about the amounts of compounds used in each one. When they were finally cool enough to touch, I brought them over to Luke's workstation, where his samples were bubbling away in an oil bath. He slid a mortar and pestle toward me, then watched as I started grinding the first sample into a fine powder.

"You must be one hell of an artist," he said suddenly.

I looked over at him, surprised. "What?"

"The fact that you're even entertaining another field when it's so obvious how much you love science…and how good you are at it…" he continued. "So where *are* you going to college?"

I shifted the pestle to my left hand and shrugged. I was running out of ways to dodge this conversation.

"Oh my God," Luke said. "You're still in high school."

"No!" I exclaimed. "No, no. I graduated. In May."

His look was piercing. There was nothing to do but tell him the truth.

"The thing is...I'm not actually going to college. I mean, I got in, I just...It wasn't..."

"What?"

"It's so boring to talk about. It's completely not interesting."

"I'm interested."

I looked up and met his eyes. There was no judgment there and, best of all, no pity.

"My mom got into debt, and she couldn't find a job, and the bank was going to foreclose on our house," I said. I didn't know why my voice was practically a whisper or why I felt like I was spilling a big, shameful secret. I hadn't done anything wrong. "So I cashed out my college savings account and used it to pay off the mortgage."

"Your mom couldn't sell it?" he asked quietly. "The house?"

I shook my head. "No. There weren't any offers, and the bank wasn't...wasn't going to wait any longer..."

"The real estate market," Luke said, nodding like everything suddenly made sense. "I've heard it was bad."

We were silent for a long moment. Then Luke leaned back in his chair and said, "Wow."

"No."

"Yes. Wow. That was an amazingly generous thing you did. So where were you going to go?"

"I hadn't decided, actually. Either New York University for pre-med, or Parsons for art."

"Those are some great schools. Pretty expensive, though."

"I know. But I'll get there eventually. I'm working two jobs right now. It'll take me a couple years to save enough—"

"And I'm sure you can get scholarships. And loans."

"Nope. No loans," I said, shaking my head vehemently. I'd seen what debt had done to my mother.

Luke's forehead furrowed. "So…you're planning to fund a private school education through part-time jobs?" he asked. "That would mean working…eight thousand hours a year for each year of college? Twenty hours a day, every single day of the year?"

I wished he would look somewhere else. I didn't know how much longer I could take the intensity of his gaze. "I don't know. I haven't done the math."

"*You* haven't done the math?"

"What is this?" I asked, anger creeping into my voice. "Why do you care?"

"Don't get mad," Luke said gently. "I'm just trying to understand. The in-state tuition here is so much less…Did you consider Newark University? Or one of the other state schools?"

I leaned down to scratch a mosquito bite on my ankle…or maybe just to hide for a moment. "So what about you? Why did you come here?"

Luke seemed like the kind of person who would keep pushing and pushing, mining for information until he learned every last thing he wanted to know, but he let me change the subject just like that.

"I have this younger brother, Liam," Luke began. "Half-brother, technically, but who cares? He's ten, and he is amazing. I mean, with a little support, that kid is going to do great things. And I just thought it would be best to…you know, stick around. In case he needs anything. Stability is, uh…it's important. I think it is, anyway."

"So he lives nearby? With your mom?"

124

"Well, he's actually spending the summer with his dad in Montana," Luke said. "And my mom..."

"What?"

Luke closed his eyes for a fraction of a second, and his whole face drooped a little. If I hadn't been watching him so closely, I might not have noticed. "She left last month," he said. "For France. The lease on her apartment was up, and instead of renewing it, she left."

My jaw dropped. "Is she coming back?"

He shrugged. "Yes. No. Maybe. Who knows? Apparently, she is searching for my dad. Who she hasn't seen in twenty-three years. Who I've never met."

"And if she doesn't come back?" I asked. "What happens to your brother?"

"He stays in Montana, I guess."

"So you chose Newark University to be close to your brother, but he might end up living thousands of miles away?"

"That about sums it up."

"Luke, that's awful," I said. "I'm so sorry. And to be stuck here for no reason..."

Luke shot me a look. "Stuck here?" he repeated. "I wouldn't go that far."

"I just—"

"This is a fine school. Yeah, maybe it's not fancy, and maybe the dorms are legendarily awful, but anybody who goes here will get out of it exactly what they put in. If you want to party and take a bunch of easy classes and mess around, then no, you won't learn that much. But if you work hard...if you take the tough classes...and you *want* it...you *want* to learn...you can get as good an education here as anywhere."

I felt like an idiot. "I know that," I said. "You totally misunderstood.

I just meant…I mean, obviously you made a big decision about your life so you could be near your brother, and I think it really sucks if he ends up in Montana now. That's all I meant. I—"

Abruptly, I stopped. I had different dreams, that was all, and they didn't include Newark University. It was that simple. I didn't need to apologize or explain myself. If Luke thought that made me a judgmental jerk, that was his opinion.

"Yeah, well…" Luke leaned down to check the thermometer in one of his samples. "My family's always been pretty unstable. Too many electrons, not enough protons, if you know what I mean."

I tried to smile. "So you guys are all negatively charged? Or do you just generally repel each other?"

"You can't keep people together if they don't want to be together."

"No. You can't." I realized that I'd been grinding the last sample for several minutes. "This must be ready."

Luke stood up pretty fast. "I'll walk you to your car."

"Oh. Thanks," I said as I picked up my bag. I would've stayed longer. I, well, wanted to stay longer. But Luke was already halfway to the door.

We didn't say much as we walked across the campus. There were about ten cars scattered throughout the parking lot, and I wondered which one had Luke's entire life packed in it.

"Good luck with your project," Luke said when we reached my car. "Maybe I'll see you around sometime."

I hope so, I thought. But I didn't say it. Instead, I smiled up at him and said, "Thanks again for your help."

He stepped away from the car and sort of waved before trudging back to the lab in the beam of my headlights. I was all buckled in, with the powder we'd made nestled in the seat next to me. I was leaving with everything I'd come for, and yet I couldn't shake the feeling that something was missing. I was as dissatisfied with what I'd said as with what I hadn't. I wanted to run after him and say, *But I'm really not a snob.*

And, *It must be a good school; you go here.*

And, *My family is all electrons too.*

The farther he walked, the more ridiculous it would be to follow him, but I still struggled with the impulse. There was something unfinished between us, and it couldn't wait until a nebulous "sometime," whenever that might be. At least, I couldn't, but the way we'd parted made me think I was running out of reasons to see him. By the time I got home, I was sure that Luke was so over hanging out with someone as stuck-up and immature as me.

Then I checked my email.

J,

I forgot to say—please let me know about the powder.

I hope it works.

L

CHAPTER 14

Dear Walter,

Your mother called on us last week and brought a cake for Liza. We were all very glad for her visit, as Liza's convalescence has not been as quick or easy as we might have hoped. She is often in a foul mood from a gnawing pain in her leg that should have receded by now. Instead, it has become transient, migrating from her leg to her hip to her other hip and then back again. Sometimes her hip seizes— no, it is more than that; it seems to lock in place and will not be coaxed into any other position, making Liza quite immobile. When this happens, she scarcely speaks. Her silence is a greater testimonial to her suffering than any words could be.

Liza also complains of a steady ache in her jaw, but if she is to see the dentist, we must orchestrate her transfer down three flights of stairs with one of her legs entirely incapacitated, and Liza assured us many a time that the ache is not so troublesome that we must summon a dentist to her bedside. This was, we now know, a mistake.

We all do our utmost to keep Liza's morale high. Of course it is tedious to spend all of one's hours in bed. The girls from the factory have been so good, visiting her on a schedule of sorts so that she might have companionship most evenings. Even before their arrival, Liza is in high spirits, brushing her hair so that it gleams and rouging her cheeks. She has a fine hand for such applications. I would never know that their rosiness is artificial if I wasn't the one to wipe them clean at bedtime. With her visitors, Liza puts on a grand show. Her laughter fills the rooms of our cozy dwelling, and so it is no wonder that she is quite exhausted afterward.

She takes great pains to marginalize Charlotte during these visits, ordering her about and treating her like a young child. One terrible night, Liza even sent her away from the sitting room, cracking wise that it was past her bedtime, in front of Helen and Mary Jane. Poor Charlotte. Walter, she was ever so embarrassed. She tries hard to act older when she is around the other girls from the factory, and I know that such treatment in front of them must smart. We have all tried to be understanding with Liza, but Charlotte has run out of patience. That night—she was still awake when the girls left, of course; it wasn't even nine o'clock—Charlotte was unusually rough when we helped Liza back to bed, so that Liza's head knocked against the doorframe to our room.

"You did that on purpose!" Liza snapped at her.

Charlotte's eyes were dark. "And so what if I did?" She let go of Liza abruptly as we positioned her above the bed, so that Liza tumbled onto the blankets. I had to rush to catch Liza's leg as she fell so that it would not be further injured, and a dreadful feeling overcame me then. My two sisters were spitting like cats, and I thought: Nothing good can come from this.

"You want me in this bed," Liza hissed at her. "You want me out of your way. You're not holding the job for me; you're keeping it for yourself."

"That is quite enough from you both," I said, in hope that I could silence them. "Good night, Charlotte."

She was still scowling as she left, and so was Liza as I tucked the blankets around her.

"You must be kinder to Charlotte," I told Liza at last. "It is not her fault that you are laid up in bed."

"Well, she needn't enjoy my suffering so."

"For shame! She is your sister!" I cried. "How can you think such a thing?"

"Lyddie, I'm so weary of this!" Liza exclaimed. Two red patches that had no connection to the rouge bloomed on her cheeks. "Every day I am in pain. Every day I am so lonesome. I want my life back. Please, Lyddie, how might I get my life back?"

"Shh, shh, don't upset yourself," I said.

"Everyone has forgotten me," she continued stubbornly, as if determined to be maudlin. Her lips quivered, which might have been for show but for the tears glistening in her eyes.

"Poor Liza," I said, stroking her hair. "I know it's been utterly tedious to be ill for such a long time."

"Yes," she said sullenly, swelling her lower lip into a pout. "Yes, it has."

Then a look of panic careened across her face, and I knew something terrible had happened. "Liza, what?" I whispered. "What?"

She shook her head, hard, then covered her mouth. It took some coaxing, but at last she pulled away her hand, building a ropy bridge of bloody saliva from her mouth to her fist. In her palm lay a single tooth, glinting like a star in a nebula of blood. I plucked the tooth from Liza's hand so that she wouldn't have to bear its weight and all that it meant.

"This," I said sternly, "is a poor excuse for a pearl."

130

She stared at me with wildness in her eyes before she laughed, but the laughter soon turned to tears, a Frankenstein of emotions stitched together with disbelief. A bloody bubble burst on her lips, splattering her face and nightclothes. This was useful, as cleaning it gave me something to do and a way to disguise my horror and alarm.

I clucked over Liza like a querulous hen, my intention being to distract her from the gravity of the situation. "Liza! We would've sent for the dentist!" I scolded. "Which one was it? From the back, I hope. Open up."

She obliged like an obedient kitten, so that I was able to peer inside her mouth. The gaping hole welled up with blood on the left side, near the front, but fortunately in the lower part of her jaw so that she can still smile without showing that she has lost a tooth.

"Here," I said, packing a clean square of linen into the weeping socket. "Bite down. Hard."

It was then that I realized she'd lost the tooth she uses for pointing her brush when she paints, the one with the convenient gap between it and its neighbor. Of course I said nothing about it, for if Liza hadn't realized that herself, then there was no reason to upset her. Painting is really her only activity of late. She shows no interest in books or sewing or even the diary Charlotte gave her, and luckily I am earning enough to keep her in canvases. When she returns to work, it will undoubtedly slow her progress to develop a new technique for pointing the brush.

I made Liza a cup of chamomile tea to calm her spirits, and when a clot finally formed in the open socket, she sipped the tea with great care. I hesitated to say what I did next, but it had been on my mind for some days, so at last I ventured to speak my thoughts. "When I visited Edna," I began.

Liza looked at me sharply, but I pressed on.

"She showed me advertisements. For Evr-Brite. She was convinced that it would be a most beneficial curative—"

"But I am not so bad as Edna," Liza interrupted me.

"No, no, no," I assured her. "Not so bad by far. But if it were able to augment the healing process, and if we could come by some Evr-Brite...I did try to get some for Edna, but was unable to do so. Of course, neither Edna nor I had the sort of connections at ARC that you do."

Liza sipped her tea, staring deep into the distance, and I decided that I had said enough on the matter. It would be up to Liza to determine her course. She fell asleep quickly, no doubt exhausted by the evening's unexpected excitement.

I was bone-weary myself, Walter, and yet sleep was elusive for me. I am more worried about Liza than I have let on to her, and yet she is no fool. She knows—she must know—that someone as young and healthy as she should feel at least some improvement in her leg as the bone mends. And now this trouble with her tooth. What could make a tooth fall from one's jaw without warning or apparent cause? We'll have to bring the dentist around, no matter what the cost. It is so mysterious.

At long last, I fell asleep in the smallest, darkest hours of the morning, though I did not sleep well, not at all. I dreamed that the earth gave way beneath my feet, and I plunged into a sudden free fall through the blackest parts of the galaxy, and all the stars were falling away as well. When I awoke, I started in the bed as if I really were falling to my doom and sat upright, gasping for breath, before I could situate myself.

"It was only a dream, Lyddie. Go back to sleep."

For a moment I worried that I had awakened Liza, but then I realized she must have already been awake, as she was sitting up in bed, writing a letter on the lap desk.

"Are you ill?" I mumbled groggily. "Can I help?"

She turned to face me, Walter, and except for her hair, every part of her was white—her nightdress and her skin—so that the glow from the painted walls and ceiling made a ghastly impression on her.

"There's nothing you can do. Go back to sleep."

Somehow, I did.

In the morning, I might have thought that my memory of Liza writing at the lap desk was merely another facet of my dream. But then she pressed a letter into my hands with explicit instructions to deliver it to Mr. Mills. Perhaps you have been curious as to the nature of their relationship, given Liza's condition? They correspond twice a week, and I serve as letter carrier for them both, and no one, not even Charlotte, knows about it. I have been sorely tempted to peek at their letters, of course, but have never done so. This morning, I was more tempted than ever, which is the most likely reason why I was so much stricter with Charlotte than usual, scolding her for nearly the entire walk to the factory.

"Liza is ill, Charlotte! She's very ill! And if you can't see how shameful your behavior was last night, then her assessment of your youth is more astute than I realized."

"Lyddie," she protested. "That's not fair. I do nothing to offend her, other than exist. But Liza goes out of her way to make a fool of me in front of everyone. I can't abide by it!"

"You are able-bodied," I told her. "And well and in full health. Do you mean to tell me that you are incapable of showing your own sister a bit of additional consideration during her convalescence? Or are you just unwilling?"

"Nothing I do is right by you," she said petulantly.

Oh, Charlotte! If I am hard on her, it is because of how much I believe in her. I cannot allow her to take the easy course—to develop a weak character, to drift into factory work and an early marriage. Not when she has such a gift with words, composing them in ways that make me see the world anew.

"I am asking you to act like the adult you think you are," I told her with all the sternness I could muster. "If that is beyond your current skills, you need only say the word, and I will adjust my expectations accordingly."

When we arrived at the factory, I tried to find an excuse to see Mr. Mills so that I could deliver Liza's letter. It grows harder and harder to slip off to his office unnoticed, and I wonder how Liza was able to manage it for so long without attracting attention.

Near the end of the day, Mr. Mills called both Minnie Johnson and me to his office, ostensibly to praise our accelerated speed, but I think the true purpose was so that he could speak to me alone, as he asked for another moment of my time after he dismissed Minnie.

"Is she still painting?" he asked, blunt as always.

"Oh, yes, sir," I replied. "She is keen to maintain her skills for that day when she may return to work."

He grunted in a way that was impossible to interpret, and then portioned out a greater supply of Lumi-Nite than usual. I knew better than to ask questions, but they must have been writ on my face.

"It's the same stuff," he said. "As in the Evr-Brite. I can't get it for her all packaged in a pretty bottle, but it's the same stuff."

His meaning slowly dawned on me. "So she should…"

"However she wants," he said. "She can drink it or eat it or apply it topically. It's magic, what it does for the body. Immortality in a powder…for those who can get it."

Mr. Mills lowered his voice and leaned toward me, as if we were conspiring on some secretive plot. "I like it in a dish of pudding," he continued. "It invigorates the blood, you see. Reverses the ravages of time. You're both too young to know about that. But I'd reckon if Liza started early, she might never age. It's a wonder, is what I'm telling you."

"Thank you, Mr. Mills," I said. "I'll see that she starts dosing herself directly."

I waited for the usual dismissal, but it did not come, and I sensed a heaviness between us, as if there were some things left unsaid.

"I should still like to see her."

I was so grateful that he stared down at his desk while he spoke, so that I would not have to see the pleading in his eyes. The longing in his voice was almost more than I could bear.

"I will convey your request" was all I said, knowing full well Liza's views on this matter.

The way he looked at me then—oh, Walter! In his eyes I saw that he knew precisely why Liza has not allowed him to call. "She is quite indisposed," I babbled, which only made things worse. "She only wants you to see her at her best, you see, not laid up in bed all disheveled and pale from pain, wearing the same nightclothes for days—"

He cleared his throat gruffly. "Very well. Tell her...tell her that I miss her."

He sat down, hard, and turned away so that he could sort through some paperwork, but there was no focus on his face. I took my leave as fast as I could.

Once home, I set to making a big bowl of pudding for Liza, and also for Charlotte, as I already regretted my harsh words. The constant stirring served as a calming agent, for by the time the pudding was thick and silky, my thoughts were settled. I sprinkled a spoonful of Lumi-Nite over Liza's serving and stirred it in. It was a very small amount, but as I carried the bowl through the ill-lit hallway, the pudding glowed like the full moon, a soft and gentle light that could guide one through the darkest nights.

I did not tell Liza about the secret ingredient until after she had her first bite. Then I recounted everything about my conversation with Mr. Mills.

She stirred the bowl languidly. "So it's in here? The Lumi-Nite?"

I nodded.

"I didn't even taste it."

"I have seen the advertisements," I told her. "If half their claims are true, you'll be well in no time. Mr. Mills himself takes a small measure of powder each day."

"Oh, I'm sure he does," she replied, and there was a tone in her voice that I did not understand.

"Liza," I began. "He wants to see you."

"No."

"But, Liza…if there is an attachment between you—an understanding—then it seems unfair that he should be denied a visit… and…if there is not, then it seems cruel that he should continue to believe—"

Liza tossed a letter at me and watched me read it while she licked her spoon. It was from Captain Lawson, who has made the same request as Mr. Mills. There was great tenderness in his letter. It led me to believe that a certain intimacy has developed between them.

"You must unburden Mr. Mills of any expectations he may harbor," I finally said. "Talk to Mother about these developments with Captain Lawson. I'm sure she would invite him to supper."

But Liza shook her head. "No, goose, it does me no good for Captain Lawson to call. Not here."

"Liza, I am confused. Do you even like either of these gentlemen?"

I will tell you, Walter, what I could not say to her—that true love enacts no such impediments to meeting. That nothing would stand in my way if the slightest opportunity to be with you should arise.

"I like them both, Lyddie," she said, giving me a hard look. "Surely you can understand why neither can call on me. Not now and not here."

I began to understand all too well. "So Captain Lawson is too good for us, and Mr. Mills is not good enough."

"You needn't be vulgar about it," she replied. "Is there any reason I should throw one to the side right now? Especially when they might both be of great use in the future?"

She licked her spoon again, and I had to wonder if Mr. Mills would give so generously of the Lumi-Nite powder if Liza severed ties with him. And if he did not, how much longer would her recovery be? And would he even allow her to return to work once she is well, or would he simply insist upon Charlotte remaining in Liza's position? Or if perhaps he would have had enough of the Grayson girls and terminate us all? Oh, Walter, these entanglements seem so needlessly complicated to me! They give me a headache, they truly do.

But all I said was, "Be careful, Liza," as I took her empty bowl. As I passed through the doorway, she called my name.

"I prefer chocolate pudding," she said.

"I'll ask Mother to buy some cocoa," I promised.

A cup of hot cocoa does sound especially good right now. Spring is so late in coming this year, and we are all weary from an endless winter. I almost feel as if the cold has seeped into my bones and settled there, as if some hollow hand rummages around in the marrow searching for something it cannot find.

But you know me; I am not interested in the grotesque. Which is why a nice hot cup of cocoa would be so welcome tonight. I am sure you would welcome one as well, wherever you may be. I wish that I could wrap all the warmth and light of home in these letters to you, Walter. My words are not enough to convey my love for you. Never enough. But tonight, they will have to suffice.

Love,
Lydia

CHAPTER 15

For almost a week, I spent every spare moment in the dark, filling a blank canvas with swirls of stars in all shapes and sizes; constellations only I could see; a glowing universe of my own making. It would take courage to cover them with an opaque night, painting heavy clouds to obscure all that light, but I wanted to believe in the promise of stars. Even when you couldn't see them, you knew that they were there.

More than that, this canvas was my last hope to find out how LG had made her paintings. I'd tried every other combination I could think of. If she hadn't used oil paint over a hidden glowing image, then I was out of ideas. That's why I called in sick on Friday; I couldn't wait any longer to find out if it would work. Not one more day, not one more hour.

I needed the lights on for what came next. Palette in hand, I swirled around blues and blacks, purples and grays. Sucking the hope out of color was a delicate kind of chemistry, but eventually I hit on just the right formulas, mixing shades that were heavy and humid, thick and bleak. Then I took a deep breath and started hiding my stars. I had most of the canvas covered with a layer of night when there was a knock, and my door swung open.

"I see the lights are on," Lauren said as she strode into my room uninvited. "That's an improvement."

"Um, hi to you too," I replied, trying not to frown. How did Lauren know that? I was about to ask when—

"Come on," she said, yanking open my closet door and walking right in as if she owned it. "It's totally gorgeous today, and I'm taking you out. But you need to change first. Let's go. Get up."

"No thanks," I said, smooshing more purple into the puddle of blue on my palette. "Maybe tomorrow."

"Up," Lauren said again, shoving a tank dress at me. "You seriously need to get out. Let's go shopping."

"I went out last night."

"What, to *work*? Not good enough. Come on, Jules. It's so *depressing* in here, all stuffy and messy and—"

"Could you not boss me?" I snapped. "For like five minutes of my life, could you *please* let me be?"

Lauren stared at me, icy and unblinking.

"I'm here for you," she said. "I'm doing this for *you*."

Suddenly I saw everything the way she did: my paint-splattered shirt, my oily hair, my messy room reeking of paint and turpentine. I closed my eyes and pinched the bridge of my nose. Pinched hard.

"I'm sorry," I said, my eyes still shut. "You're right. I just wanted to—"

Lauren's hand was gentle on my arm. "You need to get out," she said. "Come on. It'll be fun. I'll clean your brush."

"Thanks," I said as Lauren took it away. I snuck one more glance at my painting. It would be okay until I got back; oil takes weeks to fully dry. That's what I love most about oil paint. It gives you so many chances to fix your mistakes.

Lauren's promise of fun was, perhaps, slightly overstated. For six hours we shopped—or, I should say, Lauren shopped while I tried not to touch anything—at a bunch of exclusive boutiques I'd never seen before. I hovered in the margins of each store, hoping that no one would notice the broken strap on my sandal or the tiny hole in my dress. Just as I was wondering how much longer this shopping odyssey could possibly go on, we stopped at a fancy skin-care place where Lauren lost her mind over a jar of hand lotion. Pearlescent and creamy, it smelled faintly of honeysuckle or maybe sweet clover. Just a tiny dab left my skin velvety perfect.

"This stuff is uh-maaaaa-zing," Lauren crooned. "We need it."

I had to agree with her. Then I looked at the price: ninety dollars. Ninety dollars for a jar of lotion that was smaller than a strawberry.

"Ehhh, it's out of my budget," I said, helping myself to just a little more from the tester.

"I'll buy you one," Lauren replied.

"No..." I began. "It's okay. I don't need—"

She tossed her hair back and, with a triumphant smile, beckoned to the lady behind the counter. "We'll take two of these," Lauren announced loudly. "In separate bags, please."

Her gold credit card flashed, and I thought: *Is she enjoying this? No. She can't be enjoying this. But how does she not realize how embarrassed I am?*

"Seriously, Laure, I don't want it," I whispered in a rush. "The smell is kind of...too strong—"

"I don't want to hear it!" Lauren said with a grin. "You're getting one." So she was enjoying it. It was all a joke to her.

"Lauren, I really don't want it," I repeated. "You don't have to do this—"

But it was done. She was already signing the receipt.

"Here," Lauren said as she thrust a small white bag at me. "Enjoy it."

My fingers clenched the bag's satin handles. Enjoy it? How, when the scent alone would conjure my humiliation, highlighted by spotless mirrors and dazzling chrome? As soon as we got in the car, I used my foot to nudge the bag far under my seat. Maybe by the time Lauren found it, she would've forgotten about buying it for me.

I knew one thing: there was nothing Lauren could do or say to get me into another overpriced boutique today.

"Question," I began. "Do you remember Gifts of the Shepherd? On Branson?"

"Yeah."

"I haven't looked for any paintings there. Do you mind if we swing by? I know it's kind of out of the way…"

"I guess we can go," Lauren replied. "If you want." She pulled a hard U-turn and acted like she couldn't hear everybody honking at her.

We used to walk by Branson Avenue all the time in sixth grade. The neighborhood hadn't been great then, but it was a lot worse now. I'm sure that Gifts of the Shepherd was set up with the best of intentions, but in the many years that it'd chugged along as a charity shop, the place had become so run-down that it might as well have been a giant middle finger to poor people. Everything about Gifts of the Shepherd said: *We don't care anymore. We give up.*

It said: *Too hopeless to help.*

"I might wait outside," Lauren said, her upper lip curled in a sneer of disgust.

"Wouldn't do that, if I were you."

She looked over her shoulder at the iron bars on the windows and nodded without speaking. Now *that* was a bad sign. When Lauren clammed up like that, she was upset. Really upset.

"Five seconds," I said, already moving faster than normal. "Two. I'll be right back."

The tables scattered around the store held precarious arrangements of knickknacks: china kittens, travel alarm clocks, a gaudy bejeweled hairbrush that had lost most of its rhinestones. There were just a few paintings, stacked so roughly that it broke my heart to see them carelessly strewn on a table like that. Those paintings had mattered to someone once. Someone had dreamed of making them; someone had believed not only in her vision but in her talent; someone had held a paintbrush and a palette and stood before a canvas whose utter blankness held all the possibility of the universe.

And now? No one cared. These paintings mattered to no one.

Except, maybe, to me.

Focus, I told myself, *focus, focus, focus.*

Then I found a painting in that telltale frame and nearly hugged it in relief. *I came for you,* I thought, before I snapped out of it and remembered where I was, and what I was doing, and who was waiting for me in the doorway. I was just about to leave when I stopped and pawed through the rest of the pile. Just in case.

And there. There it was.

Another one.

Thrilled with my good luck, I cradled both paintings in my arms and went straight to the register. I hardly dared to hope that there might be anything else connected to them, but there was: a narrow box of antique paintbrushes with specks of caked-on paint still splattering their handles. I knew in my heart, knew beyond all doubt, that they had belonged to LG.

A few minutes later, I hurried up to Lauren with the biggest dumb smile on my face.

"Hey. Sorry," I said. "You'll never believe what I just bought. Look!"

"Show me in the car," she whispered. "I want to get *out* of here. This place is disgusting."

"Where are we going to put these?" I asked, shrugging my shoulders to raise the paintings. "The trunk is packed."

"What a good day I had, huh?" Lauren replied. "The shopping gods were *so* with me!"

"I could hold them on my lap, maybe?"

She shook her head. "I know. Put them in the car seats."

"Really?"

"Why not?"

It was actually kind of hilarious, the two paintings tucked into the twins' car seats, and then Lauren—she was in such a weird mood—started cracking up as she buckled the safety harnesses over them.

"Claude. Don't," I said, laughing in spite of myself. "What if the paint chips?"

"Excuse me, Vince. The safety of these paintings is my highest priority," she shot back. "And I happen to know for a fact that these are the best car seats money can buy."

I just shook my head as I climbed into the front seat. For the entire drive to my house, Lauren rambled about everything she'd bought that day. Her self-obsessed monologue required nothing more from me than occasional noises to show I was still listening. Which I was. Mostly. But I snapped to attention as soon as she approached my house.

"Hello," Lauren said as she peered through the windshield. "Why is there a kitchen in your front yard?"

"I have no idea," I said, staring at the fridge, the stove, and the dishwasher, just hanging out in the grass next to the For Sale by

Owner sign like they were having a party. But everything became clear when Lauren and I walked into the kitchen and saw their shiny new replacements.

"Holy crap," she said as she looked around. "Did you know about this?"

I shook my head, stunned into silence.

"Look," Lauren continued. "Tile samples. I bet she's getting new countertops too."

I still didn't say anything.

"When my parents redid our kitchen, it cost, like, fifty thousand dollars. I'm not even kidding. Where is she getting the money for this?"

"I don't know," I finally replied.

"You are a saint," Lauren said. "An absolute saint. This is a total outrage. First she blows through your college money, and now she's getting a fancy new kitchen? Does she even have a job?"

"I—I can't deal with this right now."

"You know what I did yesterday?" Lauren asked me. "I registered for my classes. Introduction to Printmaking. Figure Drawing. Survey of European Art. Sculpture One."

I flinched with every course she rattled off. "Why are you telling me this?"

"Because, Julie, it should be you too," she said firmly. "*You* should be choosing all your classes. *You* should be getting ready to move into the dorms. *You* should be going to college next month! What your mom did to you? Derailing your future? It's one of the worst things I have ever witnessed."

"Can you stop?" I snapped. "You're not helping."

"Are you mad?" she asked. "Good. You *should* be mad. I have been waiting for *months* for you to get mad. Because until you get mad

145

about it, Julie, you're not going to be able to change anything."

"I am *already* working as hard as I can—"

Lauren shook her head. "That's not what I mean," she said. "Nobody could work harder than you. Nobody could do more than you've done. But your mom, Julie, and you know I love her, what she did was way out of line. And you have to call her out, because as long as she thinks that her new kitchen is more important than you going to college—"

"Why would she do this?" I cried as I burst into tears. "Why? We just paid off all her debt!"

Lauren wrapped me in a hug. "I'm so sorry, Jules. I am so, so sorry. Don't cry."

"What am I going to do?"

"Just...tell her that she has to return this stuff. All of it. And if she somehow had the money to pay for it...well, she owes it to you, so she should give it to you."

Like it was that easy. I mean, I appreciated the support, but even Lauren had to know that this entire situation was a thousand times more complicated than that.

"Let's do something," she said suddenly. "Anything you want. We could go to a movie or...or...go get something to eat. Anything."

I didn't even have to think about it. "Let's go look at the paintings. In the dark."

There was a pause before she replied. "Okay."

With every step up the stairs, I could feel something sinister slinking toward us. The air itself was charged with anticipation, like the atmosphere before an electrical storm. My body crackled with apprehension. I gritted my teeth, once, before Lauren laid her hand briefly along the side of my jaw. We stood next to each other in heavy silence, the kind where language fails you, and even the thought of speaking, of disrupting the stillness, seems like a dangerous mistake.

The painting I'd carried upstairs was a bedroom with two beds, end to end, and a girl at each one. Through the window, a moon was rising—or setting—but it cast barely any light. The blackness of the night sky seemed to pour into the room. One of the girls had already slipped into her bed and lay there, expressionless, with her eyes wide open. The other girl knelt at the side of the other bed...praying, I think? It was hard to tell, especially with her head bowed so that her hair concealed most of her face. I wanted to pull back those dark curtains of hair and let the light shine through her eyes. I wanted to see her, to know for myself. What was in that face? Those eyes?

I turned to the other painting, a portrait of a young woman, hoping to find the answer there. *LG?* I wondered. *Is that you?*

Of course, there was no response. I didn't expect one. I mean, I'm not crazy.

But what if it *was* her?

Lauren spoke first. "So..." she said, and her voice was hushed, respectful. "Self-portrait?"

"I don't know. Maybe. I think so."

I studied the girl's smooth cheeks, the hair swept away from her face. The whorl of her ear was an infinite spiral, a wonder of design. You had to marvel at such meticulous invention. An ear: who could imagine such a thing? And yet when you thought of it by itself, say, cut from a head, sitting alone on the kitchen table, or the floor, an ear became an object of horror, a dried apricot of disgust. I was about to mention that to Lauren, to make another one of our endless van Gogh jokes, when—without warning—she turned out the lights.

Maybe it was because I wasn't expecting the sudden darkness, but I hadn't braced myself for what could appear. Or maybe it was because I was in too deep, way too deep. I was drowning in what these paintings might mean and all the questions I couldn't answer. And here it was: more horror, more mystery. I should've known by now that I wouldn't be able to look away.

At first glance, the portrait had hardly changed at all. The glow seemed to illuminate those delicate doll-features from within, turning her eyes into large, luminous moons staring at me from many light-years away. The only thing I noticed—the only real difference—was her jaw. It was gone. Only her upper lip, like half a heart, remained. Then came a great emptiness where her lower lip should've been, where her chin was missing. This was not a mouth you could kiss; this was not a face you should see. The gaping hole seemed poised to speak, but whatever it wanted to say could only be communicated by her eyes.

Look away, I thought.

But I didn't. On the street, you wouldn't stare at someone who looked like that, but here, in my room, face to half-face, looking away from her would've been rude. I might as well have said *You disgust me* and *I'm afraid of you.* And that, I think, is why I wanted to touch her—I mean, the painting. This is what I would do for the ravaged girl in the painting. I would find the beauty in her. I was admiring her pretty ears, tracing the tiny rosebud earring that had appeared, when Lauren spoke.

"You shouldn't do that."

"What?"

"You know." Lauren's voice, disembodied in the darkness. "Touch it. The painting."

"I'm not going to hurt it."

"Well, not on purpose. But your skin can harm…Come on, Julie, you know this. Don't touch the goddamn painting."

That was it. I turned on the light. "What's your problem?" But when I saw Lauren's face, saw how gray she was, her lips nearly invisible, I softened my voice. "Whoa. What's wrong?"

"What's wrong? Are we looking at the same thing? Did you see...did you *see*—"

"I just looked at the portrait. What is it, Lauren? I know it's creepy and—"

"Look at the other one."

Lauren scooched backward until she was pressed against the wall—she was as far away from the paintings as she could be without leaving my room—and then she drew her knees up to her chest and hugged herself. I was so annoyed with her. Why *now* was she freaking out about the paintings?

When I turned out the light, I understood.

I understood so much, actually, that it seemed to smack me on the head. How could I have missed it? I mean, of course the beds were graves, crowned with funereal wreaths of roses. Of course they were. And of course the girls were skeletons, so long dead that their elastic skin and gristly muscle and creamy fat had all rotted away, so that only their bones, elemental and eternal, remained. The one who'd been in the bed was clearly dead and buried. The other one— the one who'd been praying—was worse. She was crawling into her grave, dangling one foot over the side the way you might sit on the edge of a pool and skim your toes through the water. That yawning grave, so cold, so deep, so eerily empty. It was waiting for her, and worse than knowing that was realizing that she knew it too. Why else would she have painted it?

"Look," I whispered to Lauren. "Look at the moon. It's a face now...a girl...It's a girl peering in the window, watching ev—"

"It's not. It's just the moon."

"Look at how the headboards of the beds turn into tombstones.

Oh my God, can you read this? She wrote…something…God, I wish I knew…Come here, Lauren. It's okay. It's just a painting."

Moments later, I felt the warmth of Lauren's arm against mine as we knelt, side by side, and stared.

"I can't read it," she said at last. "It's too small."

I leaned closer. "There's something about the writing…"

"What?"

"I don't know. It looks…it looks different, doesn't it? Go get one of the other paintings. I want to compare."

"Can we just—"

"It's a date!" I exclaimed. "Oh, Lauren—did she know *when* she was going to die?"

"Stop," Lauren said softly. "Stop. I don't want to think about that."

"This one here," I said, reaching for one of the tombstones. "This date is…let's see…September 1916. I think."

"That's an eight," she corrected me. "It's 1918."

"It has to mean something," I continued. "She wouldn't paint a date on that tombstone for no reason. It has to mean *something*, right?"

Lauren didn't answer.

"Just imagine," I said, my breath catching in my throat. I hardly recognized my own voice. "Something terrible is happening to you…and you have to paint it. Your art is your voice. It's your story. Your sister is dying…or maybe she's already dead—"

"Seriously, can we—"

"Come on, Claude! Use your brain! I can't figure this out by myself."

"Enough, Julie! Stop!"

I blinked in surprise. It was too dark to see if Lauren was kidding. And I couldn't tell from her voice.

150

"Stop what?"

"That Claude and Vince stuff. It's so stupid. Why are we still using those old-man nicknames like we're still in sixth grade?"

"Why are you freaking out? You called me Vince an hour ago."

"Well, I don't want to do it anymore," Lauren said. "It's stupid. And completely immature."

I heard the swish of her skirt as she got up. Seconds later, my room was flooded with light. I blinked a few times as my eyes tried to adjust, as the rest of me tried to adjust to this strange shifting beneath my feet. Lauren was...she wasn't looking at me, over by the door. She was—

"Are you mad at me?"

It wasn't just a babyish thing I said. It was the way I said it, my voice high and hollow, already betraying how hurt I was.

"No. A little," she admitted.

"What did I do?"

For a moment, Lauren paused, and I thought she would tell me. Then she shrugged and looked away. "Never mind. It's nothing."

But I couldn't let it go.

"What? Seriously, tell me. I want to know what I did."

Her hands moved like she didn't know what to do with them. "It's just...Jules, what are you doing with these paintings?"

"What do you mean?"

"Like, why are you so obsessed?"

I tried to laugh it off. "I am not!"

But Lauren didn't laugh with me. "Julie. You want to compare the writing on them? Like you're some kind of detective? I'm honestly worried about you. Even your mother is worried."

"Please. She doesn't know anything about it."

"Yeah? Then how come she asked me to come over because

you've spent literally days in the dark?"

Jesus, Mom, I thought. I hadn't seen that one coming.

"So...why?" Lauren continued. "Why are you so obsessed with the paintings?"

Even if I knew the answer to Lauren's question, I doubt I had the courage to say it aloud. I turned away from her and opened the box of antique paintbrushes I'd bought earlier. Some of them were so small, with just a few hairs, that it seemed incredible that anyone could paint with them.

As I dabbed one of the brushes in oil paint, Lauren really lost it. "What are you *doing?*" she asked incredulously. "Stop trying to become her, Julie. It's pathetic."

"I am not trying to become her!" I shot back. "I'm just trying to find out—"

"What? Exactly *what* are you trying to find out?"

"You know what," I said, stalling for time as I tried to figure out how to answer. "How she did it. Why she did it. And...and...what happened to her."

Lauren shook her head. "No, that's not it. There's something deeper going on. Something darker. Besides, you don't know that anything happened to her. Maybe she was just some sick twist who was really into the macabre. Who got off on painting some really scary, really disturbing, really disgusting stuff. And, whatever, that's cool and all, but that's not who you are. Or is it?"

"Why are you attacking me?"

"I'm not—"

"You just called me sick and twisted!"

"No, I didn't, Julie. I said the *artist* was sick and twisted. Not you. But you see what I mean? You're taking everything about the paintings way too personally. This"—here she pointed at the paintings like she was accusing them of a crime—"is not interesting to me anymore. It's creepy. It's freaking me out. And, to be honest, so are you."

"Listen, you don't have to worry about me, or the paintings, anymore. Obviously you don't understand them, and that's fine. Honestly, I never expected you to."

"'Cause I'm too stupid, right?" she sneered. "'Cause I'm not a *real* artist, like you?"

I shrugged, knowing that would hurt her more than anything I could say.

"God, Julie, when did you get so mean?" Lauren exploded. "Where is your gratitude? I have been the best friend to you! But these paintings come along, and you constantly blow me off for them. You care about these stupid canvases more than a living, breathing person—"

"Listen to yourself," I interrupted. "How entitled. How spoiled. One thing in the world that was *mine*, one thing I could focus on, one thing that made my life matter, that pulled me out of this stupid, dead-end existence that's going nowhere, and it's killing you, isn't it, that maybe there's something you can't buy on Mommy's credit card."

Amazingly, she smiled, as if everything suddenly made sense. "Well, I'd rather be spoiled than jealous," she said.

"Why are you still here?" I demanded.

A heartbeat.

"I don't even know anymore," she replied. When she walked out, I didn't try to stop her.

I wasn't ready yet to see if my starscape would glow through the oil paint I'd applied that morning. Instead, I lay down on the bed and started to cry. I fumbled under my pillow for the diary and flipped through the pages.

2 April

I don't care. I don't care. I don't care. I don't care. I don't
care. I don't care. I don't care. I don't care. I don't care. I
don't care. I don't care. I don't care. I don't care. I don't
care. I don't care.

"But you do care," I whispered into the silence. "And so do I."

Why was that a bad thing, exactly? Didn't this whole hurting
world deserve—no, *need*—a little more care? Never again, I promised myself, would I apologize for caring about something, and that
was the thought that dried up my tears. Twilight shadows crept
through my room. When I rolled onto my side, I could see all six
paintings glowing. Waiting.

The skeletons at the graves—

The girl who'd lost her jaw—

The tombstones made of teeth—

The dancers with their shattered bones—

The faces in the buildings—

And the first one, the one that had started it all: the aviator and
his girl, flying away from the withered blooms.

Nothing had changed; they were the same as when I'd found
them. And yet each painting sat there expectantly, like they were
waiting for me to—

What?

"I don't know what to do," I said aloud, and still they glowed,
still they stared, until at last I turned away and realized, all in a rush,
that there was no other light in my room. My desk—and the canvas
on it—was dark.

I had failed.

All those glowing stars that I'd painted were gone now, lost forever under a sticky layer of oil paint. In one morning, I'd wasted every drop of the paint Luke and I had made. I'd never see those stars shining again. I'd never know, now, how LG made her paintings.

I turned away from my failure, couldn't stand to face it. I wanted to run from all of it, and that's probably how I found the courage to go downstairs to the kitchen. To wait in the dark, crouching like an animal, for the confrontation that had been building for months.

CHAPTER 16

Dearest Walter,

I am sorry to report that Liza is no better. Indeed, she may be worse. Though her leg troubles her less, she is still unsteady on it, and I cannot discern if she is fearful of using it because she is out of the habit, or because there is a fundamental weakness in the bone. She takes such small, tentative steps, walking gingerly like a shriveled old woman. And yet it seems like only yesterday that she could run and dance with abandon.

But her leg is not the worst of it. Not by far. It is her mouth, which does not heal. The dentist visits us twice weekly now and is baffled by the disintegration he sees. Liza lost another tooth, and then a third; the empty sockets fester and fill with a putrid cream. Dr. Mackintosh doses her with ether until her eyes cloud, and then he debrides her jaw. Using a sharp curette he scrapes out soggy chunks of gum tissue, gray with disease, until the healthy pink flesh below is revealed. For a while, each operation seems to be a success, and indeed the gums surge forward in a fine display of regeneration. Liza is in such great spirits, and her optimism is contagious, so that we are all hopeful that she will at last be returned to health.

Then, without fail, Liza wakes up one morning to find a foul discharge dampening her pillow. A sticky black paste oozes from her mouth. She swallows with great displeasure, her lips twisted with disgust. If the rotten-garlic smell is any indication, the taste must be terrible. And so we send for Dr. Mackintosh again and he examines her jaw with great concern, as there is no obvious source for this infection, and yet it continues to recur.

Each night, I prepare a bowl of pudding for Liza so that she might benefit from the medicinal properties of Lumi-Nite, but I will admit that I have begun to doubt its healing qualities. If it is such a panacea, then why is she no better? As long as Dr. Mackintosh has no better suggestions, I suppose we must continue on as we have.

There have been changes at work. Mary Jane has left employ at ARC after developing an uncomfortable swelling beneath her chin, and I sorely miss her presence. She served as a "big sister" to all, and without her, we are out of sorts. There have also been changes on the second floor, where the chemists concoct Evr-Brite. They are now sporting heavy smocks over their clothes, and fine mesh masks over their mouths, and thick glass goggles that give them a decidedly owlish appearance.

It was a startling change to see them conduct their work in such getups, Walter. For what practical purpose would they need adornment like this? I mustered the courage to ask Mr. Mills, and he told me that their "uniforms," as it were, are simply to assure the purity of the medicines they compound. So why, then, am I so unsettled at the sight of them? Certainly my discomfiture bears no small relation to the way gas masks haunt my dreams. But I think there may be another reason as well.

On payday last, I went to Dr. Mackintosh's office after work so that I might settle Liza's account, and to my great surprise, who do you think was knitting in the waiting room? Helen Anderson from ARC! How we missed each other on the walk over, I'll never know. I was very sorry to learn that Helen has been suffering from a mild tenderness in her jaw; "more an annoyance than a trouble" were her exact words. I can guess what you are thinking, Walter: that I am assigning far more importance than necessary to a mere coincidence. I tried to push any connection from my own thoughts. After all, it should come as no surprise that a couple of girls from ARC happen to share a dentist.

There was little time for Helen and me to chat before I was called to the window, and while I was there, who should come out of the treatment room but Minnie Johnson? We shared a good laugh, though Minnie less so than Helen and me, because her mouth must have been sore from the treatment she had received. Her eyes were dull from painkillers, and there was a slackness in her cheeks, as if she had forgotten how to coordinate something as simple as closing her mouth. There was not much time for more than a quick "Hello!" among us, for Helen was immediately ushered into the treatment room. Minnie gave her arm a fast squeeze of solidarity as she passed. I am sure they have delayed care, despite their pain, to receive treatment on payday.

Minnie stood behind me as I finished my transaction, and then— I cannot tell you what compelled me to do this—I dawdled as I put on my hat and gathered my things, so that I was not ready to depart until Minnie had paid her bill, at which time we were poised to leave together.

Minnie's demeanor toward Liza, Charlotte, and me has been decidedly chilly since I bested Eugenie for the job at ARC, and on any given day, I would be inclined to make sure our paths would cross no more than necessary. Yet on this day we found ourselves walking side by side in the sunset. Perhaps it was Minnie's painkillers, or perhaps she felt it was finally time to bury an old grudge, but she was ever so genial toward me. I took pains to avoid divulging too much of Liza's travails to Minnie, but I did learn that this is Minnie's third visit to Dr. Mackintosh this month, and she is troubled by a similarly slow-to-heal wound in her mouth.

As we reached my street, blistering red sunbeams spangled across my eyes so that I found it difficult to see. This can be the only reason why I did not notice Mr. Mills standing in the doorway of our building until we were nearly on top of him, for if I had, I surely would have done anything to avoid the exchange that happened next.

It would have been peculiar for Mr. Mills to pay a visit to our apartment, and that alone would have alerted Minnie to an unusual circumstance, even in her addled state. What truly captured her attention, though, was the bouquet nestled in the crook of Mr. Mills' arm—flawless rosebuds of the palest pink I've ever seen. A pretty chunk of his pay must have been spent on this fine bouquet. It was such an incongruous picture, Walter—oafish and oversize Mr. Mills, all stubby fingers and ruddy earnestness, cradling such delicate blossoms, and in our doorway, no less. Is it any wonder I was struck dumb?

Not so Minnie, I'm afraid.

She looked at me first with confusion, then with dawning understanding, and blurted out, "But what about your sweetheart overseas, Lydia? Oh, that would be a dirty trick to two-time him, and he in uniform!"

Would that I could've come up with some witty rejoinder and shepherded Minnie on her way! But Mr. Mills spoke up—why, I don't know—and said that he was here to see Liza, and would I be kind enough to admit him?

The old scheming glitter returned to Minnie's eyes. Of course there's no way to be sure, but I sensed her innocence was entirely put on when she asked, "But what about her fine captain in New York? Has she thrown him aside, then?"

My laugh was too loud. "Oh, Minnie, hush!" I said, giving her a playful pinch but using far more force than necessary, as I wanted her to take it as a warning. "You're ever so addled! Mr. Mills, if you will excuse us, I must see Minnie home. She's been to the dentist, you see, and is quite incapable of finding the way herself. I shall return in just a few moments' time, if you'll be kind enough to wait for me."

He nodded slowly, with a blankness on his face that I could not interpret. For one thing, I had not the time, as I was eager to whisk Minnie away before she could say anything else so foolish. Her chatter was idle for the short walk to her building, but I could see her eyes still flashing, and it was with a great feeling of foreboding that I bid her good night.

I returned to our building as fast as I could, and yet not fast enough, for Mr. Mills was already inside, I assumed, and all that remained was a single rose petal on the dirty stoop. I took it inside to give to Liza, though I was sure she would have no use for it with such a fancy bouquet gracing her bureau.

The apartment was strangely silent when I entered, and then I realized that Mother and Charlotte were still at the grocer. Payday is such a busy day! I wondered if Liza had admitted Mr. Mills herself, and if, oh heavens, they were alone in her room! I paced the living room, quite unsure of the best course to take, for I dared not disturb them. Yet if Mother and Charlotte returned and discovered their dalliance, there would be such a catastrophe, Walter, that I was not sure I could bear it. Nor was I blameless. After all, I had enabled Liza to carry on such an ill-advised entanglement for months now. Her poor judgment had created the situation, but mine had sustained it. My only hope was for Mr. Mills to take his leave before Mother and Charlotte returned.

Which he did not do.

They bustled through the door as darkness fell, burdened with all sorts of brown-paper parcels from the butcher and the grocer, and asked me how Liza was feeling. I fibbed that she was resting and took my leave to see if she needed anything. There was a commotion in the kitchen as they were so late in starting the laundry and had to prepare supper and unload all the packages, so I was able to slip away unnoticed.

I approached the bedroom in a state of nervous agitation and tapped on the door so lightly that I was not surprised when no answer came. Like it or not, I had no choice but to interrupt them—but then, I told myself, I should feel no shame about it. They had no right to put me in such an uncomfortable position to begin with!

So I knocked louder.

And louder still.

And finally I cracked open the door, leaned my head in with eyes firmly closed, and whispered Liza's name and said that Mother and Charlotte had returned.

At this point, of course, I expected to hear some rustling commotion, or at least Liza's or Mr. Mills's response to me, but only silence filled my ears. Then I heard such a terrible sound, Walter, that I don't think I will ever forget it: a choking sound, a strangled gurgle, a thick, wet gasp for air, and somehow I knew that Liza was in grave danger. Only later I realized that if she was, then so was I—for what would Mr. Mills do to me, if he could cause such harm to Liza?

I sprang forward at the same instant my eyes snapped open, without a plan but certain that I could somehow arrest his attack—fling myself over his back like a wild monkey, claw and scratch at him, whatever it took.

I stopped short, though, for Liza was quite alone.

Though the room was mostly dark—it never gets truly dark, not anymore, not since we painted our galaxy—there was an especial brightness coming from Liza's bed, and I looked—and looked again—to see a glowing fluid flow from her nose and mouth. And I realized with terrible clarity that Liza, lying down in the bed, was choking on the stuff.

I screamed for Mother and Charlotte and rushed to Liza's side, lifting her up. (How light she was, Walter. Since Liza has begun walking on her own more, I hadn't noticed her growing frailty. Her bones must be as hollow and delicate as a bird's.) Liza awoke, still sputtering, as Mother ran in and turned on the light.

It wasn't paint that poured from Liza's nose, of course. It was blood—rich red blood, quite ordinary in the light, and yet something had happened to her blood, Walter, for I swear what I write to you is the truth: In the dark, it glowed.

It took nearly half an hour and more linens than I could count for us to staunch the blood that flowed so freely from Liza's nose. I have no idea how she slept through the start of such an incident. Indeed, she was quite exhausted by the time it concluded, lying wanly against her pillow with all the color drained from her face save for bruise-dark circles blooming under her eyes. My poor Liza. My poor Liza.

There was a great deal of laundry to do, with all the bloodstained linens, and yet it was decided that Liza should not be alone, so I kept her company while Mother and Charlotte attended to the evening's work. She was too tired for much conversing, so I kept up a steady stream of chatter, and when we'd been alone for several moments, I crawled into bed with her so that I could lower my voice as I told her all about seeing Minnie and Helen at Dr. Mackintosh's office.

"I wonder who you'll see there next," Liza said thickly, her nose swollen with clots. It was early still, but already her head was drooping, and it was clear to me that she would soon be asleep again. So I turned out the lights, and in moments, she was unconscious. She did not even wake when I lifted her head so that I could place my pillow under her own to elevate her, should she suffer from another nosebleed in the night. There hadn't even been a chance to tell Liza about Mr. Mills's unexpected visit. (You have surely realized my folly by now, Walter. Mr. Mills was never in Liza's room. He had never even entered our apartment!)

I knew that I should join Mother and Charlotte in the kitchen to help with the various chores that would surely keep them up into the smallest morning hours, but I was afraid to leave Liza, and so I decided to lie down on my own bed for at least a little while, in case she should quickly wake and need me.

How heavy was the worry weighing upon me, Walter, as I lay beneath our glowing galaxy. I am less enamored of the Lumi-Nite paint than once I was. The yellow undertones remind me of jaundice; the greenish glow conjures thoughts of nausea and seasickness. Most of all, I long to be enveloped by pure darkness. I have a strange fear that Lumi-Nite may become so prevalent that we will never be able to enjoy the dark again—at least, not until we are dead and buried in our graves.

Liza's words kept running through my mind: I wonder who you'll see there next. I am sure that she meant nothing by it—I am sure that I assign it more importance than it merits—but really, Walter, do you think it strange that I should see two dial painters there in one afternoon? And then there is the question of Liza, still so bafflingly ill. And Mary Jane, disappearing so suddenly and visiting no one?

And even, I suppose, poor Edna Parsons, dead and gone for nearly six months already.

That is a lot of girls from the same factory, wouldn't you agree?

Or am I making a mountain out of a molehill?

If there is any chance, Walter, any chance at all, that something in the paint—or in the dial-painting studio—or perhaps some other factor of which I am unaware—could be affecting all these girls, then I must get Charlotte away from ARC. She has been in their employ a full two months already. We are running out of time. I pray that it is not too late. But Charlotte will never leave willingly. She loves it there.

If Liza were well enough to reclaim her position—

But she is not.

I am in a muddle, Walter. Please advise me. I eagerly await your counsel.

But not as eagerly as I await your return.

Love,

Lydia

CHAPTER 17

How long was I in the kitchen, lying in wait? Long enough for darkness to overtake the room; long enough for me to prowl from fridge to dishwasher to stove, loathing their shiny newness; long enough for everything inside me to crystallize into something jagged and ferocious. Lauren told me that I should be mad, but mad didn't cut it. Not anymore. A toxic concoction of rage and resentment and regret bubbled through my veins until my brain was blazing with fury, and nothing but blood or tears could quench that fire.

A beam of light arced through the kitchen, followed by the purr of a familiar engine. Mom was home. I could hear it all: the slam of the car door, the shuffly footsteps on the walkway, the key turning in the lock. I swallowed hard, gulping like something was stuck in my throat—my breath or my courage or my resolve, I guess. In my heart, I wasn't ready for what would happen next.

But I knew, then, that I never would be. So despite my shaky legs and wobbly arms I stood up and snapped on the light. It flooded through the kitchen just as she opened the door. I think we both jumped.

"God, Julie, you scared—"

I didn't say anything as I stared at her, hard and mean; harder and meaner than I knew I could stare at anyone. In the moment she realized it, when that terrible dawning spread across her face, I settled into myself and steeled myself for what was coming next.

"The hell have you done in here?"

"Please don't yell at me, Julie," she said flatly. "We can talk about this after you've calmed down."

She moved toward the door, but I was quicker, blocking her way before she could escape.

"You don't get to run away," I shouted. "Not this time! Answer my question. *What have you done?*"

Her head snapped back, and our eyes met. She seemed to realize that this was finally happening. It had been building for months and couldn't be put off for another day.

"Why do you keep asking that? You have eyes. You can see for yourself."

"I want to hear you say it."

"Well, I'm renovating the kitchen," she said, shameless.

It was too easy, the way she handed it to me like that, like what she'd done didn't matter at all.

"Oh, that's all? You're just renovating the kitchen? You're just spending thousands of dollars on crap we don't need? And that's no big thing to you?"

"Julie, please. Please don't do this."

"No. Don't turn this on me. I'm not doing anything, Mom! *You* did this!"

"Yes, I did, Julie. I did it for you!"

"For me?" I repeated. Surely I had misheard her. Surely she wasn't so deep in her own delusions that she thought a new kitchen was something I cared about in any way, shape, or form. "For *me?*"

"Yes, for you, and I'm not going to apologize for that."

"Oh, of course not, why should you apologize for anything? Not for lazing around the house all day! Not for spending thousands of dollars on a brand-new kitchen! Not for ruining my life!"

"No, no—" she started to say, again and again, but I kept talking.

"I mean, it sure sounds like a nice life *you've* got! No jobs, no responsibilities, no sacrifices—"

"No—"

"I mean even when the bill collectors were calling, like, every hour, you know, just a gentle reminder that you should maybe *pay your bills*—"

"No—"

"I still thought, well, Mom's the adult here, she knows what she's doing—"

"No, no, no—"

"But that's where I was the fool, huh? I always believed all your lies…Oh, Julie, you're so smart. Oh, Julie, you're so talented. Oh, Julie, you can be anything you want, anything you want—"

"No—"

"But that was just a big setup, wasn't it? You never had any intention of letting me go."

My words rang in my ears. I didn't know where they'd come from. I didn't know who was standing across from my mom, bellowing like a bull, sweaty and red and raging. And yet I couldn't stop. I couldn't shut up.

"Took a lot of planning, huh? No wonder you couldn't find a job, not when you were too busy unraveling my entire life. When did it start? When Dad left you? Or before?"

"Jubilee—"

"No, *shut up*. Don't even call me that stupid name. I swear, you've hated me since the moment I was born, and I was so close to getting away from you and this house, but you won, didn't you? You won."

"I've *won*?" she repeated. "You think I've won? You think I wanted this life? You think this life makes me happy?"

"You wouldn't even go to that job fair—"

"Oh, I *did* go. You said to get there early, so I went and came home before you were even out of bed. Guess how many people were there? Three thousand. For sixty jobs. Do you see what I'm up against?"

"That was just one—"

"No, it's *every* job fair. It's *every* job ad. It's not my fault that every time I apply for a job, there are hundreds of applicants more qualified than I am."

"But you—"

"You think it's so easy because you got a couple part-time jobs. Do the math, Julie. Even a full-time minimum wage job wouldn't have kept this house going. And too bad for me, nobody's interested in hiring a woman with an eighteen-year hole in her résumé. Too bad for me, I thought I was doing something good staying at home for you, making a home for you and your father—"

"Don't bring him into—"

"You already did. So let's face the facts about your dad, shall we? He's such a special guy. Such a special guy who walked out on a perfectly good home, a perfectly good family. But you already know that. What else do you know, Julie? That there was no way he could keep two households at the same standard of living? And when he had to choose one, he chose himself? Did you know that? Did you?"

I didn't respond.

"No? How about this. Did you know that he's had some hard times too? Did you know that he took me back to court so he could pay less alimony? Less child support? Did you know that?"

The look on my face gave her the answer. But I was not about to let her twist things around and distract me from everything she'd done wrong.

"So is that why you took my college money like you were entitled to it?"

Mom sucked in her breath sharply and held on to the edge of the counter. "Here it is. I've been waiting for this—"

"You had no right!" I yelled over her. "You had no right to take that money—"

"You offered...You insisted...We sat right there at that table, and I said, are you sure, are you sure—"

"It was never supposed to be some magic solution to your mountains of debt!"

"*My* mountains of debt? You know it's more complicated than that! Remember science camp? Art lessons? Prom dresses? Field trips? I have given you everything. I've made sacrifices for you that you can't begin to comprehend! That college account was just the beginning!"

"Please, tell me more about that, Mom. How did you contribute to *my* college fund when you never even had a job?"

"Because *you* were my job, Julie! I was here. Even after he was gone, I was here. I was taking care of you, I was making you thousands of meals and reading you thousands of books and listening to thousands of problems—"

"I never asked you to—"

"But I wanted to, Julie, and that's what makes the difference. I stuck around, and I gave you everything I had when he was too selfish to love either one of us."

"You're wrong!" I screamed. "Dad *does* love me. That's why he sent that extra check for my college account every month. He didn't have to, but he did. He *wanted* my dreams to come true!"

Her head was wobbling back and forth a little, and she looked so confused that I might as well have been speaking in tongues. Then her hands were on her cheeks, and clarity flooded her eyes.

"Oh, Julie," she said. "Oh, Julie. The college account wasn't your dad's doing. It was mine."

"Wrong!"

"No, honey," she said, her voice soft with pity. "I fought for that in the divorce. I wouldn't sign the papers until he agreed to fund it."

"Shut up. You did not."

"I'm so sorry, sweetheart," she said. "I thought you knew. And even after…after we went back to court…I agreed to less alimony to make sure those payments for your college account would keep coming. That was a mistake. I know that now. I never could've predicted that he would ignore the court order and just stop sending checks. That he would disappear like that. Abandon us both again. And even after he did, I thought…" She took a deep breath. "I truly believed everything would work out somehow. Financially, I mean. I was sure I could get a job. I never dreamed of touching your college account until we were about to lose everything."

All this time—stupid, stupid—all these years—stupid, stupid—I thought that those monthly checks meant something, the only shred of evidence that my dad still cared. They were, I thought, proof of his love.

And now it was gone.

"It's his loss, Julie," she said, rubbing my arm. "When he walked out on you, he made the biggest mistake of his life, and I feel so sorry for him—"

I jerked away from her. "Stop it! You're trying to distract me.

You're trying to make me feel bad. He has nothing to do with all the money you just spent on this kitchen!"

The shine of love in her eyes hardened like quick-set concrete. "Right. The kitchen. Well, if you'd given me a chance to explain, I would've told you that I had a real estate agent do a walk-through last week. She said we'd never get a buyer unless we updated the kitchen. Imagine that, Julie. No one wants to buy a house with a thirty-year-old kitchen full of broken appliances. So I found these floor models for fifty percent off.

"Did I have the *right* to buy them? Should I have asked your *permission*? Maybe. I don't know. I'm still not used to being in my daughter's debt. But I do know that I was comfortable taking this risk—this very calculated risk—because of how great the payoff would be."

We stared at each other for a long moment.

"And that's why this kitchen is for you. Because if I can sell this house and repay you, maybe, hopefully, you can get yourself to college and move forward with your life. I know how easy it is to get off track. How hard it is to find your way again. You think I want to hold you back? To keep you here?"

I swallowed hard, but I didn't answer her.

"No. I don't want that. I want you *gone*, Julie. I want you out of this house and off to college because I cannot bear to watch someone with so much promise throw it all away."

Not one more minute—not one more second—could we stay under the same roof. I pushed past her and charged up the stairs. It didn't take long at all to shove a bunch of stuff in my backpack— dirty and clean clothes jumbled together, my uniforms for work, the diary. I had no intention of coming back anytime soon.

But the paintings.

How could I leave them behind?

Making multiple trips up and down the stairs was out of the question. And to be honest, they wouldn't all fit into my little hatchback. So I tucked the smallest painting under my arm and careened downstairs, determined to leave and not look back.

CHAPTER 18

June 18, 1918

Dearest Walter,

Thank you for your wise counsel. I have acted upon it, though perhaps not entirely in the way you would expect, and though I cling to the conviction that I have done what needed to be done, I am not certain that what I did was right.

If you do the wrong thing for the right reasons, is it still wrong? I struggle with this question every day.

I will never tell anyone what I did, except for you in this letter, and if you love me less, I will understand. I feel very unlovable tonight. Still, you should know, I suppose, what sort of person I am deep inside, that I could commit such an act against my own sister.

My plan took several weeks to execute, during which I had to be exceedingly sly. I stitched nearly invisible pockets into the hems of my dresses. That was the start. And then I taught myself some sleight of hand. A watch face here, a freshly painted dial there, a case, a spring, a band. A smattering of crystals. Spindly hands. Pieces pilfered daily, hourly, secreted away in my skirts. No one noticed; no one suspected a thing.

While Liza slept away the fitful hours under the light of our stars, I assembled all those pieces to the best of my ability, slowly building for myself a fine cadre of illuminated wristwatches. I might have set up shop as a watchmaker if I had been so inclined, but that was not my intent. When I had a good number—some twenty or so—it was time to act. I feared that soon Mr. Mills would notice the missing pieces, which would surely lead to greater scrutiny of all us girls. If I were discovered as the thief—

I get ahead of myself.

On the appointed day, I snuck the assembled watches back into the factory. They were heavy, but did not weigh nearly so much as my guilty conscience. I suppose I could have called it off, but in truth I had no better ideas. So I persevered, ignoring all my misgivings, and near the end of the day, I found a moment to slip off to the cloakroom, where I deposited all the watches in Charlotte's bag.

Seven o'clock could not come fast enough, and yet when it did, Walter, my heart plunged through my chest. But I followed my plan precisely. I did not falter. Not once. In the cloakroom, I reached for Charlotte's bag before my own.

"Charlotte, your satchel is heavy!" I announced in so loud and cheery a voice that everyone turned to look at us. "Are you carrying rocks?"

Then I made an exaggerated effort to hoist the bag, and everyone laughed at my clownish antics but Charlotte, whose eyes narrowed. She alone knew how out of character such behavior was for me.

I had planned to somehow spill the contents of the bag, but perhaps Providence approved of my plan, for what happened next was even better. The seam burst from the weight, and all the watches scattered over the floor, making the most dreadful racket, Walter, which was worsened by the gasps of shock from the other girls. One of the watches split apart—my poor handiwork on display, I am sure—and all the pieces bounced across the floor, springs and crystals and those delicate hands I'd worked so hard to paint.

"Oh, Charlotte!" I cried, and I think I killed part of my soul with this. "Oh, Charlotte, what have you done?"

Mr. Mills, on the balcony, saw it all. He thundered down the stairs in such a temper, red-faced and full of rage, and grabbed Charlotte by the shoulders and shook her. "A thief!" he shouted in her face, and at once Charlotte began to cry, certainly from the trauma of it all, but her tears only made her appear all the more guilty. "A dirty little thief who repays my kindness by stealing from me! The police will know what to do with the likes of you, you miserable thief!"

Of course I interceded on her behalf. "Mr. Mills, you mustn't call the police. Just send her away. She's so young, sir. It was just an error of judgment. Charlotte will never come back and never trouble you again. Please, Mr. Mills, please, it would mean ever so much to the whole family if you could see fit to send her away without any trouble."

He took my meaning as I hoped. After raining a few more harsh words on Charlotte's tear-streaked face, Mr. Mills ordered her to get out and never return. We were hardly past the gate before Charlotte fell against me, racked by such great heaving sobs that she could not even walk.

"Lyddie, I never...I never would..." she choked out, her words strangled by the torrent of emotion.

"Shh, shh, dear one, shh," I said, holding her up with my arm. "Everyone is watching. Wait until we are home..."

With all haste I hurried her along to the sanctity of our apartment. Of all the times I had walked through the stages of my plan, Walter, this was the one I could never imagine. Or perhaps I could not bear to imagine it. Charlotte's humiliation was so great, and her pain so enormous, and to know that I caused it…

Do you remember what I wrote before? About doing the wrong thing for the right reasons?

Mother was very disturbed by Charlotte's ordeal and wanted to speak to Mr. Mills, to assure him that Charlotte had surely been set up, but I was able to dissuade her from that with ominous reminders about Mr. Mills's threat to call the police. I endeavored to remind her of the necessity that I, at the very least, maintain my position so that we might continue to enjoy our more comfortable standard of living.

Of course, Liza's medical bills are also a consideration.

Perhaps my entreaties were too strong because I caught Liza giving me an odd look. But I did not stop until I was convinced that there would be no more talk of Mother interceding on Charlotte's behalf.

That night, when I made Liza's pudding per her insistence, I realized that we had run out of Lumi-Nite. Perhaps Mr. Mills has been gradually reducing the supply he provides? The thought is troublesome to me for many reasons. I do not think that I have imagined the increasing coldness emanating from him since that evening when he waited outside our door with flowers for Liza, flowers that were never delivered.

I apologized to Liza that her pudding was nothing but pudding and promised her that I would replenish our supply tomorrow. She flew into such a temper, Walter, but for once I was glad of it. She has been so listless of late that it was a relief to see some spirit in her again.

I tried to apologize again, but Liza would have none of it. And then she did the most astonishing thing, Walter. She picked up her palette, still tacky with paint, and scraped up a gloppy mass with the spoon from her pudding.

"No! Liza!" I exclaimed. "Have you lost your mind? You can't possibly mean to eat that paint!"

"And why shouldn't I?" Liza retorted. "If I'd known that you would forget to bring more Lumi-Nite, I wouldn't have mixed up so much paint this afternoon. It's the same stuff anyway. You said so yourself."

"There is quite a difference between eating the powder in pudding and eating it in paint!" I said. "You might as well drink a bottle of glue, Liza. What if it makes you ill?"

"Look how much you've painted," she said. "Has it ever made you ill? All the lip-pointing you've done? All the brushes you've tipped?"

Then—I think this was just to spite me—she ate the entire spoonful of the paint, Walter! And afterward she looked very sick— the paint is so gritty and unpalatable—but satisfied as well. Oh, she can try my patience, Walter. Like no one else I know. I barely spoke another word to her for the rest of the night.

Then, long after we had gone to sleep, I woke with a start. There was a figure in the room, standing at the foot of my bed. I could see her in the light from the walls, and something about the cast of the greenish-yellow glow twisted her features so that my own little Charlotte was nearly unrecognizable.

"You did this to me," she hissed, her face streaked with tears. "You."

I pressed my hand over my heart in hope that I could quiet its pounding and said, "Lottie, pet, what is it? What is the matter?"

"As bad as Liza," she spat out. "Worse. Because I know that Liza never loved me. But you...you! You always pretended to. Why did you do it, Lydia? Why did you do that to me?"

If there were ever a time to admit what I'd done, it was at this moment, Walter. But the way Charlotte stood there, trembling with rage, seething with such fury that I'd never seen before…

I am not proud of myself, but I took the coward's course and feigned innocence. Because my fears may be unfounded—because my suspicions may never be proved—it seemed too great a risk to confide in Charlotte. Besides, how much would she have understood? She is very young. She looked so young, you see, bathed in the green glow, overcome with emotion. It was impossible to look at her without seeing the infant Charlotte squalling for some milk.

So I shook my head, made my eyes go wide, and proclaimed that I had no idea what she was talking about.

"It will be better this way," I promised her. "You'll have more time to devote to your writing. You can go back to school now…"

There was a long, terrible moment when Charlotte stared into my eyes without blinking. I can well guess what she saw there. Then, without another word, she exited my room.

She knows, Walter.

She knows, and she will never forgive me.

As I will never forgive myself.

I am in a bad spot either way—if I am wrong or if I am right. If I am wrong, Walter, I have subjected Charlotte to a great injustice and perhaps severed bonds with my sweet little sister forever. And it is no comfort if I am right, for the consequences—if there is a poison in the factory that is slowly killing Liza, that may be slowly killing other girls…

I hope that I am wrong.

Liza's illness takes new and horrifying turns that baffle every doctor we consult. She has lost five—or is it six? I admit that it is hard to keep count—teeth now, and the infection gnaws away at her jaw unchecked. The bone is spongy, cobwebbed with holes like a cheap piece of muslin or a slice of Swiss cheese. You can't view it without wondering what would happen if you touched her mouth. Would the slightest pressure from your fingers carve a new hole?

There is talk of a radical operation to remove a great chunk of her jaw, from just below her ear to just before her chin, in hopes that the infection may be extinguished once and for all. Liza resists with all the strength she has left, but if it is a matter of life or death— which it may well be—I am sure she can be made to see reason.

But I pray that it won't come to that.

I have begun to make the inquiries you recommended. I have written to the Board of Directors at ARC to explain my—our— concerns. I know I am just a dial painter, but I do hope that they will respond with haste. It is certainly alarming to me that Mr. Mills now dons protective articles when he arrives at the factory and wears them all day long. I ventured to ask about this change, but he told me that it was not my concern. There have been no uniform or dress requirements for the girls, so I can only assume that we are not in contact with anything hazardous.

But what sort of exposure does Mr. Mills face, then? He is not a chemist from the second floor. He is only involved with the paint— with the powder—as are we…

My thoughts run away without my consent. I counsel myself to be patient, to have faith that I will understand in time. If there were any real danger, precautions would have been taken, I am sure.

Please keep us in your prayers, Walter—Liza who is so ill, and Charlotte who is so grieved, and me—

What am I? Afraid, I suppose. Tonight I am mainly afraid.

All my love,

Lydia

CHAPTER 19

I slammed out the door and into my car and drove exactly four blocks away. Then I pulled over, parked, and turned off the engine. I had nowhere to go, but I didn't want my mother, if she looked out the window, to know that.

Then it really hit me: I had nowhere to go.

How did this happen?

How did I lose not just everything, but everyone?

It's you, a mean little voice said in my head. *No one likes you. No one loves you. There's something wrong with* you.

A sharp spasm of pain exploded through my jaw, radiating down my neck with thorny fingers. I tried to unclench my teeth, but they were locked together. It was understandable that I started to whimper, alone in my car, with no one to hear me, no one to help.

Well, no. I wasn't really alone. There was the painting in the backseat, which glowed with soft comfort. In its own small, silent way it was fighting against the darkness, pushing it back. I could curl up with it in the quiet and listen. Maybe, if it was just the two of us, it would finally tell me its secrets. Maybe I would understand at last.

Nothing.

I rummaged in my backpack until my fingers recognized the worn leather of the diary. I knew exactly which entry I wanted—no, *needed*—to read.

14 May

> I suppose the seasons are changing. I suppose the flowers are blooming. I suppose the girls are telling stories at work, stories I'll never ever know, and sharing their little jokes that will never include me. I suppose the whole wide world is a whirling carousel, aflutter with streamers and aglow with light, that keeps spinning and spinning and never even notices that I've fallen off. I suppose—

I understood, I think, why she couldn't finish her last sentence. Letting those words into the world made them real, imbuing them with a powerful freedom that was as terrifying as it was true.

Not good. My thoughts throbbed through my brain. *I should maybe not be alone right now.*

But who could I call?

Where could I go?

Then I had an idea.

I rolled down the windows and fastened my seat belt as an afterthought. It was sticky hot outside; the clouds had been creeping in since the afternoon. The air seemed to crackle with electrical charge.

Or maybe it was just me.

The whole drive I thought it might start to rain. I didn't text him to say that I was on my way. I just drove, one thought looping through my brain, loud enough to drown out all the others. I didn't realize my teeth were clenched until I was standing before that gray tower, staring up at the fifth-floor window.

There was a light on in the lab.

I thought, in the distance, that I saw a flicker in the sky. But it was gone before I could be sure.

I climbed the steps two at a time, which was a mistake because my heart was already racing. By the time I reached the door I was breathless; so not cool. I pressed my hand over my heart as I peered through the narrow window in the door. I recognized him right away, the shock of black hair falling over his face as he held his head in his hands.

Oh, Luke. He had no idea I was standing outside, watching him. I didn't want to be some weird creeper skulking around, spying on him, but I really needed another minute—just one more minute...

Of course he looked up. Of course. I tried to smile big, brighten my eyes, and wave so that he'd think I had just arrived.

Luke was so surprised to see me that I don't think he wondered how long I'd been standing there. I tried to think of something to say as he crossed the lab with long strides and opened the door. But he didn't give me a chance.

"How did you know?" he asked. His fingers, cool and slender, wrapped around my wrist as he pulled me into the lab. "Things are falling apart in here. Falling apart. I really need some help."

"Of course," I said, ducking into the closet where I grabbed some goggles and pulled back my hair. "What's going on?"

"The ice. I forgot the ice," he said. "Can you... The ice machine is on the first floor, in the lounge... Can you hurry..."

I grabbed the plastic bucket from the counter and catapulted myself back down five flights of stairs. It was dark and deserted in the student lounge; the only light came from the far corner, where three vending machines hummed in the darkness. I shoved the bucket under the ice machine and hit the button. The frosty crunch of ice tumbling down the chute set my teeth on edge.

Moments later, I was back in the lab. I don't think I'd ever moved so fast in my whole life. Luke had already fished two samples out of the oil bath. He plunged them into the ice before I could even put the bucket on the counter. It wasn't until after he had adjusted the thermometers and made sure their temperatures were dropping that he finally exhaled.

Every three minutes, we pulled another sample from the oil bath and stuck it in the ice to cool. Once the sample's temperature hit zero degrees Celsius, the reaction would halt, and Luke would have a new intermediate to run through the NMR downstairs to find out what, exactly, he had synthesized. Maybe a worthless compound. Maybe something that would change the world.

At last, he sighed and turned to look at me. In the fluorescent lights, I saw the raccoon rings under his eyes. But he looked happy at least, happy and peaceful. "Thank you, Julie. If you hadn't shown up—"

I waited for him to finish his sentence. "What?"

"It would've been ruined. That ice thing…such a newbie mistake. I've been here for, like, twenty-seven hours. I'm just so tired. I really owe you, Julie."

"No you don't," I said. "Whatever. I was happy to help."

"How can you not be a scientist?" he asked, staring at me so intently that I had to look away. "Seriously. You're so good at it."

"I don't know about that. I don't know about anything, really."

"You can get a ton of money to go into the sciences, you know," he said.

"Yes, of course people will throw tons of money at me." I laughed. "I'm really excellent at filling an ice bucket. You know what else that qualifies me for? Maid service in a nice hotel."

But Luke didn't laugh. "Don't do that," he said. "It's really annoying."

It stung more than I wanted to let on. Then again, what gave him the right? "Okay," I said slowly. "I was annoying by accident. But you were rude on purpose."

"Sorry," he said. "That came out harsher than I meant. I just hate that self-immolation crap. If you talk like that enough, not only will other people believe it, but you'll start to believe it too."

"I don't know what I believe," I said. "I think…everything is falling apart. In my life, I mean."

"You want to talk about it?"

I shook my head. What was the point?

"Can I tell you something, then?"

I looked up, met his eyes, held his gaze. He didn't waver, not once.

"Sometimes—at least in my experience—when everything falls apart, and life is worse than you ever imagined it could be…it's really a sign, you know? That things are about to get better. All you have to do is hold on, Julie. You know what I mean?"

I nodded because I wanted to believe him. His eyes were so bright. His hand was so close. If he made a move, I knew how I'd respond.

"You'll figure it out," he said. "You're so smart."

The compliment hung in the air between us. We were both waiting—for something—and then he turned back to the experiment. But there was an unexpected shyness in the curve of Luke's shoulders. If I could steer us back to where we were during the experiment, that sparkling place of connection—

The painting in my car. I could show it to him. I had a feeling, suddenly, that Luke would understand. How could he not?

"Hang on," I said, slipping off the stool. "I'll be right back."

CHAPTER 20

July 12, 1918

Dearest Walter,

Last week I received an encouraging letter from the Board of Directors. They invited Liza and me to a meeting at their offices in New York, where Liza would be examined by a specialist in occupational disease, and I felt assured by the letter that if any element from the factory was responsible for her illness, it would be identified and addressed posthaste. After the shadowy and unrelenting course of Liza's illness, there was at last a glimmer of light and hope. We both felt it dancing around our hearts. Liza is not much for smiling these days, not with her smile marred by the black gaps where so many teeth are missing, but she must've forgotten because the grin on her face lasted for the remainder of the evening. She may recover yet, Walter. And perhaps we will all awake from this bleak nightmare.

On the appointed day, Liza was more energetic than she had been in weeks, which can be explained only by the healing power of optimism. I was grateful, whatever the cause, for I knew she would need all the energy she could muster for the trip into the city. I had to caution her against exhausting herself on her first excursion outside in such a very long time, but she would not be dissuaded from gaiety, and even hummed on our way to the train!

Was it only five months ago that we took this same train to New York City? It seems like another lifetime, Liza in her velvet gown, glowing jewelry painted on her skin. Every element of her aspect then was beautiful and bright with hope.

Arm in arm, we walked through the finery of Fifth Avenue. There were carts on every corner filled with flowers, and it was something special to stroll about the city with Liza on a summer's day, as if we had not a care in the world. At the intersection of Fifth Avenue and Twenty-Third Street, we stood in the shadow of the strangest-looking structure I've seen in my life. This Flatiron Building is equal parts wondrous and odd, I think, like so much about these times in which we live. I would've stood there longer to marvel more at its peculiarity, but it was apparent that Liza was tiring already. I was glad of the elevator—very modern, it deposited us on the fourteenth floor in no time at all.

We were ushered into a fine room, with dark panels on the walls and a long, gleaming table, around which sat all the gentlemen from the board. They were quite solicitous of Liza and me, listening attentively as I told them my concerns. I had been afraid that I would stumble in my speech, perhaps stammer or lose my train of thought. But I did fine, I think. I think you would have been proud.

Then Liza and I were escorted into a small office where her examination was to take place. I helped Liza undress so that the nurse could weigh and measure her. Walter, I had no idea that the leg she broke is now two inches shorter than the other one! As if the bone continues to disintegrate! No wonder she limps. No wonder she walks with such care, as if she is liable to break at any moment.

187

Some long strands of her hair were cut and sealed in glass vials, and four vials of blood were taken from her arm. I watched with concern, but it appeared normal—red blood with no glow at all.

Of course, the room was rather bright.

Then the nurse turned to me. "Did you bring the item?" she asked.

I nodded as I produced a ring box from my bag. The nurse snapped it open to confirm that one of Liza's lost teeth was nestled inside. Then she slipped the ring box into the pocket of her uniform and left us.

Liza and I sat by the window so we could stare at the street below. From such a distance, the people seemed small and insignificant, like miniature playthings. In the bright light from the window, Liza appeared so thin that I could see not only her bones through her flesh but the shadows that they cast. Though we were not left to wait long, she fell asleep, and I couldn't bear to wake her. I just held her cold hand in mine, grateful to share the warmth of my skin.

Dr. Francis soon arrived, and he seemed a kindhearted fellow, full of reassurances that Liza was too young and too pretty to be so ill, and they'd soon find out what was wrong so that they could make it right. The exam was methodical and precise. He took great pains to listen to her heart and her lungs, to peer into her eyes and her mouth. Though his touch was light and sure as he palpated her flesh, she flinched so often that I wondered how he did not lose patience.

When the exam was over, he called for the nurse and requested that she draw my blood and take a sample of my hair as well. I spoke up at once: "But I am not ill."

"Oh no, of course not, the very picture of health, my dear," he said, smooth as pudding. "This is just for comparative purposes."

Once Liza was dressed, we were returned to the larger room. Dr. Francis stood behind Liza with his hands on her chair.

"Gentlemen, I appreciate the opportunity to examine Miss Liza Grayson, who I understand to be a dial painter at the Orange, New Jersey, factory. Recently the patient and her sister, Miss Lydia Grayson, have contacted you with concerns regarding the patient's various illnesses. I have conducted a thorough physical examination, and while we will of course have to wait for analysis of the biological samples, I feel confident that I have arrived at a diagnosis that will hopefully enable the patient to receive proper treatment so that she may enjoy improved health."

Liza grabbed my hand and squeezed it. I wanted to celebrate with her, but something tripped me even then—the phrase "improved health" was not as reassuring as I had hoped.

"The patient is suffering from an advanced case of syphilis," Dr. Francis continued. "There is no indication that her work as a dial painter has affected her health in any way."

Syphilis, Walter. Syphilis is what he said. Such an ugly word, slithering over the tongue like a venomous snake. I had never heard it spoken out loud before, just in whisper-hisses hidden behind hands when an uncharitable rumor spreads from girl to girl. Liza's head fell forward, and I was afraid that she would faint, but then I realized that she was simply trying to hide her shame.

But no. I did not believe it because I know Liza. She is not without her faults, but there is no way—no way, no way—that she could have contracted syphilis. Not my Liza, Walter. Not my sister. I was about to protest when Dr. Francis continued.

"There are chancres in her mouth, for example. These pus-filled sores are found in the nose as well, which may be indicated in the patient's recurrent nosebleeds. The patient also suffers from chronic

weight loss and weakness. She is clearly anemic—the pale translu-
cent skin, bluish undertones like watered-down milk—"

"But what about my leg?"

Brave Liza. Speaking even before I found an opportunity to
do so.

Dr. Francis, for the first time, looked inconvenienced. "That is
merely a gumma in the femur."

"Excuse me?" asked one of the board.

"It is like a tumor filled with bacteria," Dr. Francis explained. "It
eats away the bone. Terribly painful, gummas. So you see, all of the
patient's symptoms indicate a late-stage infection with syphilis."

"No," I argued. "I don't think that they do. Because Liza does
not… She is not… She has never—"

The doctor and the chairman exchanged a glance dripping with
meaning. There was much clearing of his throat before Dr. Francis
spoke again. "We must also take into consideration an important
mitigating factor," he said delicately, as if he could soften his words
to such extent that they would cause less offense. As if there were a
way to imply such a thing without utterly humiliating Liza in this
fine room, in front of these important men.

Liza probably should have grabbed my arm or nudged my foot or
done anything to signal me to stop. But she did nothing.

"What could possibly be this mitigating factor of which
you speak?" I asked. My voice trembled, but not from fear or
embarrassment.

Before Dr. Francis could reply, Mr. Chandler—the president of
the company—spoke for him.

"Miss Grayson," Mr. Chandler began. "Perhaps you are unaware
of your sister's…dalliance with her supervisor. Naturally, we contacted Mr. Mills as soon as we received your letter, for we were

gravely concerned by your speculations. We wanted to hear from him about any illnesses he may have observed in the girls under his supervision. We were relieved, of course, that he has noticed nothing out of the ordinary. Then Mr. Mills wisely chose to confide in us about his misjudgment in pursuing a most inappropriate relationship with your sister. It is highly likely that Mr. Mills transmitted this infection to her in the course of their...relations. We also understand that your sister is known for dangling her favors before a great many men, which—please correct me if I am wrong, Dr. Francis—is a common characteristic of patients suffering from this disease."

"No," I croaked, but of course there was no need for Mr. Chandler to pay any attention to me.

"Mr. Mills understands his error in judgment and has assured us that it will not happen again. And, you see, even though we had a likely cause for your sister's illness, we still showed her—both of you, I should say—the favor of an audience and a consultation with a physician to confirm our suspicions. No one could say that we did not treat this situation with the utmost consideration. Of course, given the nature of your sister's illness, there can be no expectation that ARC would be responsible for compensation of any sort. But Mr. Mills assured me that she is a fine worker—that you both are— so when Liza has recovered, she is of course welcome to apply for employment again."

As if on some unseen cue, the men began chatting quietly among themselves, and I realized that Liza and I were dismissed. The meeting was over. As the secretary escorted us out, Liza spoke not a word. She did not even look up from the floor, studying the ornate rug as if the secret answers to her troubles were woven alongside the many multicolored threads.

Midway down the hall, I stopped and laid my hand upon a doorframe to steady myself. Our exit was so rushed that I needed to clear my mind. To come to a decision. I had only a moment so there was no time to give this course adequate thought, to be certain that my decision was the right one.

I squeezed Liza's hand so that she knew I would return, then rushed back to that grand room, even as the secretary called, "Miss Grayson! Miss Grayson!" as loud as she dared.

Most of the men were gone when I burst in, flinging open the door so hard it banged against the wall. The two who remained—Dr. Francis and a young man who was the spitting image of Mr. Chandler; he must have been his son—gave quite a start to see me returned, and with such a lack of decorum in my bearing. But I felt the time for propriety had passed.

I willed my heart to calm. And I told them my secret.

"My tooth," I said. "It is loose. At first I thought it my imagination, but—"

Neither of them looked at me.

"It—wobbles—in the socket—"

I took a deep breath.

"How can you explain—"

The younger Mr. Chandler's eyes met mine then, and I felt like I could drown in the pity of his gaze. "The best advice for you, Miss Grayson, is to make note of everything your sister has done and do the opposite."

This, Walter, this was too much. After the assassination of Liza's character, and the way she'd sat in her chair, so helpless, so defeated, well, whatever it took, I would not allow these men, in their fine suits, to say the same about me. One of the Grayson girls would speak up for herself, no matter how impolitely.

"How dare you," I said, my voice sharp as a razor, as if it could slice through the air between us and draw blood from his face. "How dare you—"

"What I mean to say," he spoke over me, "is you should reflect on where and how she has spent her days, and what sort of pastimes have occupied her hours, and then you must do the opposite."

"But you know where she has spent her days," I said. "We told you. She spent them at the factory until she became too ill to work."

"Then you already have your answer," he said, scooping the papers into his arms and escorting the doctor away, leaving me alone and gasping like a fish that has been ripped from the water, snagged on a hook that it never saw coming.

I turned around to leave and saw Liza standing in the doorway.

It was clear that she had heard every word.

Her eyes were watery with tears on the brink of falling, and yet so much more—unspoken apologies and unforgettable defiance and, ultimately, a terrible realization that seemed to sink into us both at the same time. There was no need to speak of it. We linked arms, like we have so many times before, and each helped the other down that hall, into that elevator, onto that street. That the sun keeps shining and the birds keep singing and the people keep living when our world is crumbling is a marvel to me.

We stopped to rest on a park bench on our way to the train station. Liza closed her eyes and let the sun fall across her face. She did not smile, but I could tell that its warmth pleased her. There was something that I desperately wanted to ask her. Though the better part of me knew that I should refrain, I was unable to do so.

"Liza?" I asked. "Did you ever...with Mr. Mills..."

"It doesn't matter if I did or I didn't."

"But if you didn't, we must tell them," I said. "We must go back and tell them. It's not fair that his word should hold more sway than your own. Did you know…that he was…"

She opened her eyes, and I saw, just once or twice, those familiar sparks flash through them.

"Of course I knew," she said. "Why do you think he doses himself with Lumi-Nite?"

"If you knew," I asked, feeling ill, "then why did you—"

"I didn't," she interrupted me. "Of course I didn't. I'm not stupid, Lyddie. I saw the sore on his—"

"Stop."

"What does it matter now?" she asked, closing her eyes again. "I'm going to die either way."

"No," I said firmly, squeezing her hand so hard that she flinched and tried to pull away. "You mustn't talk like that, Liza. Even the doctor said that you would get well again—"

Still she didn't open her eyes, but a resigned smile flickered across her lips. "Yes, of course," she said. "Of course you're right. The sun feels so good on my face, Lyddie. Tilt your head up to the sky. Do you feel it? I don't think I've ever felt anything so warm or good in all my life. I'm so glad to feel it…"

"We have to hurry," I said. "We don't want to miss the train."

"Of course," she said again, slipping her arm into mine. Her bones were sharp even through her dress.

I have exhausted myself in the writing of this letter, Walter. Forgive its abrupt conclusion. There is not much left to tell of this tale anyway, besides the meekness that settled over Liza on our train ride, so that by the time we reached Orange she was gentle like a lamb, allowing me to shepherd her this way and that. It is hard to think that in some secret part of her heart, Liza hasn't given up. That her spirit hasn't melted away like the muscle from her bones.

I will write more as soon as I am able. I miss you most tonight and pray that you are cloaked in safety. I cannot bear to imagine anything else.

I love you.

Lydia

CHAPTER 21

"Hey," Luke said, standing as I entered the lab, cradling a canvas in my arms. "What's that? Did you paint it?"

I shook my head. "This has been my summer project. I've been collecting these old paintings…Just wait till you see…They're amazing…"

Luke stood directly behind me. I thought I could feel his breath on my neck, but it was probably just my imagination. Together, we stared at the painting. In the light, it seemed pretty ordinary, almost unremarkable, but it was one of my favorites. After all, I'd been there; I'd walked through that room. I'd recognized that long table and those large windows the moment I saw them. In the painting, a row of young women sat side by side at the table. Each one held a slender paintbrush—I recognized those too—and a tiny pot of paint.

There were watch faces scattered on the table in front of them, with needle-thin numbers marking the time in miniature. It was something I had never thought of, that actual people had once painted those tiny numbers that circled the face of a watch. The girls at the table looked so familiar, especially the one whose hair was swept back with a cluster of roses. I was pretty sure they were the same girls from the dance-hall painting, but it was hard to know for certain.

"It's…nice," Luke said. He smiled wryly at me. "Sorry. I'm not much for art appreciation. Am I missing the amazing part?"

"You bet," I said. "Is there someplace…dark…we could go?"

He raised an eyebrow at me, and I blushed.

"Or here is fine," I said quickly. "If I can turn out the lights?"

I ducked out from under his gaze and walked across the lab, my sandals slap-slap-slapping on the tile floor. My toes were cold.

After the lights were out, I had to get back to Luke by touch. My steps were tentative until I reached the counter. Then, with one hand holding on, I made my way to the painting. It cast a green glow over his face. The lab was so dark that I could've stared at him and he never would have known.

But I didn't. My gaze dropped to the painting instead. It wasn't as gruesome as some of the others I'd found, but it was definitely weird. In the dark, the paint and paintbrushes glowed, and the glow seemed to seep into the girls' hands and arms, illuminating their bones like an X-ray. Spindly finger bones, knobby knuckles, plated wrist bones linked like puzzle pieces. The glow crept up their arm bones, inching toward their hearts.

The only other part of the painting that glowed was the girls' faces, but not how you'd expect. They lacked lips and noses and eyes, their faces wiped clean of expressions and emotion. Instead, a parade of numbers marched around their featureless faces, *one two three four five six seven eight nine ten eleven twelve*, glowing watch faces painting glowing watch faces.

Oh, and the French, of course: *On est à court de temps.*

We are running out of time.

It was creepy and all, but like I said, she'd painted worse. But I guess Luke didn't know that. I guess that was why his voice sounded so strained when he said, "Hold on," and moved away from me. I mean, from the painting.

I sat in the dark for a few minutes. When Luke came back, he flipped the switch, flooding the lab with light. In his hand he held a small gray device, about the size of a remote control. I searched Luke's face for answers, but it was closed to me.

The device had one glowing green light—a power indicator?—and another light that was dark. As Luke approached the painting, there was a flash of red. Then another, and another, and another, blinking in a rapid and unstable pattern, until the red light stopped flashing and stayed lit. Static hissed from the device; it sounded like it was spitting.

"What is that?" I asked. Luke's face had darkened; the creases in his forehead were enough to tell me that something was wrong. Something was very, very wrong.

"My God, Julie. Where did you get this?"

"This? I just…at a consignment store," I said. "What? What's wrong? You're kind of freaking me out. Can you…"

I paused, distracted by the crackling clicks. "Can you turn that thing off?"

"I don't know what to say," Luke replied, staring at me. "Julie, this is a Geiger counter. It measures radioactivity."

"What? No." I tried to laugh. "You just have one of those lying around? Do you have a lot of experience with mutant superheroes in this lab? Any, uh, radioactive spiders I should look out for?"

Luke didn't laugh.

"I don't think you realize how serious this is," he said. "This painting is *radioactive*. Radiation is poisonous, Julie. Radiation *kills*."

"No. That's not…that's not possible—"

"It is. This painting is clearly radioactive," he repeated. "That's why it's glowing. Exposure to radiation makes people radioactive too...you know, by touching it. Or breathing in the off-gases."

"Off-gases?" I repeated stupidly.

Luke sighed like he was frustrated, but his hands shook ever so slightly, like he was afraid. "The radioactive material. As it breaks down, particles of it get into the air. It turns into radon gas, and if you breathe it in, you can get cancer."

"*Cancer?*"

"That's what I'm trying to tell you, Julie! Radiation is no joke. We're talking, like, atomic bombs here. This is really, really dangerous stuff. I mean highly toxic. It can kill you. How much of it have you been exposed to?"

My mouth opened and closed, opened and closed. I don't think I even really understood what he was asking. All I could think of were the paintings—all seven of them—and I had *touched them with my hands*—and I had *slept with them near my bed*—and *carried them around in my arms*—and *shared them with Lauren*—

And *Luke*—

And oh God, *the twins' car seats. I put the paintings in their car seats...*

"If I could figure out how much you've been exposed to," Luke was saying, mostly to himself. "If I could calculate the amount of radiation the paintings are emitting and the time you've spent in their presence...There must be some formula for this..."

I didn't hear anything else because at that point I jumped up so fast I knocked the stool over, and I ran out of the lab, my hands over my mouth, my stomach heaving. I had to get outside, fast, because I was going to throw up—and also because I couldn't bear to hear another word. I heard Luke calling my name as I careened down the stairs, but nothing could stop me running from the building, across the rough concrete of the quad, over the rolling slopes of the lawn, past the towering lights around the perimeter, to the place where the campus was swallowed up by the dark row of trees leading to the woods. I would throw up—get that over with—and fall into the dirt, under the trees, and maybe, hopefully, die, because I deserved no less.

But I didn't deserve to die, either, because what I really deserved was punishment—punishment for putting everyone I love at such risk, punishment for being such a thoughtless, careless fool. If I lived a thousand years, I could never, ever apologize enough.

Waiting to throw up was interminably awful, kneeling in the dirt, gagging on stomach acid. And every time I heaved I saw a detail from a painting—the shattered bones, the crumbling teeth, the disappearing jaw, the *graves*—

Was that my future, foretold a hundred years ago? The bone-deep ache in my jaw, an early symptom? My body, a toxic waste site?

What had I done to myself?

At some point I lay down, hugging my knees under my chin. I don't know how long I lay there in the dirt, curled up and quivering. It could have been minutes; it could have been hours. I know time didn't stop—I know that's not possible; the laws of physics forbid it—but it might as well have. Thunder rumbled in the distance. It was too dark to see the clouds gathering overhead, but I could feel them. I could feel the pressure building outside me, in the air, and inside me, in my heart.

And that's when I realized that you cannot will your heart to stop, not even when it's in your best interest. It beats and beats and beats, even as it breaks. The blood pumps out of it—you think, maybe you hope for the last time—but that heart of yours won't quit. It won't give up on you, not yet. In the rhythmic pulsing you can hear it saying *get up, get up, get up;* and there is an even deeper whisper under that, a long-buried secret that you almost forgot to remember. I was so close to wrapping my brain around it when I heard footsteps crunching across the brittle grass.

Luke.

He said nothing but knelt next to me in silence. Then he placed his hand in the center of my back with just enough pressure to tell me that I could still feel something. When he started to talk, I paid more attention to his voice than his words, letting soft notes of reassurance wash over me. There were apologies falling from his lips—*too sudden, too harsh, should've explained it better, I'm so sorry*—

I rolled over, taking him by surprise. I was practically in his arms. I didn't care. I didn't analyze. I just leaned up and kissed him. His lips were as soft as I'd imagined they would be.

He closed his eyes but I kept mine open; that's how I saw the streak of lightning rip through the sky, white-hot power hitting somewhere close. We'd been waiting so long for a really good rainstorm; I could hardly believe that it was here at last.

I wrenched my brain away from the weather so I could focus on more urgent matters here in the dirt, Luke's body heavy on my own, his mouth tasting of coffee and a faint tingle of peppermint. Had he expected this? Did he follow me down here, sucking on a breath mint, working on a plan?

I didn't care.

Because oh, his kisses were so good, just what I wanted, just what I needed, tender and eager and strong. My hands cupped around his head, my fingers ran through his hair, and it was so soft, so silky. I couldn't help pulling his face closer to mine, and I think he liked that. He kissed me harder, deeper, and I couldn't breathe, and I know I liked that.

The sky lit up again, purple clouds billowing like a bruise. I counted the seconds until the thunder—

one—two—three—four—

I couldn't wait.

My hands fluttered down Luke's neck, across his broad shoulders, down, down, to the narrowness of his waist. Luke's T-shirt was thin but not thin enough. I wanted to feel his skin. My fingers plucked at his shirt, fistfuls of cotton in my grip. With my hands pressed against his back, I pulled him to me, and I don't remember how this happened, but my legs split like a peach, curling around his hips, holding him close.

My face was wet, but not with tears. The first raindrops fell shyly, and I was ready, so ready, to let it all go. My body wanted what it wanted, and why shouldn't I have it? And Luke—he wanted it too. I could tell from the way he was breathing, from the urgency in his mouth. This was happening. I was making it happen. I tugged at his jeans, fumbled for the button, for the zipper. Luke was poised above me. I was ready. He was ready.

And then—

He pulled away.

My mouth followed him before my mind understood what he'd done.

"It's okay," I mumbled through a sloppy kiss, pulling him back to me.

But his shoulders were stiff with resistance.

"It's okay."

Luke shook his head. "Julie. This…this isn't a good idea."

"Yes." My mouth on his neck. "Just do it… I don't care—"

"Well, I care," he said. "You might not think you're worth more than this, but I do."

Something snapped between us, and I fell back, landing on my elbows in the mud. The rain was harder now, stinging my face. My hair was plastered to my skull. *Why would he want you?* that hateful voice jeered in my head. *You're a toxic waste dump. Forget a condom. He'd need a hazmat suit to be with you.*

I couldn't look at Luke as he pulled me to my feet. He talked the whole way back to the lab, but I could barely understand a word he said.

He didn't want me to take the painting.

But how could I leave it with him?

He wanted to bring me to the emergency room.

But how could we spend another minute together?

He followed me all the way out to the parking lot. In the headlights, in the rain, I could see his lips moving.

Then I drove away.

CHAPTER 22

August 31, 1918

Dearest Walter,

I have received your letters, and I apologize for my lack of response. I also apologize, in advance, for the curtness of this letter. I will try as best I can to answer all of your questions in the time that I have.

Shortly after our trip to New York, Liza agreed to the radical surgery that had been proposed. The procedure took the better part of a day, during which I made so many errors in my work that it is a marvel that Mr. Mills did not fire me on the spot. It was decided, of course, that it would be imprudent for me to miss a day of work and the pay that I could earn, especially as Mother and Charlotte would be able to wait at the hospital for word of Liza's condition as soon as the procedure was over. Charlotte has not been able to secure other employment since her termination from ARC.

I had not anticipated what the scandal would do to her reputation; a thief is quite unwanted in even the lowest sort of positions. If I am honest, I can confess to you and you alone that it has harmed the laundry services. There is not nearly the number of patrons that once there was. So you see, Walter, it is simply impossible that I quit my position, though I assure you that I have given the matter a great deal of thought, and that your impassioned pleas have made a deep impression on me. If I left ARC, how would we pay for our barest living expenses? Not to mention the medical bills that accumulate daily? I learn from Liza's example that it is very expensive to die.

But shame on me, Walter, for even thinking such a thing. For Liza has had this surgery, and we have placed all our hopes in the surgeon's capable hands, and God willing the procedure will, at long last, offer the cure that has remained so elusive these past months. If the surgeon has to remove all her jaw, so be it; whatever it takes to rid her body of the insidious infection that consumes her.

The factory is not as pleasant a place to work as once it was. Mr. Mills treats me with great indifference—no more teasing, like when first we met, and no more respect, like after I discovered his feelings for Liza. He offers me no more Lumi-Nite, and I ask for no more. I have not made pudding in a month, and I doubt that I will ever be able to do so again. I think of those glowing crystals, and I worry, Walter. I think of stirring the powder, ethereal like heaven and gritty like earth, into Liza's nightly bowl of pudding, and I worry. What if Mr. Mills—what if everyone—was wrong? What if it is not so much panacea but poison?

If that is the case—if I have hastened her demise—

I cannot bear to think on it.

Liza has only made requests for Lumi-Nite once or twice since our trip to New York. She must assume Mr. Mills withholds it out of anger. But I have a different suspicion. If he still harbors feelings for Liza, mightn't he try to protect her? Sometimes I catch him, wearing his protective outerwear and looking at me with remorse, and I wonder if there could ever be a time for me to speak to him. If only there were a way to know if Mr. Mills still ingests the Lumi-Nite himself, or if he has abandoned all the faith in it that he once had.

Liza has not abandoned her faith. Sometimes, late at night, I hear a scratch-scratch-scratch at the walls. It is not a mouse, though. It is Liza. With her brittle nails, she scrapes at the glowing stars on the wall near her bed, and when she manages to peel off a flake of paint, she places it, still glowing, on her tongue, an unholy Communion born of desperation. What more does she have to lose?

As I was saying, the studio is not as friendly a place as once it was. The other girls are still quite chummy, but I am of necessity on the fringe of that circle. Minnie Johnson sits and stares at me, stares with a hard smile of triumph. There is little doubt in my mind that she told Mr. Mills all about Liza's flirtation with Captain Lawson. Which has ended with an anticlimactic sigh and then silence. One day Liza received a letter from him with no indication that it was to be the last, and yet another one never came.

Oh yes, I was telling you of Minnie Johnson's mean little smiles, and how pleased she is with herself these days, especially since her sister Eugenie has joined her as a dial painter, taking the position vacated by Charlotte. I look at Minnie and Eugenie, and I remember how Liza and I raced them to the factory that gray September morning, how Liza slammed the metal gate closed to throw an obstacle into their path, how I was able to secure the position through— what? Fortune? Or fate? I look at them and wish that my shoe—and not Eugenie's—had fallen off as we ran. I look at them and think that it's not so grand to work here. I look at them and hope that they won't someday harbor the same regrets that I do.

No one is overtly unkind to me, but I hear the whispers when I pass, and I know what they say—her sister Liza the whore, her sister Charlotte the thief—and the great injustice of it is like a poison in me. It is a cruel thing to condemn my sisters like that, to dismiss all the good in them for the convenience of a label that holds no truth. I tried to tell the other girls, before I understood in what low esteem they held my family, about my fears—specifically the powder in the paint—but all my concerns were ignored. I understand why. Sometimes even now, with all I know—with all I think I know—I find myself gazing on the powder's quiet luminescence or the stars shining on our walls at night, and still, after all, I find myself drawn to it.

At least I know I told them. I warned them, at least. I remember that thought when I start to imagine what they whisper about me, what they whisper as they paint their nails and their faces, as they paint their buttons and their teeth. Lydia the lunatic.

When at last the long workday was over, I went directly to the hospital. The possibility that Liza had not survived the operation did not occur to me until I stood before the hospital's doors and felt such dark clouds of dread settle upon me. Like a child, I wanted to run from this hulking brick building of death and disease, but I found some tarnished mettle within me and entered the hospital to make inquiries about my dear sister. To my relief, Liza did survive the operation.

Though perhaps, knowing what I know now, it would have been better if she had not.

I found Liza recovering in a large postsurgical ward, just one of ten patients confined to white iron beds, with Mother and Charlotte by her side. The disease had burrowed deeper into her jaw than expected, Walter, and so more of it is gone than expected—past her chin and nearly to her ear: gone. Gone. There is, I guess, just three-quarters left of her face. I made my best estimate, for much of her head remains wrapped in layer upon layer of fresh linen bandages.

Eventually a thin rust-colored fluid seeps through the bandages, and with great care, we change them, layering strips of linen as lightly as we can over the gaping hole in her head, where the teeth that remain rattle in their sockets from even the slightest motion. After Liza recovers, when sufficient healing has occurred, the surgeons tell us that she will be fitted for a prosthetic tin mask of sorts, modeled in the image of her face. This mask will cover the scars and empty spaces so that her countenance will not be so fearsome. After she recovers.

Of course, Liza's jaw is not the only thing she lost. Her lips are gone, and her voice as well, for she cannot speak with her face so bandaged. She should not move what is left of her mouth when there is so much regenerative healing for her body to perform. I had not thought of that, Walter, that she would be struck mute. How could I have known that I would not hear her sweet voice again?

On the third night following the operation, while Mother and Charlotte toiled on the small amount of laundry work at home, I sat by Liza's bedside in the hospital and held her hand. No one will even look at her anymore, and yet I cannot look away. She is so beautiful, Walter, still so beautiful to me. I wish I had a photograph of her from before because already I fear that my memory ebbs. I could never paint her, never do justice to the gentle hills and valleys of her face that have been ravaged by bacteria and curettes. I look at her with the heavy fear that soon I will no longer be able to do such a thing. How wrong that is. I want to always see her.

She opened her eyes, her yellowing eyes, and looked at me for the first time as if she remembered who I was. She even tried to open her mouth—to speak, I think—before the lightning bolt of pain struck her, searing though what remains of her face. I placed a pen in her hand and held a notebook beneath it.

Please, she wrote.

Take me home, she wrote.

I want to die under the stars, she wrote.

"Don't be silly," I whispered. "We knew you would feel worse before you got better. You have to give the operation time, Liza. You have to give your body time."

Please, she wrote again.

And then the pen slipped from her hand and clattered to the floor.

"You'll tire yourself out," I told her. "Rest, my sweet. Rest so that you may heal and be strong again."

She would not look at me, Walter, and she would not close her eyes.

So I spoke to Mother, and at the earliest opportunity, we brought Liza home, to her room, to her bed, to her stars. She seems more comfortable, at least, and the doctor comes every day. When she is hungry, I unwrap some of the bandages from her face, and she tilts back her head like a baby bird so that I may dribble some broth down her throat. It is good broth that Mother makes, rich and gold from boiled bones and bright vegetables. I am sure it is nutritious. Then Liza holds up her hand when she is finished, and we dress her face with fresh bandages, and she drifts back into a dense fog of morphine. Sometimes her eyes don't close and I can watch them move back and forth. I wonder what she sees.

It is still too soon to gauge the operation's success, but I thought, as I replaced the bandage this evening, that I noticed that old familiar scent of decay wafting from her face. I made a note to tell the doctor tomorrow. I pray that I am wrong, and it was merely the memory of the smell as I viewed the wreckage of her face. For if the operation was for naught...if whatever eats at her continues to devour her...

If she has gone through this great swath of suffering only to suffer more…

Only time will tell.

How precious are these moments with my Liza; how hopeful I still am for her recovery. There will someday exist a world without her, yet it is not one that I have ever known, and I hope that I never will.

As for my last letter, where I believe I mentioned a problem with my tooth, well, that was just a very silly little complaint of mine, and certainly nothing for you to worry about. I have seen the dentist, and he has assured me that all will be well. I apologize profusely for causing you even a moment of worry.

I just want to apologize once more. For everything.

All my love,

Lydia

CHAPTER 23

I drove for hours through rain-slicked streets, bleary candy-stripe lights glinting off every raindrop the windshield wipers missed. I didn't have any destination in mind. I didn't know where to go, but it felt good, at some elemental level, to keep moving. Body in motion and all that. I knew the truth, though. There was no way to outrun radioactivity.

I think it comes for me.

If it was in me, it was in me deep, in all the dark places of my body—hibernating in the marrow, sailing through the blood, burrowing in the teeth. Inside, was I a shining supernova of imminent disease, a ticking time bomb of radioactive decay?

Before you break, the cracks will show.

And if I was? What would that mean? I tried not to ask myself questions I couldn't answer. Luke's eyes had already told me more than I could bear to know.

Nothing good can come from this.

I had made a mess of so many things—more things than I could even count—and yet some small, strong part of me wanted to believe that there was still a way to fix them. That there was still a chance to make amends. Maybe it wasn't too late.

We are running out of time.

Then I was coasting on fumes. Then I was so tired that my eyes were slamming shut, and I could feel the steering wheel swerve under my hands. I was about to do something really, really stupid. I had to get off the road. I had to stop running. I had to find somewhere to go.

Only one place came to mind.

It wouldn't be so bad to go home, I told myself. I could slip in, and she might not notice. I knew how to be so quiet.

The front light was on. I went upstairs, so silent, like a shadow, like a ghost. I stopped at the top of the stairs and took a deep breath. The house still smelled like home to me, or maybe it was my imagination working overtime. Clean clothes hot from the dryer, sugar cookies shining with sunbursts of jam, and, faintly, a hint of my mom's perfume, carrying a lifetime of memories: the softness of her hugs, the whisper of her kisses, the smell of her hair. Her fierce mama-bear protectiveness when I'd been wronged by a teacher or hurt by a friend. All those times I'd fallen, how she always helped me get back up. When I was small, no matter what went wrong, she always knew how to fix it. She used to know. Maybe she still did.

Her bedroom door was ajar so I nudged it with my foot until I could see her sleeping silhouette. I watched the way the old quilt moved up and down, up and down, with her breathing. Every part of me was willing her to wake up—*Mom, I need you; Mom, I need you*—but I couldn't remember how to say the words.

Still, I thought I'd better try.

"Mom?"

Nothing.

I tried again.

"Mom?"

"Mommy? I—"

My voice caught in my throat, but she didn't move. I sank to the floor and wondered how I'd ever find the energy to get up again.

She suddenly lunged in the bed. "Julie?" she asked, panic in her voice. She fumbled for the light, and I blinked in the sudden brightness.

"Julie, oh my God, what happened?" Mom asked. She was at my side in an instant. "Oh, Julie, who did this to you?"

My clothes were crusted with mud; my hair was stringy and damp. No wonder she was freaking out. I started to cry. "My mouth hurts. I don't want to die, Mom. I don't want to die."

She wrapped her arms around me. They were stronger than I remembered. When was the last time I'd hugged her? Or let her hug me? Sitting on the floor of her bedroom, she held me while I wept. The story stumbled out of my mouth in fractured phrases. Sometimes the words were wrong, and even I could tell that I wasn't making much sense. But she understood. She understood enough.

Mom didn't say anything as she pulled me to my feet and led me into the bathroom. She filled the tub with hot water and lowered her eyes while she helped me undress. While I sat in the bath, I heard her moving around in my bedroom, and then there was a long silence, but I didn't care. Then she was talking to someone on the phone in a low voice, and I also didn't care. My body, distorted by the rippling water, was equal parts wonder and revulsion. Who could say what lurked under my skin?

"Ready to get out?" Mom asked from the doorway.

Maybe I nodded, or maybe I just thought about nodding. Or maybe she made the decision for me. I was all fuzzy—in my eyes and in my head and in my body, which went limp as my mom helped me to her car. She drove east, where the pink light was rising. From the backseat, I wished we could drive straight into the sunrise: rose-colored obliteration.

That's not what happened. Instead, Mom pulled into the ambulance bay at University Medical. I didn't realize that the entrance was wrapped in reams of paper for my benefit, or that the cluster of nurses and doctors, all cloaked in yolk-yellow suits, were waiting for me.

Time got all screwed up then. I know the car had stopped only for a minute, but it was long enough for Mom to grab my hand and squeeze it. "I'm not going to leave you," she said.

But that was not a promise she could keep.

Our cocoon cracked open then as someone yanked on my door.

"Let's get her into Decon," he said.

I walked down the paper aisle all by myself, like a big girl.

"She shouldn't even be here," one of the nurses hissed. "Eighteen isn't peds. Why is she in the peds ED and not the adult ED?"

"Too late now," someone whispered back. "No sense contaminating both departments."

"In here, Julie," another voice called, and her eyes were blue and kind. That was all I could see of her, kind blue eyes behind a clear plastic screen. The rest of her was wrapped in plastic—purple gloves, goldenrod suit, rubbery green boots, all with the waxy sheen of a new box of crayons. I followed her into a plain cement room. The panels of lights overhead tried to brighten it, but the grayness was overwhelming, as if it could drain all the color and hope from anything that entered.

"Put your clothes in here," the nurse said, holding up a red biohazard sack. "Then stand under the shower and scrub every bit of you. I'm sorry the water will be cold. It's better that way."

"But I just had a bath," I said, surprised that I didn't choke on the words. "It was hot. Is that—"

"Shower anyway, Julie," she said. "That's what the decontamination room is for...decontaminating."

She left then, and when I heard the soft click of the door, I wondered if I'd been locked inside. If anyone would ever come back for me.

✳ ✳ ✳

I spent two long, terrifying days alone in an isolation room, marking time in six-hour spaces between blood draws, blinking back tears as a nurse in a protective suit scanned my body with a Geiger counter. I strained my ears for the clicking static, but this machine must've been better than the one in the lab. It had a digital display kept carefully hidden from my spying eyes.

There were thick binders with the words Radiation Emergency Protocol blazing on the cover. There were doctors who examined every inch of my naked body. There was my dentist peering into my mouth and finding a hairline crack in one of my teeth. It wasn't from radiation exposure, though. It was from all the grinding. I could hear Lauren saying, "I told you so!" before I remembered that I'd be lucky to ever hear her voice again after what I'd said.

Scientists from the Environmental Protection Agency came to see me, twice, asking the same questions for hours: Where did I find each painting, and when, and who did I expose, and how? Lauren. Luke. My mom. Anyone who had been in the presence of the paintings had to be tested too, their blood whirled through a centrifuge, separated to reveal any secret contamination. I was way more worried about their test results than my own.

Colorless liquids dripped into my veins through long snakes of tubing. Monitors with blinking lights and red numbers kept me company through the loneliest parts of the night, times when I refused to sleep because of what I saw when I closed my eyes: the girls in the factory...the people at the dance...the paintings, always the paintings. They lurked in the darkness behind my eyelids, glowing through the perpetual night.

That left nothing for me to do but look long and hard at the person I'd become. Last spring, there had been this one bright, true moment, looking at my mom's crumpled face, when I knew that I would give—that I would do—anything for her. Something mean and ugly had happened to me since then, gnawing away at what was most important until it started to consume me too. Now I had to wonder, though—what did it really matter? Maybe this wasn't the life I expected to live, but it was still a life I loved. There had to be a way to fix everything I'd wrecked. I would claw myself out of this crater of self-pity until my fingers started to bleed, if that's what it took.

I just had to get out of this hospital first.

* * *

On the morning of the third day, Dr. Margolis came into the room with her nose buried in my chart. My mom followed her and perched on the edge of the bed. I noticed right away that Dr. Margolis wasn't wearing a protective suit. For the first time, a spiral of hope coiled inside me.

"Julie," Dr. Margolis said. "How are you?"

I had to think for a moment before I realized the easiest answer would be: "Fine."

"And the pain in your jaw? Does the temporary crown help?"

I ran my tongue against my teeth. "Yeah. I think so."

She made a note in the chart. "I'd like you to follow up with your dentist as soon as possible," she said. "Perhaps he has an appointment today so you can be seen for a permanent crown fitting."

"Today? So I get to—"

"You're discharging her?" Mom interrupted me.

Dr. Margolis looked up. "Julie's test results have stayed normal over the last forty-eight hours," she said. "That's exactly what we hoped to see."

"So…I'm going to be okay?"

There was a pause. "At this time, there is no indication that you are suffering from any of the immediate effects of radiation poisoning," Dr. Margolis said carefully. "We'd be very concerned if you had burns or sores, or if your hair was falling out, or if you had severe gastrointestinal upset."

I waited, breathless, for her to continue.

"However."

And again, that killer pause.

"There's no safe level of radiation exposure, Julie. And even if there were, everyone responds differently to radiation. You might never have any problems. I might have half the exposure you've had and get cancer in five years."

"So I could still…?" I couldn't even say it.

"It's possible. But remember that everyone is exposed to radiation, every single day. Ever eat a banana? They're radioactive, you know. In fact, some people have suggested we stop using the sievert to measure exposure to radiation and replace it with the BED—the banana equivalent dose!"

Dr. Margolis was the only one who laughed. She quickly cleared her throat. "You'll need to be particularly vigilant with your medical care for the rest of your life, Julie. Complete physicals every six months, including blood work and thorough cancer screenings. I'm happy to provide your follow-up care. We'll watch for anemia and signs of skeletal weakness. Call me right away if you break any bones.

Or if you have any symptoms of anemia—exhaustion, weakness, lack of energy, fainting…"

She stood up then and shook my hand. "Julie, without a doubt you've been the most excitement this hospital has seen in a long time. Before you came, we'd only gotten out the radiation emergency protocol during drills, thank God. Please take care of yourself. And if you have any questions—any concerns at all—don't hesitate to call."

"Thanks, Dr. Margolis," I managed to say.

The doctor hadn't even left the room before my mom reached for me, and I clung to her in a cloud of relief. Suddenly I was four years old again, and we were always going to be on the same team, and nothing could break us, nothing could tear us apart. I held on longer than I should have; I held on tighter than I needed to; because I already knew that this togetherness wouldn't—couldn't—last.

* * *

When we got home, I moved slowly, tentatively, like a guest who didn't want to intrude. But Mom ricocheted between the kitchen and the living room, talking nonstop.

"Are you hungry? You must be hungry. Hospital food, yuck," she said. "I went to the store, and I made chicken soup. The kind you like, with fresh noodles. And I got everything to make Nana's macaroni. Does that sound good? I could make it right now. It doesn't take too long. Or maybe a sandwich? We have hummus and lettuce and tomatoes or, um, sliced turkey? And cheese? Or what about something sweet? I bought cupcakes. Chocolate-chip cookies?"

"I'm not…" I started to say. And then she stopped moving for a moment, hovering in the doorway with her eyes all watery. They were pleading eyes, maybe even begging eyes, and I realized that it didn't matter if I was hungry or not.

"Mac and cheese sounds good," I finished. "If that's not too much trouble?"

It was the right answer. Her whole face brightened as she ducked back into the kitchen, still carrying on both sides of the conversation. I took a deep breath and tried to figure out how I could start to apologize in the middle of her monologue on the price of whole chickens. It was hard to focus through her rambling and the cacophony of my own thoughts, but it's not like I could go to my room, where all those radioactive paintings were lying in wait. Or were they? I wondered if I'd ever see them again.

Then my cell phone buzzed. I glanced at the screen, but the number was unfamiliar. "Hello?" My voice was so leathery that I had to clear my throat.

"Is this Julie Chase?" a man asked. "My name is Bert Rawlings. The owner of Lost & Found called me. About your letter? Those paintings you bought...They used to belong to me."

I sat down hard.

"You had a question?" he continued. "About technique? I'm afraid I can't really help with that as I don't know much about art. I inherited these paintings from my father—"

I started talking fast. "I have other questions about the paintings. About the artist... If you know anything about her...or why she was painting them..."

I held my breath, waiting. Hoping.

At last, he spoke. "I know a little bit."

"Oh my God, for real? Can I...can I ask you some questions?"

"Uh, sure. Go ahead."

My voice dropped to a hush. "Do you want to get some coffee? Are you anywhere near the Panera on Elmwood?"

"Sure," Mr. Rawlings said. "When? Now?"

"That would be perfect." I hung up and started thinking fast about my car and how it was out of gas. About the way Mom's hands kept capping my shoulders, guiding me here and there, and how I'd let her, like I was a little kid. About the look on her face if I said, "Gotta go meet some stranger about the paintings that could've killed me!"

There was only one thing to do.

I slunk into stealth mode, slipping on my sandals, picking up my bag in slow motion to silence the loose change clanking around in it. I crept toward the door, pocketed Mom's keys, and eased outside, shutting the door so carefully that the click was nearly noiseless. Then I was in the sunshine, and in her car, and driving down the street before the adrenaline could even kick in. At the corner, I passed a news van and wondered idly what it was doing on our street. And then I wondered about coincidences—like why would this Bert Rawlings call me today, when I'd given up hope that I'd ever hear from him.

What I didn't know was that the fallout had barely begun.

* * *

The Panera was pretty empty at two o'clock on a Tuesday. I chose a table with a clear view of the door so that I could watch for Mr. Rawlings. I could tell it was him the moment he walked in, from the way he glanced around like a twitchy rabbit, looking for me. I raised my hand like I was in school.

"Are you Julie?" he asked. "You're younger than I thought you'd be."

I tried to smile. What could I say to that? *You're older than I thought you'd be?* He was, with sparse hair and a furrowed forehead; there was a grayish cast to his skin. Mr. Rawlings didn't look like someone who got out much.

"Thanks for meeting me," I said.

He nodded once, fumbling with his hands on the table. "You have some…questions?"

"I do. I want to know…well, *everything* about the paintings. Everything you can tell me."

"I'm afraid that's not much," he replied. "They belonged to my grandfather. Of course he's been dead since the sixties. It was my father who died three months ago. That's when I got the paintings."

His grandfather, I thought, stung by the knowledge that I'd been wrong all along: LG wasn't a girl. "So your grandfather painted them," I said slowly. "Do you know why? Or how? I mean…what techniques he used?"

Mr. Rawlings shook his head. "He didn't paint them. Someone gave them to him…someone who was no relation. Her name was Lottie."

"Do you know how she got the paintings?"

There was a pause. "I believe one of her sisters painted them. But I can't say for certain. They've been locked in the attic of my father's house for decades."

He cleared his throat, and I perched on the edge of my chair, jittery with anticipation.

"So this is really my fault," Mr. Rawlings continued, staring down at the table. "Honestly, I had no idea they were radioactive. I owe you an apology, I suppose."

"Oh. It's okay," I replied. "I mean, you didn't know. Who would've known, right? But…ah…the artist…one of Lottie's sisters? Do you know anything about her, anything at all? Like her name or anything?"

"She had two sisters, Lydia and Liza," Mr. Rawlings said. "No one ever really talked about them. But I do have…"

He reached into his backpack and pulled out a stack of wrinkled envelopes, yellow with age. The spidery cursive on the front was hard to read.

"These letters might interest you," he continued. "One of Lottie's sisters wrote them to my grandfather, around when the paintings were made, I think. My grandmother hated that he kept these letters. She never understood why he wouldn't just throw them away."

"Can I read them?"

"You can keep them." Mr. Rawlings shrugged. "I don't have any use for them." He glanced at his watch. "Is there anything else I can do for you?"

I shook my head slowly, torn by my eagerness to dive into the letters and a nagging, pinching sense that I was forgetting something. But I couldn't figure out what it was. "Thank you for…" I waved my hand over the letters. "For these. For meeting me."

"Sorry I couldn't be more help," Mr. Rawlings replied as he pulled himself up.

I watched him shuffle toward the door and walk outside. Then lightning crackled through my brain, and I ran after him.

"Mr. Rawlings!" I shouted. "Wait!"

He was stepping into his car, but he turned around to face me.

"Who told you the paintings are radioactive?" I asked breathlessly. "How did you find out?"

A wrinkle of confusion creased his forehead. Then, like an afterthought, he said, "Oh. That woman from the consignment store who called me. On account of the EPA had been to her store and taken my contact information."

"The EPA," I repeated.

He chuckled. "She sure has a nose for business, doesn't she? Asked me if I'd be interested in doing any media interviews. Said she'd be happy to set something up…manage any appearances for me. For a small 'cut,' she said."

"Media?" The news van on my street. Driving toward my house. *Oh my God,* I thought, sparkles of panic exploding at the corner of my eyes. *Everyone will know. Everyone.*

"Well, yes," Mr. Rawlings said. "But they're not going to get anything from me. You have those letters now. You can decide what to do with them."

He got into the car, waiting patiently for me to remove my hands from the hood. It was too hot to touch, really, but I didn't know how else to steady myself. I couldn't go home. That was certain. Not with the news van lurking on my street, satellite ready to broadcast my horror story on the six o'clock news. So I'd have to read the letters somewhere else.

And I knew who should read them with me.

CHAPTER 24

Dearest Walter,

Liza died Tuesday last.

To the end, we all pretended—even she pretended—that she could yet recover, even when she struggled so to breathe, even when the pus and blood flowed down her neck and soaked her nightdress. It was the last, worst lie of her life; may it be mine as well.

When it was so horrible, I thought often of how great our relief would be when her suffering was finally over. In the earliest hours of Tuesday morn, when all the world was still and dark, Mother and I held Liza's hands as she exhaled—no soft, gentle sigh; it was the wet rattle of a gutter overburdened with fallen leaves—and a terrible silence followed. We waited, electric with tension, for a breath that never came, that would not come again. As Mother started to weep, softly so that she wouldn't wake Charlotte, I realized how wrong I had been when I imagined that we might feel relief. Because all that I feel is the enormous hole her passing has left in my life. In my heart.

I have always mapped my course to follow Liza and find myself adrift in uncharted waters without her.

Charlotte is gone, which is as it should be. Better for her, really. Whatever happens next, I would rather she not be here to see it. She disappeared after the funeral, and we found a note in her room explaining that she has volunteered for service as an army nurse. I cannot explain it, but I have a strong conviction that your paths will cross overseas. If so, please give her my love and the enclosed letter addressed to her. I always wanted my Charlotte to have adventures; somehow, through the heavy cloak of grief, it is a great comfort to imagine all the wonders of the wide world unfurling for her.

I come now to the most difficult part of this letter, Walter, which is informing you that it will be the last one you receive from me. I want you to know that I must stop writing to you not for lack of love, but for a surfeit of it.

I am sure that you remember, my dear Walter, the summer before last, when the war had scarcely just begun, and you told me of your intentions to enlist. I am sure you remember what we discussed that soft summer night on the rooftop as we watched for shooting stars. I cannot keep the promise that we made, and I do not expect you to keep it, either. Therefore, with this letter, I release you of all your obligations to me.

The time may come when you hear unkind words spoken about me. I hope that you will remember that you have always, always, always had my steadfast fidelity, and you must never doubt for a moment that I have, in all my words and deeds, been true.

I would ask of you one favor, Walter. If you have saved my letters, please burn them…or bury them. Do whatever you must do to destroy them, but do not keep them. The ones that glow, the ones with the secret messages painted in the margins, are the most dangerous of them all.

I still have hope for a brighter world. I imagine a world without war, where no one needs a watch that glows so that he will be better coordinated for killing in the dark. I imagine a world where Liza wears white not for her burial but for her bridegroom. I imagine a world where we dance at her wedding.

I imagine a world where I wait for you on the rooftop. As the first stars appear, I see you approach. I climb into the back of the airplane, and together we fly away, fly away, fly away from all the things that are broken and dying to that brighter world that still gives me hope.

All my love,

Lydia

CHAPTER 25

We sat side by side on Lauren's bed, hunched over each letter, speaking only when one of us had trouble reading Lydia's elaborate cursive. By the time we finished the last letter, I felt as fragmented as a Picasso. Like a balloon with a slow leak, all the exhilaration and anticipation seeped out of me, leaving me hollow and deflated and terribly, terribly sad.

"So," Lauren finally said.

"So," I repeated.

"So this guy you met today," she said. "How was he connected to the letters?"

"He got them from his grandfather," I said, trying to piece it together. "So his grandfather was...Walter?"

"Then how did Walter get the paintings?"

"From a woman named Lottie," I said. "Who was...Charlotte?"

"What about the letter Lydia wrote to Charlotte?" Lauren asked, looking in the last envelope again.

I shook my head. "It's not here. He must've given it to her. Oh, Lauren, do you think Walter and Charlotte really saw each other during the war?"

"Maybe," she said doubtfully. "Or maybe it just got lost. It's been, what, a hundred years?"

"The diary belonged to Liza," I said. "And the love note…that must've been written by Mr. Mills."

"Weird, isn't it?" she asked. "He sounded like such a creep when Lydia wrote about him. Hard to believe the same guy could write a letter like that."

She started rustling through the letters. "These letters bring up more questions than they answer. What happened to Lydia? And Charlotte? And Walter? Mr. Mills…did he really have syphilis? Or did he get sick from the radium too? I want to know what happened next!"

But that's not how life works. I thought briefly of Dad. *People enter and leave your life when you least expect it. You don't always get to know the whole story.*

But what I said was: "Well, we have their names. We can google them. We can google radium watches. And find out more about the American Radium Company."

"These letters are practically useless. I mean, you still don't even really know who did all those paintings you found," she pointed out. "It sounds like Lydia and Liza were both working on canvases, right?"

"Right," I said slowly.

"Then again, when would Lydia have had the time?" Lauren asked. "She was working, like, eighteen-hour days. But after she got sick, Liza was home all day with nothing to do. And they had the same initials. Liza Grayson and Lydia Grayson. So some of the paintings could be Liza's, and some could be Lydia's."

"I guess."

"Or even Charlotte's! With her nickname and all."

"It had to be Lydia," I insisted. "Like what she wrote in the last letter, about the airplane flying away? That perfectly matches the first painting."

"True," Lauren acknowledged. Then she started folding the letters, matching each one to its correct envelope by comparing the letter's date to the envelope's postmark. I took a deep breath. I had already told Lauren how incredibly relieved I was that her blood tests were normal, but there was still something big I had to say... and just one chance to say it.

"So these letters. They're not the only reason I came over."

She looked at me with her eyebrows arched.

"Wait. Turn around. I can't look at you."

Lauren scooted around so that we sat back-to-back. I could feel all the knobby bumps of her spine grazing against my own.

"That stuff I said?" I began. "Awful. Unforgivable. I'm sorry."

"No, wait," Lauren said. "I'm going first. You have to let me go first. You were right. I was attacking you over the paintings."

"I deserved it."

"I'm not done." Lauren shifted uncomfortably. "I was...*ugh*, this is hard to say. The way everything fell apart for you...I didn't know what to do. How to fix it. So I pretended like nothing had happened...which probably made it harder."

"It did," I admitted in a whisper. "And you were right. I was jealous."

"Are you still mad?"

"Are you?"

"I don't think so."

"Then neither am I."

She shifted on the bed and winced a little.

"Okay, what is up with you?" I finally asked, turning around.

"Are you okay?"

"Yeah, I'm fine," she mumbled, looking away.

"Uh-uh," I said. "Spill it."

Two pink circles flushed on her cheeks while I waited. Finally, Lauren sighed. *Here it comes,* I thought.

"So, you know how I was gonna get that tattoo?" she said.

"Oh. My. God," I exclaimed. "You did it! Oh my God! Where? Show me!"

"Nope," she replied, shaking her head. "It's, uh, it's on my butt."

"What?" I shrieked. "I cannot even believe you! God, I really want to see it. At least tell me what it is."

She smiled a little. "It's a laurel wreath," she said. "You know, like in ancient Greece? For victors? And, you know, my name...comes from the word *laurel*—"

"Nice," I said. "Very symbolic. Did it hurt? Like, a lot?"

"Honestly? It was like getting bit in the ass by a sparkler," she said. "And I haven't been able to sit down right since!"

I burst out laughing so hard, for maybe the first time all summer.

Lauren's phone started to ring. She glanced at it and passed it to me. "It's your mom."

"Do I have to?"

"Just get it over with."

"Hello, Mom," I said into the phone. "What's up?"

"Where are you? I've called you five times."

"I'm at Lauren's. Sorry. My phone must've died."

"You need to come home now."

"Is there, um, a news van outside?"

Mom paused. "Not anymore."

"Okay. I'll be there in a while."

"Julie."

"Fine. Ten minutes."

I handed the phone back to Lauren. "So when do you move into your dorm?" I asked as I dug around in my bag for my own phone. Once it finally powered up, I realized that my mom had called nine times, not five. But who's counting?

"A week from tomorrow. I'm never gonna finish everything I have to do."

"Well, I can come over and help you pack. If you want me to."

"Maybe," she said. "Thanks. I'll call you."

"Okay, then," I said as I slipped the letters into my bag. "See you?"

"Yeah," she said. "And, you know, if I don't see you again before I leave—"

In the pause that followed, I looked right at Lauren, almost unrecognizable to me with her newly dyed chestnut hair, chopped to her chin; ice-blue eyeliner making her eyes even bigger and paler. But there was still so much about her that was familiar—the ghosted scar above her right eye from that time we got wasted and she walked into a door; the freckle near her lip that looked like a tiny smudge of chocolate. I had to believe that our friendship was like that, that somewhere beneath all the quicksilver transformations, there was a foundation that would never change. No matter what.

"I really hope you'll visit me in New York," she finally continued. "Whenever you want. Anytime."

"Anytime," I repeated.

Then I gave her a little wave, and I left.

✳ ✳ ✳

When I got home, Mom was waiting for me in the living room with two glasses of soda. I knew this routine. We were about to have a Talk. I perched on the far end of the couch, staring at the tiny bubbles dancing through my glass. There was no gradual way to do this; I had to steamroll my way into an apology.

"I'm so sorry, Mom," I said. "I didn't mean any of those things I said. I know how much you've done for me. I know how much I owe you. I—"

"No, Julie, you don't owe me anything," she interrupted. "I just want you to sit and listen for a few minutes, okay?"

I nodded.

"I'm doing everything I can to sell this house. I don't know how long it will take. It could take months. Maybe even years. But when it does, you'll get all your money back. I promise."

"I don't want it back," I mumbled. "I just want to tell you…how sorry I am—"

"Julie. Look at me."

She didn't speak until I raised my eyes to her face. "I said something that I didn't mean… Well, I meant it in a way, but it came out wrong," she tried to explain. "When I said that I wanted you gone—"

"Mom—"

She held up her hand. "From the first second I held you, I've always known that the most painful moment of my life would be the day you left," she said. "And yet I knew that my job—my only job—was to get you ready for that day. To give you everything you could possibly need to soar on your own. So it came as such a surprise this summer to realize that it was even more painful to see you left behind. And to know that I was to blame.

"So yes, I suppose I do want you to go," she finished. "But only because you're ready, Julie. I hope you know that anywhere I am will always be your home. Always."

"I know," I whispered.

"I want to tell you something else," she said, framing my face in her hands and staring into my eyes with such ferocity that I didn't dare look away. "The day you were born was the happiest day of my life. *Of my life.* I held you in my arms and marveled at you for hours: how perfect you were in every way, how much I wanted to give you the whole world and everything in it. I wanted every day of your life to be full of this unspeakable, uncontainable joy, my precious child, my reason for everything, and that's why I named you Jubilee.

"That's why I will sell this house," she continued, wiping tears from my face, then hers. "It's time you went out in the world to find your joy."

My phone rang then, as phones do at the worst possible time. I didn't recognize the number. I had to let it ring again, had to pause before answering the call that would change my life so that the person on the other end wouldn't know I was crying.

"Hello?"

✳ ✳ ✳

Almost two weeks passed before I saw Luke again; it took me that long to work up the courage to return his texts. When I thought about how ready I'd been to sleep with him, in the mud, on the worst night of my life, I wanted to pull my hair over my face and hide. I wanted to die of shame.

But. His texts had been so kind. He'd sounded so concerned. And he was on my list, the mental one I'd made in the hospital. He was owed an apology too. That's why I'd asked him to meet me at Morningdale Cemetery. I got there early, but he was already waiting for me at the entrance, his head hidden by a foldout map. But I didn't need to see Luke's face to go all wobbly in my legs.

"Hey," I called, sounding braver than I felt.

He lowered the map. "Julie!" he said. His smile seemed genuine.

"Uh, thanks for coming," I said lamely, like I was having a party.

"Morningdale Cemetery on a Friday afternoon? Always a pleasure," he replied. Then, to my astonishment, he cupped his hand around my elbow. "I got here a little early so I looked up the graves. I think they're this way."

We fell into step along a gravel-lined path that twisted through the rolling hills of the cemetery. Every step I took felt like a free fall. Every time his shirt brushed against my arm, it almost brought me to my knees, but he didn't seem to notice any of this. I stared straight ahead, not trusting myself to look at him.

There's a pull in graveyards that my body instinctively tries to resist. Maybe it's from all the times I held my breath driving past one when I was a kid or all the spooky stories at sleepovers, but I think it comes from somewhere deeper, more elemental. Some part of you knows what's coming, if not when, and a cemetery is the ultimate, inescapable reminder.

But I owed it to her to pay my respects. I owed it to them both.

"Okay," Luke said at last. "They ought to be in this row."

"Both of them?"

"Yeah. They were, uh, buried next to each other."

We didn't speak as we stepped off the path. This part of the cemetery was older than the area where we'd buried my grandpa; the stones here were weathered and hunched from decades of exposure. You had to look pretty closely to read some of the names.

Archibald Cooper

Elodie Evans

Myrtle Kowalski

Then I stopped short.

Liza Hazel Grayson

Lydia Rose Grayson

Side by side, identical headstones, identical graves.

"It's them," I whispered, sinking to my knees.

Luke reached into his backpack and pulled out the Geiger counter. "Sorry," he said quickly, seeing my dirty look. "I wanted to be sure."

But to me, there was never any doubt.

It only took a moment for the machine to start flashing and spitting static again. Luke nodded, satisfied, as he put the Geiger counter away.

"So even after all this time," I said, "their…remains…are still radioactive?"

"Well, the half-life of radium is roughly sixteen hundred years," Luke said. "So even after that much time passes, only half of the radium has decayed."

"Thanks, I know what a half-life is." My smile softened the snark.

Luke grinned back. "Apologies. Of course you do."

There was a pause before he spoke again.

"Radium is a bone seeker," he continued quietly. "It mimics calcium in the body, accumulating in the bones and in the—"

"Teeth."

"Yeah."

I thought about the darkness underground, the blackness of being sealed in a box six feet under the dirt. But maybe that was not the case for Lydia and Liza. Maybe their bones were still glowing, a night-light for their eternal sleep. In that airless place, where there was no life, the hum of radioactive decay would keep them company long after my own life was over. For centuries. For millennia.

I closed my eyes and let my thoughts whisper an apology to the sisters underground. For how sorry I was. For how wrong it was.

For how they should've had more, more of everything—more time for painting and more time for laughing, more time for kissing and dreaming and wishing. More time for misunderstandings and mistakes, for adventures, for learning, for reaching and trying and hoping and never giving up. More time for falling in love and out of love and in love again. More time for forgiveness. More time. More *time*.

I didn't know how much time waited for me, but I was sure of one thing. You could give me a hundred years, and it wouldn't be enough. I didn't want to waste a moment.

My fingers trailed through the soft grass, finding their way to Luke's hand. The lightest touch, my skin brushing against his, an unspoken question emitted from my cells. His answer was loud and clear, in the pressure of his grip, in the way his fingers twined through mine. The warmth of his hand had me plunging in a free fall again.

"It's too bad we'll never know." Luke finally broke the silence. "Which one painted them, I mean."

"Yeah."

A cloud shuddered across the sun, casting us in shadow. I pulled my hand from Luke's and rummaged in my backpack for the butcher paper and charcoal I'd brought.

"I just want to do a quick rubbing," I explained as I taped some paper to Liza's tombstone.

Though the charcoal was smooth in my hand, it left sooty residue everywhere, fingerprinting me as I rubbed it across the paper. Then came my favorite part: as the smudges darkened the paper like gathering rain clouds, the words carved into the tombstones appeared like magic.

Liza Hazel Grayson
Beloved daughter, dearest sister, loyal friend
May 3, 1899 – September 9, 1918
She dwindled, as the fair full moon doth turn
To swift decay, and burn
Her fire away.

And then:

Lydia Rose Grayson
Beloved daughter, dearest sister, loyal friend
February 18, 1901 – August 22, 1919
The stars rise, the moon bends her arc,
Each glow-worm winks her spark,
Let us get home before the night grows dark.

When the rubbings were finished, I carefully rolled them up and tied them closed with a snippet of black satin ribbon. Then I reached into my backpack again. I wasn't going to take from these graves without leaving something in return.

Luke watched me as I placed one of the antique paintbrushes on each grave. *So much more than what it seems,* I thought to the sisters underground, *but you already know that. It doesn't matter which one of you painted them. What matters is that you did.*

I stood for another moment in silence. Then it was time to go.

"Classes start a week from Monday," Luke said as we walked back to our cars. "So parking's going to suck whenever you stop by, but I hope you'll—"

"Actually, I'll be part of the problem," I interrupted him. "I'm... matriculating. I'll be a first-year student. I'm moving into the

Grantley dorm next Thursday."

Luke stopped. "What?" he asked in surprise. "How did that happen?"

"It was the paintings," I explained. "You know they were on the news, right? Because the EPA had to check out all the places they'd been...for radioactive contamination..."

"Sure. Of course."

"And then I got a phone call. The same day I got out of the hospital. It was this woman, Gloria Mendoza—she's the director of the Museum of American Women's Art. She wanted to buy the paintings for an exhibit they're doing on women's activism in the workplace. It wasn't a ton of money, but it was enough to pay for my first year of college. Lucky for me, Newark University has rolling admissions. And next year I'll apply for financial aid and scholarships and loans. Whatever it takes."

"I'm amazed," Luke said bluntly. "You were so set on your original plan."

I shrugged. "I guess I changed my mind." *Or had it changed for me,* I thought, remembering the quiet graves, the ticking clocks, and all the great unknowns of the future.

"Congratulations, then," Luke said, grinning broadly. "Tell me about the exhibit."

"So the dial painters realized that they were all being poisoned by their jobs, and they got organized. They demanded that people pay attention to how they were dying so young. They found this reporter—his name was Charles Graham, I think; Gloria was telling me about it—who wrote a series of articles about the Radium Girls for the *New Jersey Sentinel.* And that blew everything up—people were horrified and outraged to learn the truth about what was happening to those poor girls. Eventually, in the 1920s, there were lawsuits against the companies that made radium watches…for not protecting the workers, even after the bosses knew that radium was deadly. And it set one of the first precedents for workplace health and safety protections."

"Wow."

"Yeah. It was too late for Liza, though. And Lydia. And a bunch of other women who died in terrible ways. But generations of people have worked in safer factories and jobs because of them. Now the paintings are going to hang in a museum, behind this thick glass wall so that no one can get sick from them. And more people will know about the Radium Girls. Those paintings—they're a chronicle of what happened, proof that art can tell a story long after the artist is gone." Then I had an idea. "We could go see them sometime. The paintings. If you want to."

The pause before he spoke was long enough that I wanted to sink under the unnaturally green grass of Morningdale Cemetery's manicured lawns.

"Listen," Luke began. "About…that night…"

"No. Don't. I'm so sorry about that. I was so—"

"No, listen," he insisted.

"Really, it's okay—"

"Julie. Let me finish, please."

I looked down. Luke lifted my chin with two fingers and tried to look into my eyes, but I couldn't. I just couldn't.

"It's not that I didn't want to, you know, with you," he continued. *Oh God.*

"Because I did. I absolutely did. It's just…I didn't want to be one of your regrets."

I found a single strand of courage somewhere deep within and climbed it, fist over fist, until I could meet his eyes.

"Anyway, I feel like I should give you some advice about registering for classes," Luke continued.

"Oh?"

"Yeah. I'd like to, uh, *strongly* encourage you to not take Section 2 of Chem 101. Because I'm going to TA that one. Which would make things…awkward."

I was pretty sure I knew what he meant by that. "Don't worry," I said. "I placed out of Chem 101. AP credit."

"Oh good," Luke replied. "And completely unsurprising."

This time, he reached for me.

✳ ✳ ✳

Mom helped me carry four boxes, my suitcase, and my backpack to the car. After the trunk was full, we crammed the rest into the backseat.

"I guess that's it," I said, squinting in the sunlight.

"I guess so," she said. "Wait. I forgot something inside."

I followed her back into the house. In the kitchen, Mom was filling a brown paper grocery bag with stuff—a box of pasta, a carton of cereal, two cans of Diet Coke. Half a bag of rice cakes and an open box of granola bars. "You should have some food in your room, Julie," she said, her voice muffled from inside the pantry. "In case you don't like what they serve in the dining hall. Of course, if that happens, just call me, I can bring you something to eat—"

"I'll be fine," I said. "They'll have pizza, right? And cereal?"

"You should take this," she said, pulling the colander out of the cupboard. "For when you want to make pasta. And one of the pots—"

"But what about when you want to make pasta?" I asked, pushing the colander back to her.

Mom shook her head and shoved it into the bag. "What else?"

she said, almost to herself. "What else?"

"I don't need anything else. I'll be fine. Promise."

"Just one more thing," she said, opening her purse. She held out two twenty-dollar bills, so new and crisp that they must've just come from the bank. "Take this, okay?"

I held up my hand. "No, no, you keep it."

"I want you to have it. In case you need it."

"But what if you need it?"

Mom gave me one of those crinkly smiles then, like whatever she was feeling was so big and so heavy that it dragged down the corners of her mouth, no matter how much she fought it. Then I understood what she was doing with all this random stuff—what she was really trying to give me. There was never any way to be ready for this moment, though we'd been hurtling toward it for our entire lives.

"Thanks," I said, shoving the money into my pocket. "I guess I better go."

Mom nodded. "Call me when you get there. I mean, when you have a minute. I mean, when you want to."

"I will," I said. I stepped forward and gave her a long hug. She surprised me with the urgency of her embrace, as if she wanted to crush a lifetime of hugs into it. At last, I pulled away. I had to get out of there before one of us started crying. Otherwise I didn't know how I'd ever leave.

"Love you," I called over my shoulder as I walked down the hall for the last time.

"Love you too," she called back.

Things I didn't let myself do: look in the rearview mirror as I pulled away, wonder what she was doing at that moment, give in to the tears prickling at my eyes. It was time to focus on a deeper thrill, a singing kind of freedom, a dizzying anticipation. Something big was about to happen.

Newark University was completely unrecognizable, no longer the quiet concrete haven it had been over the summer. The swarming-antness of the students and their parents had me crawling through the parking lot, jostling over every speed bump. The lot closest to my room in Grantley was nearly full. Suddenly the idea of moving in all by myself seemed pretty dumb when I realized how far I'd have to lug my stuff.

During the five trips it took to empty my car, the sun started to dip below the trees where I had first kissed Luke. Every day, darkness came a little earlier. You could feel the shifting of the seasons in the chill that whispered *hurry, hurry, hurry* at the extremes of daylight. Back-to-school cool, in every sense, and all that promise, all that potential waiting to unfold.

There was a gang of guys—frat boys, probably—clustered near the door, somehow keeping a dingy hacky sack orbiting their circle even though their eyes never left the girls arriving with suitcases and back-packs and bulging nylon laundry bags. Every so often, one of the guys would say something in a low voice, and they'd all laugh together.

Room 212 was on the second floor, in the corner. It was maybe the blandest place I'd seen in my life, with wiry rust-colored carpeting and empty white walls. *Think blank canvas,* I told myself, *not mental institution.* There was a small living room with a couch and a table; a tiny kitchenette; and a bedroom with two narrow twin beds that reminded me, for one sharp moment, of Lydia and Liza, and the painted beds that were also graves.

"Hey."

I spun around to see a stranger standing in the doorway. She was taller than me, with a rainbow of multicolored braids spilling around her shoulders, some woven with metallic thread that glinted when she moved. I made a mental note to tell Lauren about that the next time she went on a Manic Panic kick. It would be an awesome look on her.

"I'm Kira," the girl continued. "I guess we're roommates?"

"Hey. I'm Jubilee."

"Jubilee? That's cool," she said. "So…which bed do you want?"

"Oh. Um. Doesn't matter. Whatever."

"You want the one closer to the window? I like it really dark when I sleep, so…"

"Yeah, sounds good," I said, dropping my backpack on the bed to claim it as my own.

Then another girl poked her head into the room. "Hey, ladies! I'm Rachel, but you can call me Rach. I'm the RA for this floor… That's short for resident advisor. It's soooo great to meet you! Listen, just dump your stuff, and we're gonna meet up in the common room down the hall for a floor meeting, okay? I bet you have a ton of questions. See you in ten!"

Kira rolled her eyes. "Ugh, I thought I was coming here to get away from chicks like that."

I laughed a little. "You can't escape. They're everywhere."

"Like zombies after the apocalypse."

"Worse. Zombies aren't that perky."

This time, Kira laughed. "Listen, I heard there's gonna be a bonfire tonight. You want to check it out after our floor meeting?"

"Yeah, maybe," I said. "I might have this other thing going on. I have to check."

"Sure, whatever."

While Kira stretched teal-colored sheets over her extra-long mattress, I unrolled the two grave rubbings I'd made and taped them to the wall next to my bed.

"Hey," I said over my shoulder. "Does this creep you out? If I hang these grave rubbings here?"

Kira glanced up as she shook a pillow into its case. "Nope," she said. "Who are they? Relatives of yours?"

I shook my head. "No. It's, um, kind of a long story—"

"Oh! *Goblin Market!* I love that one."

"The what?"

Kira pointed at the rubbings. "The verses? On the graves? They're from a poem. *Goblin Market*. I did my senior project on it for English last year."

"Yeah?"

"Yeah, it's about these sisters, and also these evil goblins that sell poisonous fruit, and one of the sisters eats it, and the other has to save her life and almost gets killed. It's really creepy and beautiful."

"It must be old, huh?" I asked. "The poem? Because these sisters died a long time ago—almost a hundred years."

"Yeah, it's from the eighteen hundreds," Kira replied, and went back to making her bed.

The mattress creaked as I sat down under the grave rubbings, wishing—just for a moment—that I still had the paintings. I missed them more than I wanted to admit. They'd become such a big part of my summer…such a big part of *me*, keeping me company, coaxing my future to unfurl in such unexpected ways.

My phone pinged, notifying me of an email. *Mom,* I thought, smiling and shaking my head as I dug around in my bag. I wondered why she hadn't just texted.

But when I looked at the screen, I realized that the email wasn't from Mom at all.

It was from Gloria at the Museum of American Women's Art.

Julie,

This morning, we started removing the paintings from their frames to do a bit of restoration before the exhibit opens. On the back of one of the canvases, we found— well, I'll let you see for yourself (images attached). Please call me when you can. This changes everything.

All best,

Gloria

I tapped on the attachment and discovered, for the last time, a secret painting. There was a girl sitting before a pair of gravestones, a half-finished canvas on her knees. She had a paintbrush in her gloved hand and a stiff apron over her dress. She had a canteen and a cup and a tiny jar filled with a liquid that cast its own light. She had everything she needed for plein air painting with poison.

I knew this painting had just been discovered. I knew I'd never seen it before, but it felt so familiar in ways that I couldn't explain… until I looked closer and realized that I recognized those graves.

And I recognized that girl.

I'd seen her face in the moon, watching the skeletons climb into their graves.

Charlotte? I thought in astonishment. *It was* Charlotte?

Once I'd read the letters, I'd been so sure that the paintings were Lydia's work. But if Charlotte had painted them—

After her sisters were already dead—

In the same cemetery where Luke and I'd sat together—

It was too unbearably sad to think about.

Then I remembered the second attachment. I clicked on it, expecting another hidden painting.

Wrong again.

It was a poem.

> Sisters, lost to shadows,
> I promise you this:
> The world will know
> how your light ebbed so mine could shine.
> I will pick up your paintbrush;
> I will pick up my pen.
> Yours is the only story I can ever tell.
> May the incandescent beacon of my love
> illuminate the truth
> as it keeps your memory alive.
> —Charlotte Grayson/Charles Graham

And now I understood what Gloria meant when she said that this changed everything. If Charles Graham was really a pseudonym for Charlotte Grayson, and those articles exposing the truth about the Radium Girls were really written by *her*, in memory of her sisters and what they had suffered—

If Charlotte's words had played such a pivotal part in unmasking the toxic corruption at the American Radium Company—

And if Charlotte's role had been to finish the paintings, using her sisters' paintbrushes to complete the canvases that Liza and Lydia had left behind—

Would there ever again be a reason to doubt what love could achieve?

Did it feel like this for Charlotte? I wondered as the charge settled over me, became part of me, until everything else melted away. To not just recognize but understand the sacrifices that had been made for me and all the ways, big and small, in which I'd benefited from them: that my every advantage was born from someone else's selflessness. Saving our home—the home my mom had made for us, the home that had helped me become the person I was today—was the very least I could do, considering all she had done for me. What could I—what *would* I—build on that foundation of love and sacrifice? I didn't know yet, but I was certain about this: I wouldn't let anything else stand in my way.

I reached up and rested my hand briefly on the rubbing of Lydia's tombstone. *She did it, Lydia,* I thought. *She accomplished great things, just like you dreamed she would.*

The window by my bed offered an amazing view of the campus, like a photo from the prospective student brochure. I could see the quad and the long concrete paths that connected the buildings. I could see the sloping fields and the trees, smudged with darkness now that the sun was setting. Already there was a group of guys building a pyramid of fallen wood for the bonfire. I watched them for a while, sauntering in and out of the forest. Then, a spark, an orange flame licking up the wood, consuming it, and a cheer from the frat boys rose with the first plume of smoke.

If I looked to the right, I could see the science building. There was a light glowing in the fifth-floor lab; a light that kindled in me the wonder of discovery. No doubt I could join Luke tonight, if I wanted; the two of us keeping vigil together, making observations, jotting notes in the margins, flirting with exhaustion and anticipation as the experiment progressed.

Or would I wander down to the bonfire with Kira, sandwiching myself between the blistering heat of the flames and the creeping chill from the woods so I could start navigating this weird new world of roommates and RAs and frat boys?

I could even stay here on my own, maybe make up my bed like Kira had made hers. Maybe I could start unpacking—the smallest box, the one with my watercolors and my brushes and the brand-new pad of watercolor paper I'd bought after I left the cemetery.

All of me tingled with hope for what was to come: all the bright days and dark nights that were waiting for me. I was hungry for each and every one. I wanted them all. I already wanted more.

It turned out the decision wasn't hard after all.

I smiled, in the darkness, for myself alone.

And I made my choice.

AUTHOR'S NOTE

This manuscript is a work of fiction based on a series of events that transpired during and after World War I. The Radium Girls, as they came to be known, were a group of young women who were hired to paint watch faces with glow-in-the-dark radium paint. Today, people know how deadly radioactive exposure can be. The Radium Girls were among the first to teach us that lesson.

Marie and Pierre Curie's discovery of radium in 1898 changed the course of human history. This pale, metallic substance inspired great hope and lofty ambitions. An entire industry sprang up to locate, mine, process, and ultimately profit from this strange and mysterious element. Doctors hailed radium as a miraculous panacea, adding it to tonics and injecting it directly into their patients. They marveled at radium's ability to decimate cancer cells. What they failed to realize, however, was that radium also killed healthy cells, and too often, the patient as well. Since radium's chemical structure is similar to calcium, the human body deposits radium directly into the bones and the teeth, where it emits alpha particles that cause catastrophic damage.

Radium soon made its way into everyday life, but it was hardly the benign element that scientists, doctors, and the public assumed. Powdered radium and zinc sulfide were added to paint to create a beautifully luminous substance that could be applied to almost any object. The United States' entry into World War I in 1917 caused great demand for luminescent wristwatches and airplane control panels, but radium paint was also used on clocks, light switches, keys, medicine bottles, telephones, and even toys. With young men fighting overseas, young women—including teenagers and girls as young as eleven—were hired as dial painters to paint millions of watch faces. For many, it was their first opportunity for paid employment, and they took great pride in their contributions to the war effort.

Since paintbrushes were easily flattened by the sticky, radium-laced paint, dial painters were taught to point the brushes with their lips. Supervisors assured them that the paint was harmless. Hour after hour, day after day, dial painters licked radioactive paintbrushes, continually ingesting small amounts of deadly radium. They also painted glowing jewelry on their skin and used radium paint to illuminate their nails, hair, and teeth. Company officials encouraged the dial painters to practice with the paint on their own time to improve their technique. One dial painter applied it to the walls of her bedroom, though what she painted there has been lost to history.

By the early 1920s, some dial painters were suffering from bizarre and terrifying ailments. Their teeth began to fall out, leaving holes in their jaws that festered and would not heal. Their bones weakened and broke spontaneously, which happened to one dial painter when she attended a dance. They developed severe anemia and strange cancers that often led to amputation of their limbs. Even worse than the disfigurement was the agonizing pain the young women suffered as they marched toward a slow death from incurable radium poisoning.

A woman named Amelia "Mollie" Maggia became the first known dial painter to succumb to radium poisoning in 1922, although her death was attributed to syphilis at the time. Years later when her body was exhumed, not a trace of syphilis was found—but her bones emitted shocking levels of radiation. The symptoms of syphilis are extremely varied (its nickname is the "Great Imitator"), making it an easy diagnosis for any collection of odd ailments. The stigma of the disease, though, could have certainly influenced other ailing dial painters against coming forward. This seemed to be the goal of two major companies: the US Radium Corporation in Orange, New Jersey, and the Radium Dial Company in Ottawa, Illinois. There was no connection between these companies, yet each engaged in reprehensible behavior when the dial painters became ill.

A scientist on the US Radium payroll examined the young women without informing them that he wasn't actually a physician. In fact, he didn't even have a medical license, but that didn't stop him from telling the girls that they were fine. Later, he furthered the syphilis rumor by publishing a paper suggesting the disease was a potential cause of their ailments. The vice president of the company also posed as a doctor, assuring the girls that they were in excellent health. After inspections of the factory revealed extensive radium contamination, the president of US Radium forged a report claiming the opposite and filed it with the state. When New Jersey officials finally demanded that US Radium institute basic safety practices, the company refused, preferring to shut down their New Jersey plant and relocate to New York, where they could get away with the same unsafe working conditions that were killing their employees.

The Radium Dial Company, which opened a few years after US Radium, was well aware of the risks posed by dial painting.

Rather than institute safer practices, Radium Dial did little to protect its employees, although they eventually offered dial painters a glass stylus instead of a paintbrush to reduce "lip pointing." Later, the company arranged for frequent medical exams of the dial painters, which revealed that they were becoming increasingly radioactive from their work. Radium Dial kept these results secret, but when the dial painters asked to see their medical records, a supervisor told them, "My dear girls, if we were to give a medical report to you girls, there would be a riot in the place." The company's callousness was matched only by its cruelty. Catherine Donohue was still employed when she began wasting away from radium poisoning. Company officials eventually fired her because they thought her presence would frighten dial painters who hadn't developed symptoms...yet.

What compelled these corporations to act with such wanton disregard of the dial painters' health? Certainly profit was a motive. Radium was used in many consumer products and medicines, and no one with a vested interest in the radium business wanted to scare the public by acknowledging its dangers. Perhaps their denials were also borne from fear. Before the dangers of radium were widely known, top scientists and company officials treated radium with cavalier indifference. Admitting that radium was killing the dial painters would mean admitting that they were potentially facing a similar fate.

Despite relentless pain, severe deformities, public shaming, and being ostracized from their communities, the dial painters persevered. Meeting in doctors' and dentists' waiting rooms, they were the first to realize that something in the factory was killing them. They fought for recognition of their illnesses and compensation to ease their final days. In New Jersey, Grace Fryer found a lawyer who would represent her in a lawsuit. Four other dial painters, including two of Mollie's surviving sisters, Quinta and Albina, joined her suit.

The media latched onto the horrors of their ailments, sensationalizing the lawsuit and enraging the public on their behalf. US Radium tried all sorts of legal maneuvering to get the case dismissed. It was widely believed that US Radium was dragging out the case in hopes the dial painters would die before a verdict could be reached. Public outrage was so enormous that US Radium was forced to offer a settlement to the five dial painters, though the company refused to accept responsibility for its role in their illnesses.

Residents of Ottawa shunned the dying dial painters from Radium Dial, worried that the community would be stigmatized by their horrible illnesses. As a result, Ottawa doctors refused to diagnose radium poisoning and Ottawa lawyers refused to represent the dial painters in court. Eventually, a Chicago lawyer named Leonard Grossman agreed to take their case. Once again, the press exploited the dial painters' plight, granting the "Radium Girls" membership in the "Society of the Living Dead." When the time came for Catherine to testify, she had to be carried into the courtroom. She brought with her a jewelry box containing pieces of her own jawbone. Though the Illinois Industrial Commission ruled in Catherine's favor, Radium Dial appealed the ruling all the way to the US Supreme Court. Catherine died without receiving any of the compensation to which she was entitled.

There were no happy endings for the Radium Girls whose illnesses were so highly publicized, but a century later, their legacy lives on. Publicity about the dial painters' demise raised awareness about the dangers of radium. Their lawsuits resulted in new regulations for workplace safety. Decades-long studies of the surviving dial painters helped scientists establish limits for radiation exposure. When World War II began, the need for luminous watches and dials exploded once more, but thanks to the sacrifices of the first dial painters, the second generation was at far less risk. Advances in laboratory safety equipment were based on devices that were specifically invented to protect the dial painters. The last radium glow-in-the-dark products were made in the 1960s, when radium paint was replaced by safer compounds.

Even today, the dial painters' remains are so highly radioactive that they emit measurable radiation from the grave. You can visit their final resting places with a Geiger counter to know if you've found the right place. This faint signal is the last message that the doomed dial painters can send. It is our duty to remember them, their struggles and sacrifices, and how valiantly they fought an entrenched system that was rigged against them. We remember Mollie and Grace and Quinta and Albina and Catherine and all the other dial painters, known and unknown. We remember.

ADDITIONAL READING

Bellows, Alan. "Undark and the Radium Girls." Damn Interesting. December 2006. http://www.damninteresting.com/undark-and-the-radium-girls/.

Blum, Deborah. *The Poisoner's Handbook: Murder and the Birth of Forensic Medicine in Jazz Age New York.* New York: Penguin Books, 2010.

Brown, Carrie. *Rosie's Mom: Forgotten Women Workers of the First World War.* Boston: Northeastern University Press, 2002.

Clark, Claudia. *Radium Girls: Women and Industrial Health Reform, 1910–1935.* Chapel Hill, NC: The University of North Carolina Press, 1997.

Farabaugh, Kane. "'Radium Girls' Remembered for Role in Shaping U.S. Labor Law." Voice of America. September 2011. http://www.voanews.com/english/news/usa/Radium-Girls-Remembered-for-Role-in-Shaping-US-Labor-Law-129169888.html.

Glassmire, Charles. "The Radium Girls." Tales from the Nuclear Age. September 2010. http://talesfromthenuclearage.wordpress.com/2010/09/13/the-radium-girls-2/.

Grossman, Leonard. "The Case of the Living Dead Women." The Modem Junkie's Portal. October 2009. http://lgrossman.com/pics/radium/.

Irvine, Martha. "Suffering Endures for 'Radium Girls' Who Painted Watches in the '20s." Hartford Web Publishing. October 1998. http://www.hartford-hwp.com/archives/40/046.html.

Moore, Kate. *The Radium Girls: The Dark Story of America's Shining Women*. Naperville, IL: Sourcebooks, 2017.

"Radium: From Wonder Drug to Hazard." *The New York Times*. October 1987. http://www.nytimes.com/1987/10/04/nyregion/radium-from-wonder-drug-to-hazard.html.

Redniss, Lauren. *Radioactive: Marie & Pierre Curie: A Tale of Love and Fallout*. New York: It Books, 2010.

ACKNOWLEDGMENTS

Jamie Weiss Chilton is technically my agent, but that word doesn't begin to convey all the roles she really plays: advocate, advisor, inspiration, motivator, confidant, and most of all, dear friend. She saw the promise of *Glow* when it was scarcely more than an idea and has championed it—and me—at every stage, and I will be forever grateful.

When I thought I'd explored every possible direction this story could take, Wendy McClure came along with such outstanding editorial feedback that she inspired all kinds of new ideas and made the revision process a joy. I'm grateful to Wendy and the entire team at Albert Whitman—Annette Hobbs Magier, Jordan Kost, Alex Messina-Schultheis, Tracie Schneider, and Laurel Symonds—for their expertise and professionalism. Thank you for transforming my manuscript into a beautiful book.

I've been fortunate to work with many excellent editors on previous books, and I'm especially grateful to Kelli Chipponeri, Siobhan Ciminera, and Kara Sargent, whose insights and encouragement have helped me become a better writer. I'm also grateful to Debra Dorfman, who said the first "yes" of my career.

I am lucky to live in a particular time and place where the written word is celebrated, and so I am deeply indebted to the incredible team at Bookmarks, especially Ginger Hendricks and Jamie Rogers Southern, as well as Ed Southern at the North Carolina Writers' Network. Receiving the North Carolina Arts Council's support at a pivotal moment in the writing of this book made its completion possible. I'm also fortunate to be a member of Writers and Illustrators of North Carolina and have benefitted tremendously from the wisdom and generosity of my colleagues.

Many professionals took time from their busy schedules to answer questions during my research. Dr. Nita Eskew patiently explained laboratory procedures to me and researched the availability of certain substances for use in lab experiments, as did Dr. Matt Melvin. Dr. Eskew also connected me with Dr. Christa Colyer and Dr. Willie Hinze, who helped me learn about the production of glowing paint today. Dr. David Brenner answered questions about radiation exposure. Dr. Gary Ljungquist was kind enough to provide French translations. Kathy M. Barnes, Associate Dean of Admissions at Salem College, explained the finer points of the admissions and financial aid process. Dr. Alison Gardner and charge nurse, Karen Meitlowski, gave me a tour of a hospital emergency department, including its decontamination room. Katherine Mahler advised me in art. Historian Dr. Daniel Prosterman, who was the first to introduce me to the Radium Girls, provided essential historical context and suggested many excellent sources for my research. Any errors in this book are mine alone.

I am grateful every day for my Highland Presbyterian Church family.

For their support, encouragement, and always knowing just what to say, I thank my friends: Connie Brake, Siobhan Ciminera, Raegan Dalbo, Carol Eickmeyer, Nancy Ellwood, Alicia Faerber, Kristen Holder, Elizabeth Jackson, Penelope Jackson, Kelly Starling

Lyons, Meg Mason, Stacy McAnulty, Gabbie Serang Hellinger, Virginia Sparkes, Nova Ren Suma, and Heather Wood. Special commendation goes to Siobhan and Stacy for their camaraderie as I've navigated the wild, wonderful, and utterly unpredictable world of publishing.

I've been nurtured by my family's unwavering belief in me, and for that I am grateful to my father, Chris Bryant; my bonus mom, Sally Bryant DeChenne; and my brother and sister-in-law, Mike and Miranda Bryant. I am only a writer today because my mother, Judith Bryant, spent countless hours reading to me when I was a child. The lessons she taught me about love and sacrifice have guided the writing of this book and the course of my life. I had the good fortune to marry into the Prosterman family, which brought Louis Prosterman, Vickie Hagan, and Dianne Floyd into my life. I wish my father-in-law, Louis, had lived to see the publication of this book. I would have loved to share it with him.

My children, Clara and Sam, illuminate my life with their wonder, curiosity, and love. Thank you, darlings, for sharing me with *Glow* and giving me the space—physical and mental—to write it.

My husband, Dan, offers me the kind of unconditional love and support that makes anything possible. Thank you for making my tea every morning. Thank you for all the times you've prioritized my work. Thank you for discussing plot points during dinner prep. Thank you for reading every word, again and again and again. Thank you for making this life we share such a breathtakingly beautiful adventure. Thank you for loving me just as I am. Thank you.

Megan E. Bryant has written more than 250 books for children. She lives in the City of Arts and Innovation—also known as Winston-Salem, North Carolina—with her family, where she teaches writing at Salem College. *Glow* is her first novel for young adults.